n
nov
Aga
the a
life
hon
Prett

D0492240

By Danielle Steel

Fairytale • The Right Time • The Duchess • Against All Odds
Dangerous Games • The Mistress • The Award • Rushing Waters
Magic • The Apartment • Property Of A Noblewoman • Blue
Precious Gifts • Undercover • Country • Prodigal Son • Pegasus
A Perfect Life • Power Play • Winners • First Sight • Until The End Of Time
The Sins Of The Mother • Friends Forever • Betrayal • Hotel Vendôme
Happy Birthday • 44 Charles Street • Legacy • Family Ties • Big Girl
Southern Lights • Matters Of The Heart • One Day At A Time
A Good Woman • Rogue • Honor Thyself • Amazing Grace • Bungalow 2
Sisters • H.R.H. • Coming Out • The House • Toxic Bachelors • Miracle
Impossible • Echoes • Second Chance • Ransom • Safe Harbour
Johnny Angel • Dating Game • Answered Prayers • Sunset In St. Tropez
The Cottage • The Kiss • Leap Of Faith • Lone Eagle • Journey
The House On Hope Street • The Wedding • Irresistible Forces
Granny Dan • Bittersweet • Mirror Image • The Klone And I
The Long Road Home • The Ghost • Special Delivery • The Ranch
Silent Honor • Malice • Five Days In Paris • Lightning • Wings • The Gift
Accident • Vanished • Mixed Blessings • Jewels • No Greater Love
Heartbeat • Message From Nam • Daddy • Star • Zoya • Kaleidoscope
Fine Things • Wanderlust • Secrets • Family Album • Full Circle • Changes
Thurston House • Crossings • Once In A Lifetime • A Perfect Stranger
Remembrance • Palomino • Love: *Poems* • The Ring • Loving
To Love Again • Summer's End • Season Of Passion • The Promise
Now And Forever • Passion's Promise • Going Home

Nonfiction
Pure Joy: *The Dogs We Love*
A Gift Of Hope: *Helping the Homeless*
His Bright Light: *The Story of Nick Traina*

For Children
Pretty Minnie In Paris
Pretty Minnie In Hollywood

Danielle Steel
FAIRYTALE

MACMILLAN

First published 2017 by Delacorte Press,
an imprint of Random House,
a division of Penguin Random House LLC, New York.

First published in the UK 2017 by Macmillan
an imprint of Pan Macmillan
20 New Wharf Road, London N1 9RR
Associated companies throughout the world
www.panmacmillan.com

ISBN 978-1-5098-0056-8

Copyright © Danielle Steel, 2017

1 3 5 7 9 8 6 4 2

A CIP catalogue record for this book is available from the British Library.

Printed and bound by CPI Group (UK) Ltd, Croydon, CR0 4YY

Visit **www.panmacmillan.com** to read more about all our books
and to buy them. You will also find features, author interviews and
news of any author events, and you can sign up for e-newsletters
so that you're always first to hear about our new releases.

To my beloved children,
Beatie, Trevor, Todd, Nick, Sam,
 Victoria, Vanessa, Maxx, and Zara,

May all your fairytales be real,
May evil never touch you,
May you be strong, wise, and brave, if it does,
 and may all your stories have happy endings,
 and may you always know
 how much I love you,
 with all my heart and soul,

 with all my love,
 Mom/d.s.

Foreword

Dear Readers,

We all need a bit of magic in our lives, and most of us secretly or openly believe in fairytales—that a certain amount of magic can happen to us. Fairytales have a useful and powerful message in today's world, to give us hope that things will turn out right in the end. I loved the idea of translating a modern-day story into a fairytale of sorts, even without magic wands or fairy godmothers, but populated by real people who turn up at the right time, lend a helping hand, stand up for what is right, and help us turn things around when necessary, no matter how overwhelming the circumstances, or how bleak the outcome may seem at times. Like all fairytales, it is essentially a battle between good and evil. And there is no denying that evil does exist and raises its ugly head at times, in all of our lives and worlds.

Wily, cunning, clever, greedy stepmothers exist even in today's real-life world. A naive parent can make an unfortunate choice of mate for a remarriage, putting their children in some pretty nasty circumstances. We've all heard those stories, and sometimes lived them. Add unpleasant stepsiblings, and you have a recipe for some very unpleasant times, and even ugly battles. Without an ally or protector, we can end up fighting the forces of evil on our own. And for lack of a fairy godmother to solve the problem with some magic dust and a wand, we have to be brave and creative to fight the battles that face us and to fight for what is right, and justice in the end. With luck, unexpected allies can appear, and with perseverance and courage, and right on our side, good can in fact prevail over evil—not always easily, but the battle for the forces of good can lead to victory in the end. It's good for all of us to be reminded of that.

With a blissfully easy childhood, in the gorgeous, lush, peaceful setting of the Napa Valley, we don't expect tragedy and evil to rear their ugly heads, but hard times can happen anywhere. And then the battle begins . . . there are no pumpkins or white mice in this fairytale, but a fascinatingly stylish, charming French evil stepmother, an innocent father who believes the lies he has been told by a bewitching woman, and an accident of fate leave a young woman fighting for what is rightfully hers, and even fighting for her life . . . while a funny, cozy, red-headed, clever, eccentric grandmother comes as close to being a fairy godmother as any of us will ever need . . . and as it should be, Good prevails over Evil in the end, which should remind us all to stay on our path, persevere, never give up, and do what we know is right, to the end! May all your fairytales end with Happily Ever Afters.

Love, Danielle

FAIRYTALE

Chapter One

It was March in the Napa Valley, just under sixty miles north of San Francisco, and Joy Lammenais's favorite time of year. The rolling hills were a brilliant emerald green, which would fade once the weather grew warmer, and get dry and brittle in the summer heat. But for now, everything was fresh and new, and the vineyards stretched for miles across the Valley. Visitors compared it to Tuscany in Italy, and some to France.

She had come there for the first time with Christophe twenty-four years before, while she was getting her master's in business administration at Stanford, and he was taking graduate classes in oenology and viticulture. He had painstakingly explained to her that oenology was everything about making wine, and viticulture was about planting and growing grapes. His family had been making famous wines in Bordeaux for centuries, where his father and uncles ran the family winery and vineyards, but his dream had been to come to California and learn more about the wines and vineyards and vintners in the Napa Valley. He had confided to Joy that he wanted a small winery of his own. It had just been a vague hope at first, a fantasy he would never indulge. He assumed that he would go back to France to follow the expected path, like his ancestors and relatives before him. But he fell in love with California and life in the States, and became more and more passionate about the vineyards in the Napa Valley during his year at Stanford. His father's sudden death at an early age, while Christophe was at Stanford, left him with an unexpected windfall of money to invest, and suddenly made establishing his own winery in the United States not only enticing but feasible. After they both finished graduate school in June, he had gone home to France in the summer to explain it to his family, and came back in the fall to bring his plan to fruition.

Joy was the most exciting woman he'd ever met, with a diversity of talents. She had a natural gift for anything related to business or finance. And at the same time, she was a painter and artist, had taken classes in Italy over several summers, and could easily have pursued a career in art. She struggled with the decision for a while in college. Her teachers in Italy had encouraged her to forget business. But in the end, her more practical side won out, and she kept her painting as a hobby she loved, and focused on her entrepreneurial goals. She had an instinctive sense of what the best deals were, and wanted to work in one of the Silicon Valley high-tech investment firms, before starting her own venture capital firm one day. She talked to Christophe about it constantly.

She knew nothing about wine when they met, and he taught her during the year they spent together. She wasn't really interested in vineyards and wineries, but the way he explained it all brought it to life for her and made it seem almost magical. He loved making wine as much as she did painting, or her fascination with creative investments. Agriculture seemed like risky business to her. So much could go wrong, an early frost, a late harvest, too much rain, or too little. Christophe said that was part of the mystery and beauty of it, and when all the necessary ingredients came together, you wound up with an unforgettable vintage that people would talk about forever, that could turn an ordinary wine into a remarkable gift of nature.

When she visited the Napa Valley with him, again and again, she began to understand that making wine was in his soul and DNA, and having a respected label of his own was the ultimate achievement to him, and what he hoped for. She was twenty-five then, and he was twenty-six. She had been fortunate to get a job with a legendary venture capital firm right after they graduated and loved what she was doing. And when Christophe came back from France at the end of the summer, looking for land to buy, and vineyards he could re-plant exactly the way he wanted them, according to everything he had been taught in France, he asked her to go with him. He respected Joy's advice about all the financial aspects of any deal. She helped him buy his first vineyard, and by November, he had bought six, all of them adjoining one another.

The vines were old, and he knew exactly what he wanted to plant there. He told her he would keep his winery small, but he would have the best pinot noir in the Valley one day, and she believed him. He explained to her about the fine points of the wines they tasted, what was wrong with them and what was right, how they could have been different or better, or should have been. And he introduced her to French wines, and the wine his family made and had exported from Château Lammenais for generations.

He had bought an additional piece of property on the hill over-looking his vineyards and the Valley, and said he was going to build a small château there. In the meantime, he was living in a cabin with one bedroom and a comfortable living room with a huge fireplace. They spent many a cozy night there on weekends, while he shared his hopes with her, and she explained to him how to make the business side of it work, and how to design his financial plan.

They spent Christmas together in his cabin, and stood on the small porch in the early mornings, admiring nature at its finest. With his father gone then, and his mother many years before, he didn't want to go back to France for Christmas with his uncles, he wanted to spend it with Joy. She had no family to go home to either. Her mother had died young, of cancer when Joy was fifteen, and her much older father had been devastated and died of grief three years later. She and Christophe created their own world in the place he had brought her to, and he had cooked a remarkable Christmas dinner for her of goose and pheasant, which set off the wines he had chosen to perfection.

In the spring, he began building his château, just as he said he would. She learned that Christophe was a visionary of sorts, but remarkably he always did what he said he would, and turned his ideas from the abstract to concrete reality. He never lost sight of his goals, and she showed him how to get there. He described what he saw in the future, and she helped him fulfill his dreams. He had beautiful plans for the château.

He had the stone brought over from France, and said he didn't want anything too imposing or too large. He based the design loosely on his own family's four-hundred-year-old château, and gave the architect countless sketches and photographs of what he had in mind, with the alterations that he felt would work on the property he had chosen, and he was relentless about the proportions. Not too big and not too small. He had picked a hill with beautiful old trees surrounding the clearing where he wanted to build his home. He said he was going to put red rosebushes everywhere, just like they had in France, and laid it all out with a landscape architect, who was thrilled with the project.

The house was well under way by summer when he asked Joy to marry him. They had dated for well over a year by then. He was constructing his winery amid the vineyards, at the same time he built his château, which was a jewel. They were married at a small ceremony in a nearby church at the end of August, with two of his vineyard workers as their witnesses. They had no real friends in the Valley yet. They had each other, which was more than enough, for a start. They agreed that the rest could come later. They were establishing their life together, and she had great respect for Christophe's passion for the earth and his land. It was in his bones and in his veins and in his heart. The grapes he grew were living beings to him, to be cherished and nourished and protected. And he felt the same way about his wife. He cherished her like a precious gift, and she blossomed and thrived in the warmth of his love, and loved him just as deeply.

The château wasn't yet complete on the first Christmas they were married, and they were still living in his simple cabin, which suited their quiet life. Joy was three months pregnant by then, and Christophe wanted their home finished in time to bring their first child there when it was born in June. Joy had quit her job in Silicon Valley when they married, since she couldn't commute that far, and she worked hard at helping him set up his winery. She handled the business and he dealt with the vines. Her belly was round and full when they moved into the château in May, just as Christophe had promised. They spent a month there, while she painted beautiful frescoes and murals at night and on the weekends, waiting for their first child to arrive, and she worked in the office of their new winery every day. He had named it after her, and called it Château Joy, which was the perfect description of their life.

They woke up excited to go to work every day, and had lunch together at the house, to discuss progress and the problems they were solving. He had planted their vines, using all the precepts he had grown up with, and two of his uncles had come to visit them, approved of everything they were doing, and said it would be the best winery in the Napa Valley in twenty years. The vines they had planted were growing well, and the château already felt like home to them. They had furnished it with old French provincial antiques they had found at country auctions and antique stores and picked out everything together.

The baby arrived as gently and peacefully as the rest of their plans had taken shape over the past two years. They went to the hospital in the morning when Joy told him it was time, shortly after breakfast. They drove down the hill and to the hospital, and by late that afternoon, Joy had a beautiful baby girl in her arms, as Christophe looked at Joy in awe. It had all been so easy and simple and natural. The little girl had her mother's pale blond hair and white skin, and her father's deep blue eyes, from the moment she was born. It was obvious that her eyes would stay blue, since her mother's eyes were blue as well. And her skin was so creamy fair that Christophe said she looked like a flower, and they named her Camille.

They went home to the château the next day, to begin their life together. And Camille grew up with two adoring parents, in an exquisite small château, amid the beauty of the Napa Valley, looking out over her father's vineyards. And Christophe's uncles' prediction proved to be true. Within a few years, he was producing one of the finest pinot noirs in the entire region. Their business was sound, their future secure, they were respected and admired by all the important vintners in the Napa Valley, and many of them sought advice from him. Christophe had years of family history behind him along with his own nearly infallible instincts. His closest friend was Sam Marshall, who owned the largest winery in the Valley. He didn't have Christophe's history or knowledge of French viticulture, but he had an instinctive sense for growing great wines, was brave and innovative, and owned more land than anyone else in the Valley, and Christophe liked exchanging ideas with him.

His wife, Barbara, and Joy were friends too, and the two couples often spent time together with their children, on weekends. The Marshalls had a little boy who was seven years old when Camille was born. Phillip was fascinated by the baby when the two families had lunch together on Sundays. Christophe would cook a big French meal for them, while he and Sam talked business and the women watched the children. Joy let Phillip hold Camille when she was two weeks old. But most of the time he preferred climbing trees, or running around the fields, picking fruit in the orchards, or riding his bike in their driveway.

Sam Marshall had been a local boy who had worked hard for everything he had and took his business seriously, as Christophe did, which Sam admired him for. It had always annoyed Sam when successful businessmen from the city, or as far away as LA, or even New York, bought a piece of property, planted a few vines, called themselves vintners and winemakers, showed off without any real knowledge, and were pretentious about it. Sam called them "Sunday vintners," and couldn't tolerate them, and neither could Christophe.

Although Christophe believed the secrets of making great wine had to be handed down for generations, he respected Sam for learning everything he knew in one. But Sam was so hard working, so hungry to learn, and so respectful of the earth and what they eked from it, that Christophe had a deep affection for him, and both of them preferred the company of the serious vintners like themselves, who had valuable information and experience to share. The wine business attracted a lot of amateurs. People who had money and bought established wineries, mostly newly rich, who wanted to show off. And the Old Guard aristocratic social set from San Francisco had come to the Valley over the years too. They kept to themselves, gave elaborate parties within the confines of their elite group, and snubbed everyone, although they occasionally acknowledged the more important vintners, including Christophe, who had no interest in them.

Camille grew up in the happy atmosphere her parents created around them, among the wine-making dynasties in the Napa Valley, and a few close friends. Their land grew as her father bought more of it, planted more vineyards, and added an Italian vineyard manager named Cesare, from Tuscany, whom Camille knew her mother didn't like, because she made a face every time he walked into the office or left the room.

Joy had continued to take care of the business end of the winery as Camille grew up, and hung out around the winery or played in the vineyards after school. And she always said she wanted to be like her mother and father and work at their winery one day, and go to Stanford just like them. She thought everything they did was perfect, and she wanted to continue in the same traditions. She'd been to Bordeaux many times with her parents, to meet her cousins and great-uncles and aunts, but she loved being in the Napa Valley, and thought it was the most beautiful place on earth. Like her father, she didn't want to live in France, and Joy agreed with both of them. The Marshalls remained their closest friends, and Phillip alternated between being Camille's nemesis and her hero as he grew up. Seven years older than she was, he teased her a lot. He was a senior in high school when she was only ten. But more than once, he had protected her if he saw anyone bullying her when he was around. She was like a little sister to him and she was sad when he went away to college and she only saw him during vacations after that.

Joy was forty-four, and Christophe a year older, the summer Camille turned seventeen, when Joy discovered she had breast cancer in a routine mammogram, and it rocked their world. The doctors decided to remove only the lump and not the breast, and thought they could cure her with aggressive chemotherapy and radiation for a year. Christophe was beside himself, and Joy was desperately ill after her treatments, but she went to the winery for a short time every day, and Camille did everything she could to help her. Joy was incredibly courageous, and determined to beat the dreaded disease. There were some very dark times that winter, but Joy never lost her will to live, and did whatever she had to do to be cured. She said afterward that she did it for Camille and Christophe, and a year later, she was cancer free, in remission, and they could all breathe again. It had been a harrowing year, and the fact that Camille had been accepted at Stanford meant nothing to any of them until after they knew that Joy was healthy again.

She and Christophe celebrated Camille's high school graduation, and gave her a party just before school ended, on her eighteenth birthday. All was right in their world again. The party was for young people Camille's age, mostly her classmates, and a group of parents had come to enjoy the party with Joy and Christophe. The Marshalls were there and they said Phillip was traveling constantly now, working on promoting their wines and doing well. He had spent six months in Chile, working at a friend's winery, and he had been in Cape Town the year before, since both were grape-growing regions often compared to the Napa Valley. He was learning the business all around the world.

They were relieved to see Joy looking so well, and after dinner, Sam's wife, Barbara, confided to Joy in a whisper that she had made the same discovery as Joy had a year before, and was having surgery in San Francisco the following week, in her case a double mastectomy. She was ten years older than Joy, and very worried about what lay ahead. The two women talked about it for a long time, and Joy insisted that she would be all right. Barbara looked as though she wanted to believe her but didn't quite. She was very much afraid and so was Sam. At first, they had decided not to tell Phillip, they didn't want to worry him, and had put it off as long as they could. But with Barbara's surgery imminent, they were going to share the bad news with him when he got back from his latest trip.

Joy had been very open with her daughter, and Camille had seen how sick her mother was during chemo. Joy had been concerned about her family history, since her mother had died of breast cancer at forty, but Barbara had no family history of it at all. Lightning had struck her randomly out of the blue, and no matter how successful her husband was, or how much money they had for treatment, or how much they loved each other, Barbara was very sick. She was a beautiful woman and admitted to Joy that she was worried about being disfigured, and the pain of reconstructive surgery. Their marriage was as solid as Joy and Christophe's, and this was the greatest challenge they had ever faced, just as it was for the Lammenaises. And they knew that other marriages in the Napa Valley were not all as wholesome as theirs. There was always a lot of gossip about the local community and who was sleeping with whom. It was a small, very competitive area with a lot of social ambition, and many extramarital affairs among the people they knew.

Joy and Christophe had never been part of any of the racier local groups, and didn't want to be. Nor had Sam and Barbara. They were down-to-earth people, in spite of Sam's massive success. Barbara had been a flight attendant before they married. And now he had the biggest, most profitable winery in the Valley, which was a lure to the social climbers and nouveaux riches. There was a lot of money invested in the Napa Valley, and many vintners making big fortunes, like Sam and Christophe, and several others. The Marshalls' only concession to their position and the empire Sam had founded was the Harvest Ball they gave every year in September. More as a joke, after a trip to Venice they'd taken, Barbara did it as a masked ball one year, in elaborate costumes, and everyone they'd invited liked it so much that the Marshalls continued doing it as a masked ball and established an annual tradition. Joy and Christophe had gone every year despite Christophe's protests about how ridiculous he felt in a Louis XV costume with satin knee breeches, a wig, and a mask.

"If I have to do it, so can you," Sam had told him repeatedly. "Barbara would kill me if I didn't," he said ruefully. He indulged her willingly to make her happy, and she looked beautiful in whatever costume she wore each year. "We should have given the party as a barbecue the first year, then we wouldn't have to dress up like fools every time now," Sam grumbled good-naturedly, but it was always a spectacular evening with fabulous buffets, dancing to an orchestra they brought in from San Francisco, and fireworks over their endless vineyards. Unlike Joy and Christophe's elegant little château, their house was vast and high-tech modern, had been built by a famous Mexican architect, and housed their world famous collection of contemporary and modern art. They had seven Picassos they lent frequently to museums, numerous Chagalls, and work by Jackson Pollock, which thrilled Joy to see, given her profound love for fine art.

Camille spent the summer after her high school graduation working in the winery office with her mother, as she had every summer since she turned fifteen. It was her fourth year, and her parents were excited about her going to Stanford, and so was she. She planned to go to business school to get an MBA after she worked for her parents for a few years, to take a break before grad school. She had no intention of ever working anywhere else, although her father said that a year with his family in Bordeaux would do her good, and help her French, which was useful in their business, but she never strayed far from them, and didn't intend to. She was happiest at Château Joy, with her parents, working and living with them.

Joy visited Barbara Marshall regularly over the summer. Once she started chemo, she was desperately sick, and her husband and son looked terrified whenever Joy or Christophe saw them. She was sicker than even Joy had been. And once Camille started Stanford, she came home on weekends more often than her mother thought she should. She told Christophe that Camille was too attached to them, and her life more insular than was good for her at her age. Joy thought she should venture into the world, at least for a while.

"She wants to be here," he said, smiling at his wife, and then kissed her. "She's our only child, don't chase her away." He loved it when Camille was with them, and the fact that she wanted to be there. They had often talked about having another child when Camille was younger, but their life had seemed so perfect as it was, and after Joy's cancer was cured, it was too late.

Christophe always said he didn't mind not having a son. He wanted Camille to run the winery one day when they were older, and he was certain she'd be good at it. She had her mother's head for business, and he had kept the winery and vineyards at a manageable size intentionally. He didn't want an empire as large as Sam Marshall's, and he kept Château Joy special, small, and exclusive by choice. What they had seemed the perfect size to them, and he and Joy ran it with ease, with the occasional battle with Cesare about the vineyards.

Cesare had been with them for years, and Joy still treated him like an interloper and never trusted him. He was sloppy with his petty cash accounts, and thought accounting to her for the money was unnecessary and an imposition. She was merciless about challenging him, which enraged them both, and they argued constantly. He rarely left her office without slamming the door. Christophe suspected he pocketed small amounts from his expense account, but Cesare knew their grapes and vineyards intimately and treated them like his children. He had flawless instincts for what needed to be done, and Christophe valued him as the best vineyard manager in the Valley, and tolerated his sloppiness with money in exchange. He cared more for their grapes than their petty cash. Joy had no patience with Cesare and was unwilling to let it go, and she argued with Christophe about it too.

Christophe forgave Cesare his small transgressions easily, knowing his deep love for their winery and how knowledgeable and conscientious he was about their grapes. A few lost dollars on his expense account didn't seem like a deal breaker to him, balanced with all the rest.

Christophe was the brilliant vintner of Château Joy, who had made it the success it was, and his wife was the practical side of the business, and handled all the nuts and bolts and kept their accounts in good order. They were a perfect team.

Camille was happy at Stanford, and met many people from around the country and the world, but the minute she had a chance to go home, she did. She was an econ major, as Joy had been in college. And most of the students she met hoped to find jobs with high-tech finance firms in Silicon Valley, or planned to head to New York for jobs on Wall Street. All Camille wanted to do was finish school and help her parents at their winery. She had three months left before graduation, her senior thesis to finish, and final exams to get through, when she was in Napa for a weekend, and noticed a medical slip on her mother's desk, to remind her that it was time for her mammogram. It brought back instantly to Camille the terrible time five years before when her mother had been diagnosed with cancer, and she had gone through treatment for a year, but she'd had no recurrence since.

Barbara Marshall hadn't been as fortunate. She had wasted away on chemo, as the cancer continued to spread, and died eight months after she was diagnosed. Sam and Phillip were devastated. She had been gone for a little over three years when Camille was almost ready to graduate from college. Phillip was running the winery with his father, had a lively reputation in the Valley, and went out with a lot of different girls. He liked fast, expensive cars and pretty women, and Camille saw him often in his red Ferrari, never with the same girl twice. She teased him about it, and he still treated her like a little sister, but the seven years between them made a big difference at twenty-two and twenty-nine. He was part of an adult world, among the serious vintners in the Valley, their sons were close to him in age, and they had in common the responsibilities they would have to take on one day. They had much to learn in the meantime, which Phillip took seriously, and his college days were long behind him. He pointed out that Camille had time before she had to take her place in an adult world, and his attitude annoyed her. She knew as much about their winery as Phillip did about his father's, but Phillip didn't act that way with her. He still treated her like an adolescent and not the grown woman she felt she was.

Camille had heard her parents say that Sam had been dating a congresswoman from LA for almost two years now, but she had never met her, and Sam was always alone or with Phillip when she saw him. Losing Barbara had aged him and he looked more serious than before. It had been a sad loss for them all, and always made Camille nervous for her mother when she thought about it.

"You still get your mammograms twice a year, don't you, Mom?" Camille asked her after she saw the notice on her desk.

"Of course," Joy said, sitting down with one of their enormous ledgers, as she smiled at her daughter. "I can't wait to turn some of this over to you when you come home." She was well aware of how capable Camille was, how organized and efficient. She had learned it from her mother. And Camille knew a lot more about the intricacies of making wine than her mother did. Christophe had taught her a great deal, ever since she was a child, far more than Joy had learned after years in the business. It was in Camille's DNA too, just like her father's. Joy was involved in operations and finance. Camille and Christophe were in love with the wine.

"Hang on, I'll be here in three months." Camille smiled at her mother. Joy had cleared an office for her, and was excited at the prospect of seeing her there every day. It was the last part of their dream coming true, having her work at the winery side by side with them, from now on. And she would take over one day when they were ready to retire, although that was still a long time away. Joy was forty-nine, and Christophe had just turned fifty.

Joy was busy for the next month, after Camille's visit home, with a multitude of projects that landed on her desk, and Christophe was choosing labels for a new wine, and wanted her help selecting them. Joy designed their labels herself, and he was having trouble deciding between the two he liked best. Camille had already cast her vote when she was home.

It was four weeks after Camille's last visit when Joy found the reminder in a heap of papers she'd shoved in a drawer, and called the hospital for an appointment for the mammogram. It was cursory, since she had just passed the five-year mark and was considered cured, but it made her nervous anyway, lest lightning strike again. Her own mother had died when she was younger than Joy now, but as Christophe said, they led a charmed life, and nothing bad was going to happen to them. She always tried not to think of Barbara Marshall's sad fate when he said it.

Joy made the appointment, and used the opportunity for some

other appointments in the city, since she didn't go there often. It was an hour and a half away, but San Francisco felt like it was on another planet when she was in the Napa Valley. She had no desire to go anywhere, although Christophe had to travel periodically to promote their wines, and went to Europe and Asia, and he was anxious to take Camille with him when she came to work full-time.

The hospital had Joy's history, and the mammogram was routine. The technician asked her to wait to put her clothes on until a doctor had checked the film, but the woman who performed it smiled as though everything was fine, and Joy was relieved, as she sat alone in an exam room, and answered text messages for work.

The doctor who came into the room was young and she didn't know him. She couldn't read anything in his eyes as he pulled up a stool and sat down facing her. He had her mammogram films in an envelope in his hand, and spoke to her as he went to put them up on a light box on the wall. He pointed to a gray area on the breast where she hadn't had a problem, and turned to look at her with a serious expression.

"There's a shadow here I don't like, Mrs. Lammenais. If you've got the time, I'd like to do a biopsy on it today. With your history, I don't think it's smart to wait. It won't take long, but I'd really like to know what that is." Joy felt as though her heart were going to leap out of her chest or stop entirely. She had heard those same words five years before.

"Are you worried about it?" Her voice sounded like a croak to her own ears.

"I'd be happier if that shadow wasn't there. It could be nothing, but we should know what's going on." After that, his voice was a blur, and she heard him from a great distance, and followed the technician like a robot to another room, where they took off her gown and covered her with a drape, she lay on the table, they numbed the area, and did a biopsy which was painful, and her heart was pounding the entire time. She kept thinking of the hellish year she'd had of chemo, of Barbara Marshall dying after eight months, of her own mother, dead of breast cancer at forty. There were tears sliding out of her eyes, while they did the biopsy, and she was sobbing as she ran out of the hospital when it was over and hurried down the steps. They said they'd call her with the results, but she didn't want to hear them. She could sense what was coming. They said that lightning didn't strike twice, but she already knew it had. She could feel it in her soul. And what was she going to tell Christophe and Camille if she had cancer again? She couldn't imagine, and she felt like she was already dead when she got into her car and drove back to the Napa Valley, blinded by her tears. Joy tried to focus on her driving, but for the first time ever, she felt sure she was going to die. How could she be lucky twice?

Chapter Two

They called her five days later with the results of the biopsy, and Joy felt as though she was hearing it through a wall of cotton. She knew all the language and the terms. The biopsy showed a malignancy, they told her all the pertinent details, and this time they recommended a mastectomy, even a double one to be on the safe side, given her history. And they wanted to do it as soon as possible, and start chemo after she recovered. It felt like a death sentence, and she remembered Barbara Marshall when she told Joy what was happening to her.

"I'll let you know," Joy said vaguely to her doctor and hung up. She didn't want anything to spoil Camille's graduation from Stanford, and if she told Christophe, he would be so worried that Camille would sense it. It could wait three months. What difference would it make? If the cancer had come back, Joy feared she was probably doomed anyway. She needed time to face the reality of it, and called her doctor back three days later. She scheduled the surgery for the week after Camille's graduation, and the doctor offered a compromise. He suggested three sessions of radiation before the surgery, to shrink whatever was there, and she agreed, and said nothing to her husband or her daughter. She went to the city when Christophe was in Los Angeles for the day. The second time, she went when he had to fly to Dallas, and the third time when he was at a vintners' conference at Sam Marshall's, so she had all three sessions of radiation before Camille's graduation, and no one ever knew.

She was dreading the mastectomy, and debating reconstructive surgery. The doctor told her they were going to use a more aggressive form of chemotherapy this time, and he was cautiously confident that with the surgery, chemo, and radiation, that would do it. She wanted to believe him, but she didn't.

When Camille came home for a weekend with two friends before graduation, Joy acted as though everything was normal, but she felt as though she was moving underwater. She had to get through the graduation, the surgery, and a year of chemotherapy and radiation after that.

The graduation ceremony was beautiful and everything Camille hoped it would be, and it reminded Joy of her own. There were tearful goodbyes with her college friends, and a long ride back to Napa, with all her belongings in the winery van they'd brought with them. They gave a dinner for her the next day at L'Auberge du Soleil. And two days later, Joy told them, and they looked like she had dropped a bomb on them, the same one that had dropped on her with the bad news of the malignancy in her right breast. Christophe and Camille cried and were shocked. Joy tried not to fall apart, for their sakes, and they all promised each other that she'd be fine, and no one mentioned Barbara Marshall. Christophe clung to Joy in bed that night, and she felt his tears on her face.

"I'm going to be okay," she promised him as she held him.

"I know you will. You have to be. Camille and I need you." She nodded and couldn't speak, and then she lay awake while he slept, thinking about how much she loved them, and how unfair life could be at times, how cruel. They had such a wonderful life, and this horror had come to spoil it, for the second time. She just prayed that they were right and she'd be cured again. She had to be. For their sakes.

The surgery went as smoothly as possible, and Joy was home at Château Joy in a week, moving slowly, but within another week she was back in her office. There was so much she wanted to teach Camille now and show her, just in case, so she could help her father if she had to, and while Joy was sick.

Camille was a quick student, and learned her lessons rapidly. She knew what her mother was going through, and thought it would help ease the burdens on her during chemo.

Four weeks later, the treatments began. She had them at the hospital in Napa again, so she didn't have to waste time going into the city. And she was just as sick as last time, and started losing her hair shortly after she began chemo. She brought out the wig she'd worn before, which depressed her profoundly. It was a long, painful summer, and by mid-August, Joy couldn't go into the office. It was all she could do to get out of bed for a few minutes and wander around her bedroom at the château, but Camille assured her mother that everything was in control at the office. It was, but Christophe's mood was dark and gloomy, which he never admitted to Joy.

In September, she was too weak and too sick to go to the Harvest

Ball, and Christophe made a rueful comment that he was off the hook, and Joy strenuously objected.

"You can't do that to Sam," Joy said firmly, sounding stronger. "He expects us to be there, and he needs your support now. He continued the ball to honor Barbara, he told me so last year. You have to go. You can take Camille. We're the same size, she can wear my dress. You'll have fun together." He groaned but knew that Joy was right, and Joy had Camille dress in her room, where she could watch her, and helped her with the costume. She looked exquisite when she left with her father, seeming like a young Marie Antoinette. It touched Joy's heart to see them. They drove to the ball in Christophe's Aston Martin, his pride and joy, and Camille suddenly felt very grown up, being out with her father in her mother's costume.

Sam was visibly relieved the moment he saw them arrive. "I'm so glad you came," he said to Christophe, grateful that he had made the effort, and he smiled at Camille, recognizing her even with the mask, and then he looked seriously at her father. "How's Joy doing?"

"It's pretty rough right now, but you know how she is, she's a strong woman. She'll get through it," Christophe said and Sam nodded, hoping he was right.

They ate from the buffet, and there was an amazing seafood bar, champagne and caviar, and vodka for those who preferred it. A roast suckling pig, a table of Indonesian cuisine, and Kobe beef flown in from Japan that you could cut with a fork. The food was superb, and the wines Sam's best. The guests were dancing to the ten-piece orchestra, and it was difficult to recognize people when they wore their masks.

Camille had taken hers off when Phillip came up to her. She had seen him with a gorgeous girl who looked like a model, but he left her for a few minutes to talk to Camille, whom he hadn't seen in months, since her mother got sick and even before. He had been away helicopter skiing over Christmas when she was home, and other than occasional chance meetings in St. Helena, their paths didn't cross often anymore. He was busy, so much older, and they moved in different crowds, and Camille had been at home helping her mother, and driving her to chemo all summer. She hadn't even been into town to do errands, she hated to leave her.

"I'm sorry your mom is sick," Phillip said kindly. "Congratulations on your graduation, by the way. Welcome to the working world." He always teased her and she smiled, but he noticed she seemed tired and worried, and he felt sorry for her. "I'll have to come and visit one of these days," he promised and smiled back at her. His father had said he wanted to visit Joy too, but didn't want to intrude while she was so sick. Camille noticed that his date, standing several feet away, appeared impatient and annoyed at their exchange. Camille was no threat. Phillip still thought she was a baby and saw her that way, even in her mother's elaborate costume. She felt like a little girl play-ing dress up around him. "I'd better get back," he said, with a glance over her shoulder to his date, and Camille nodded.

She danced with her father once, and then they left the ball and drove home. It had been tiring more than fun, with five hundred people there. The property looked beautiful with decorations and lines of topiary trees they'd rented, and so much going on. Her father had greeted a lot of people he knew, and he seemed tired too. They were both worried about Joy, and she was fast asleep when they got home. Camille kissed her father good night, and went to her own room down the hall, happy to get out of the costume, take off the white wig, and put on her nightgown.

Joy wanted to know all about it the next day, and Christophe made it sound like more fun than it had been. After giving her mother breakfast, and helping her tie a scarf to cover her bald head, since she didn't wear the wig all the time, Camille went to her office, even though it was Saturday. She wanted to catch up on work, and it was a good distraction from the reality of what they were living. Joy was fading away and there was nothing they could do to stop it. Christophe was in denial and kept telling Joy she was winning the fight, but she didn't look it. She had lost a shocking amount of weight, and as the harvest continued in their vineyards, she slept most of the time. She had no idea what was happening outside her room.

She had another chemo treatment scheduled, but her white blood count was too high and she was too weak, so they postponed it. She kept remembering things to tell Camille, and kept a little notepad next to her bed so she wouldn't forget them. It was as though she was trying to empty her mind into Camille's, everything she knew about the winery and how to run it, and all the things she needed to do to help her father. And finally, for the last few days, nature took over and Joy slept all the time, and one by one her systems shut down. She spent her last night dozing and smiling in Christophe's arms, as Camille came in and out of the room to check on them. She was sitting quietly next to her father, holding his hand, when her mother took her last breath, and then she drifted away, as Christophe held her, and Camille sat next to her on the bed and cried silently. And then they held each other, but Joy was at peace by then, she was gone.

The funeral was serious and dignified, in the church that Camille had filled with white flowers. Every important vintner in the Valley was there, and many lesser ones, along with their friends, employees, and vineyard workers. The men wore suits, and the women proper dresses. Sam Marshall was one of the pallbearers, and after the service, Phillip came over and hugged Camille with tears running down his cheeks. There was nothing he could say to her, and they clung to each other like children who fully understood how much pain the other was in. It didn't need words.

"I'm so sorry," he whispered before he left her, and he drove away with his father in the red Ferrari. It brought back their own loss when Phillip's mother died nearly four years before.

Hundreds of people came to the château afterward. Camille had had the winery caterers set out a buffet of sandwiches, salads, and light food, and Christophe opened their best wines, which everyone appreciated. It was a terrible day for Christophe and Camille. Neither of them could imagine life without Joy. She had been the strength and the backbone of all they did, and he recognized that she had not only been the foundation of everything he did, she was the inspiration and magic too. Camille realized why her mother had rushed so frantically to teach her everything she could. She had known that she was dying, and now it was up to Camille to take care of her father and help run the winery. Whether she wanted to or not, she had to follow in her mother's footsteps. The future of Château Joy rested on her now too. It was an awesome burden to carry, and she would have to find a way to do it, no matter what it took.

Chapter Three

On the Monday after her mother's funeral, feeling like she had lead in her bones, Camille forced herself to get out of bed, shower, and put on clothes, and went downstairs to make breakfast for her father, the way her mother used to before she got sick. Christophe had been making his own, while Camille took care of her mother. But now she wanted to do it for him. Raquel, their housekeeper, would be in later to clean and leave dinner for them, but she had to get her children off to school in the morning, and came to work at ten o'clock.

Camille handed her father the newspaper and poured him a cup of coffee, and he looked up at her in surprise. He hadn't expected her to be downstairs yet, and was impressed to see her so wide awake and organized. She was so much like her mother, it always made him smile.

"I have a lot to do in the office today," she said quietly as she set a plate of scrambled eggs down in front of him, just the way he liked them, with two crisp strips of bacon and whole wheat toast.

"Did your mom tell you to do this for me?" he asked with tears in his eyes, and Camille shook her head. She hadn't. She didn't need to. Camille knew what she had to do. There was no one else to take care of him now.

Camille made herself a piece of toast, and wrote a list of everything she had to do that day. She had let some of the ledger work slide the week before. And she had promised her mother she'd check Cesare's accounts again.

She knew how painful it was going to be, being in the office and not seeing her mother. And her father looked like a ghost. In the last few days, her mother had whispered to her several times "take care of him," before she drifted back to sleep, and Camille intended to do that, and be diligent at the office. She felt as though her childhood was over. She had to be a grown-up now, and be there for her father. He was used to a strong woman at his side, and Camille knew he would be lost without Joy.

They walked to the office together after breakfast. Her father disappeared to his part of the building, and Camille went to her office next to her mother's, which was silent and empty now. When she walked in, she found Cesare going through some papers on her mother's desk, and he jumped when he saw Camille.

"What are you doing in here?" she asked him bluntly, and he shrugged and said that he was looking for his expense accounts.

"I gave them to her last week, and I can't find my copy of them. I was going to copy hers."

"She hasn't been here since August," Camille corrected him in a firm voice. He always lied, which drove Joy crazy.

"Well, then I gave them to her before that. You know what I mean." He looked irritated, and tried to sound intimidating when he spoke to Camille, as though she was just a kid. But she was far from it, especially now. She owed it to her mother to keep things in good order, and she had the know-how to do it, whether Cesare believed it or not.

"No, I don't know what you mean. And don't just come in here and dig around on her desk. If you want something, ask me for it. A lot of her files are in my office now anyway, including the expense accounts. They're in my safe," she said, which wasn't true, but she didn't want him snooping through the papers on her desk either. It was a presumptuous thing for him to do, and typical of him. Because Christophe valued him so highly, Cesare took full advantage of it.

"Then give me my expense account," he said rudely. "I want to add some things to it, and get paid out. I haven't been reimbursed in months."

"Yes, you have. I saw her sign a check to you the last time she was in the office."

"It was only part of what she owed me," he said stubbornly, trying to bully Camille, and raising his voice. He was agitated and waving his arms as he talked to her, just as he often did with Joy.

"I'll go through my files. But if you have additional expenses, I need the receipts." She was matter-of-fact about it.

"What did she do? Teach you how to drive me crazy, just like her? Receipts, receipts, always receipts. You think I'm stealing from you? That's what she thought." Camille suspected her mother was right. Not big amounts, but small ones from the vineyard expenses which seemed okay to him.

"Don't you think it's a little soon to be complaining about your expense account? The funeral was on Saturday. I'll get everything squared away this week. Just give me the receipts," she said coldly.

He glared at her, stomped out of the room, and slammed the door, just as he had with her mother, and Camille smiled after he left.

Some things were apparently never going to be different, like Cesare not having receipts to justify his expenditures, and Camille knew her father let him get away with it. It was unlikely to change now.

Camille checked on her father several times that morning, and went through some of her mother's files that afternoon. Christophe had lunch with two new vintners, and Camille ate a salad at her desk.

The week seemed endless without her mother, and the nights were long and sad. Her father went to bed every night at eight o'clock, and she lay in her bed reading some of the files she brought back from the office. But by the end of the week, she was caught up. She hadn't let herself fall behind, even when her mother was sick. Work was how she had kept her sanity while her mother was dying.

Thanksgiving was difficult, and Christmas was awful. They had Thanksgiving alone in their kitchen. Christophe said he didn't want turkey, and had turned down all the invitations they'd had. He said it was too soon for him to want to go out, and Camille didn't want to either, so she made a leg of lamb, French style, with lots of garlic and mashed potatoes and string beans, it was surprisingly good. Her father had taught her how to make it years before, while she watched him cook. And somehow they got through the day. Christmas was even worse.

Camille bought the gifts they needed for their employees, and she got a number of small, thoughtful gifts for her father, the kinds of things Joy would have found for him, and a cashmere sweater that Camille knew he'd love. She had two of the vineyard workers help her set up a tree at the château, and Raquel helped her decorate it. Her father looked miserable when he got home and saw it. And he had been mournful at their office Christmas party. Sam Marshall had invited them to join them on Christmas Eve, knowing how hard this

Christmas would be for them, having been through it, but Christophe declined that too. He hadn't accepted any invitations to Christmas parties this year. Joy had been gone for two and a half months, and the wound was very fresh, for Camille too. But she was so busy taking care of her father that she had no time to think of anything else, except work. The mission given to her by her mother was to take care of him, and she was trying to.

They went to midnight mass on Christmas Eve, and for a bike ride the next day after they exchanged gifts, and Camille was relieved that the holidays were almost over. They were agonizing this year. She knew it would get better, but these early months were hard to live through, and she missed her mother too. She knew her father was trying to make the best of it, but he had been loved and cared for by an adoring wife for twenty-three years, and getting used to being on his own again was excruciating for him, even with Camille trying to anticipate his every mood and need.

She would have liked to catch up with her old friends home for the holidays, but didn't want to leave her father alone, and even on New Year's Eve he wound up going to bed at nine o'clock and she watched TV alone. The next day, he said he was going to have to start traveling again for business in January. It was a relief to hear him say it. He had neglected all their big accounts since Joy got sick. Camille knew she would miss him while he was away, but it was better for him to keep busy, and get out in the world again. It was healthier for him than remaining plunged in his mourning day after day.

His first trip was to Britain, Switzerland, and France, and he stopped to see his family in Bordeaux for a weekend. He looked better to Camille when he got back, and seemed more alive than he had in months. He had even picked up a new account in London. They had salesmen and reps to handle the more ordinary accounts, but for all the years they'd been in business, Christophe visited the most important accounts himself, and it served them well. He was a charming, intelligent man, and knew everything there was to know about viticulture. He had lived it all his life, in France and in the States. And no one promoted their wines better than he did. He was planning a trip to Italy and Spain in March, Holland and the Low-lands sometime in April, and was thinking about Japan, Hong Kong, and Shanghai in May. He had a lot of catching up to do with their big foreign clients.

He was just back from his trip to Italy in March, which had gone well, when he was invited to a big dinner for the more important vintners in the Napa Valley, and Camille asked him at dinner in their kitchen that night if he was going. It had been lonely while he was away, but she had her hands full with all the work she was trying to keep up with. She had a lot on her plate, and she was exhausted and had a bad cold when he got home.

"I'm jet-lagged, and I don't want to go," he said, helping himself sparingly to Raquel's tacos, which he usually loved. He had lost a lot of weight since Joy died.

"It would be good for you, Papa," she said, encouraging him. "I'm sure Sam is going, why don't you go with him?" It pained her to see him so sad all the time.

"I'm sure he'd rather take a date than go with me," her father said glumly, tired after the trip.

"Is he still dating the congresswoman from LA?" She knew about it vaguely, but never saw him with her, although Barbara had been gone for a long time now. Sam Marshall was an attractive man, but he kept his private life to himself and out of sight.

"I think he is, but he doesn't talk about it," Christophe commented. "Why do you think that is?"

"I think she's careful to avoid the press, and she stays away from the social scene up here." Even though they were good friends, he and Sam never discussed it and Christophe didn't want to pry. They talked about their grapes, not his love life. "She's about his age, and a very nice, intelligent woman. I don't think she wants her involvement with him in the press. I've seen him in St. Helena with her a couple of times, but it's always very low key. He introduced me to her, just by first names, but I knew who she was."

"Do you suppose Phillip knows?" She wondered how he felt about it, and if Sam would marry again.

"Probably. She's not the kind of woman who wants anything from him, which must be a nice change." Every gold digger in the Napa Valley had been after him since his wife's death, and he had become proficient at avoiding them, and a congresswoman from LA sounded impressive to Camille and interesting for Sam. She wondered if her father would find someone like that eventually, but he was still too much in love with his late wife to even want to go out to dinner with friends, let alone start dating. Joy was a hard act to follow, and would be for a long time, Camille knew.

"You should go to the vintners' dinner, Papa. It would do you good."

"Would you go with me?" he asked cautiously.

"I'm sick, my nose is red, and I have a ton of work to do." She hadn't been social since her mother's death either, but her father was more depressed than she was, and she was worried about him. At least he was traveling again.

"I'll think about it," he said vaguely, and didn't seem like he would. "We should go away for a weekend somewhere one of these days," he said kindly. "You haven't had any fun in a long time either." She was touched that he had noticed. He had been totally absorbed in his own misery for the last five months but she was managing and busy with work. She'd been emailing and texting with her friends from school to stay in touch, particularly with those far away. It was hard to believe she had graduated only nine months ago. It felt like an eternity.

The next day her father surprised her when she got home from work and saw him leaving the house in a suit and tie. All she wanted was to climb into bed. Her cold had gotten worse.

"I'm going to the vintners' dinner," he said, embarrassed. "You were right, Sam is going. I said I'd meet him there." Camille's face broke into a broad smile. He had listened to her after all.

"I'm glad, Papa. You look terrific. Great tie."

"I just bought it in Rome." It was a vivid pink Hermès tie, and unlike him to wear anything so bright, but it made him appear upbeat and young, which was a major change after the last five months, when he had looked like he had dressed blindfolded every day, and pulled something old and tired out of his closet, mostly in black and gray, which suited the way he felt.

"Well, have fun at the dinner," she said cheerfully, as he headed toward his car.

"I doubt it. Just a lot of boring old vintners talking about chemicals, barrels, and their tonnage last season. I may fall asleep." He smiled at her.

"Tell Sam to wake you up," she said, blew him a kiss, and closed the door to the château as he drove away in his racy sports car.

But the party wasn't at all what he expected when he got there. It was the usual crowd of important vintners, all of whom he knew, mixed with one or two smaller ones. There were a few members of the Napa social scene, whom he also knew and didn't care for, and some new faces he'd never seen before, who seemed like pretentious wannabe wine connoisseurs to him. He felt suddenly uncomfortable once he got there, and realized that he'd have to talk to people he didn't know, and make a social effort that seemed beyond him for the moment. It was a seated dinner, with escort cards indicating which table you were placed at, and he saw from the chart on an easel that his seat was between two women he'd never met, which felt awkward to him. The party was at the home of one of the older vintners, and he saw Sam talking to their host across the room when he walked in, and didn't want to interrupt.

Christophe accepted a glass of the host's white wine from a waiter with a silver tray, and he stood there for a moment, sipping his wine and feeling lost. It was the first time he had gone to a dinner without Joy, he missed her fiercely as he wished he hadn't come and had gone to bed instead.

"What a wonderful tie!" a female voice with a French accent said. Christophe turned and found himself gazing at a tall, thin woman who was very fashionably dressed. She had dark hair pulled tightly back in a bun, was wearing a severe black suit, and she looked very stylish for the Napa scene. She had bright red lips, a broad smile, dancing eyes that appeared to be full of mischief, and she was undeniably French. He hadn't seen a woman like her in a long time. She had a heavy gold bracelet on one arm, and was wearing sexy stiletto heels.

"Thank you," he said politely for the remark about his tie, with no idea what to say to her after that. He had been married for a long time and he felt stiff and strange being out without his wife. He wondered what Joy would have thought of the Frenchwoman as she smiled at him. "I just bought it in Rome," he said, for lack of something better to say.

"One of my favorite cities. All of Italy in fact. Venice, Florence, Rome. Were you there on business?" He nodded. He felt foolish speaking English to her since they were both French, but her English was quite good, and after twenty-five years in the States, his was excellent, with only a slight accent.

"Are you visiting the Napa Valley?" he asked, switching into French, and she smiled.

"I just moved here from Paris. Where are you from?" she asked, curious about him.

"Originally, Bordeaux. I've lived here for a long time."

"You must be a vintner if you're here tonight," she said admiringly. "Would I know which one?"

"Château Joy," he said modestly, and her eyes opened wide.

"My favorite pinot noir. What an honor to meet you," she said with just the right amount of effervescence. She was seductive without trying to be, and very French. American women didn't flirt like that, nor did American men. They talked about business and sports. Men and women were more provocative in their conversations in France and their style in addressing each other. But he was out of practice and didn't want to play the game with her. He hadn't flirted with a woman since he met Joy.

"What made you move to the Napa Valley?" He wasn't really curious about her, but it seemed the right thing to say, and put the conversational burden on her.

"My husband died six months ago," she said simply. "We had a château in Périgord, but it's too sad in the winter, and I needed a change of scene."

"That's very brave of you," he said and meant it. "It's not easy moving somewhere you don't know anyone."

"You must have done it, when you came here from Bordeaux," she said easily, wanting to know more about him.

"I was twenty-six years old when I moved to Napa. Everything is easy at that age. I came here at twenty-five to take some classes, and decided to build a winery here." She smiled at what he said.

"That was brave of you too." It had been, but it hadn't felt that way at the time, especially with Joy's help.

"I lost my wife five months ago," he said and then regretted saying it, but she had mentioned being widowed for six months, which had opened the door for him.

"It's a tremendous adjustment, isn't it?" she said gently. "I'm still feeling rather lost." She lowered her eyes for a moment and then looked back up at him. She seemed suddenly very vulnerable despite her stylish appearance, and he knew just how she felt. "My husband was a great deal older, and he was in ill health for the last few years, but it's still a terrible shock." Christophe nodded, thinking of Joy, and he didn't speak for a moment, and then Sam came over to say hello to him, and greeted the woman Christophe had been talking to.

"Good evening, Countess," he said, almost in a mocking tone, and chatted with Christophe for a few minutes, while he ignored her.

"You two know each other?" Christophe asked them, and Sam nodded.

"We've met," the woman he had called "Countess" said coolly, with a mildly flirtatious glance at Sam that he pointedly ignored and walked away.

They were called in to dinner a few minutes later, and Christophe found himself sitting next to her, with a very elderly woman on his other side, who was talking to the person next to her, and didn't speak to Christophe.

"Do you have children here with you?" Christophe asked her after they sat down.

"I have two sons in Paris, who are coming over this summer. But they have lives in France. One is a banker, the other is at university. They don't want to move here. My husband had children my age, but we're not close," she said with regret, and Christophe didn't question her about them. It seemed like a painful subject to her, and if she'd been that much younger than her husband, maybe they were jealous of her. She was a very attractive woman, and appeared to be in her mid-forties or possibly younger, but in fact, she was his exact age. "Do you have children?" she asked him, seeming interested in everything about him. She was socially adept, and very smooth.

"I have a daughter. She just graduated from college last year, and she works at the winery with me. Her mother did too. It's a family run business."

"How wonderful for you, to have your daughter close to you." He nodded and noticed that her place card said "Countess de Pantin," so she was using her title, which must have impressed people in the States, although it didn't affect him one way or another, having grown up with lots of titles around him. He was more impressed by how open, warm, and intelligent she was.

They talked about his recent trip to Italy, she asked lots of questions about the winery, and said that she had been a model at Dior in her youth, and had met her husband then, when he was shopping with his mistress and fell in love with her. They both laughed, the scenario sounded very French. She politely turned to the man on her other side after that and chatted with him, and Christophe lapsed into silence for a while, musing about their conversation then inevitably thinking of Joy again, wishing he was there with her. He and the countess chatted briefly over coffee, and she said that she was starting to give little dinner parties, to get to know people in the area, and make some friends. It sounded admirable to him, and more than he could have done at the moment. Entertaining alone seemed unbearably depressing to him.

"How would I get in touch with you?" she asked him as they left the table, and he mentioned the name of his winery again. "Of course." And then she disappeared and he talked to Sam for a few minutes, thanked the vintner who had hosted the dinner, and then left. He saw the countess in the parking lot, waiting to get her car from the valet, as she lit a cigarette, which surprised him, but she was French, and he was used to Frenchwomen smoking, whenever he visited his family in France. They had left Christophe's Aston Martin out front, and he got in it with a wave to her, as another valet brought her car, a Mercedes. The countess smiled at Christophe as he drove away, and she thought about him on her way home to the house she had rented for six months. It was a showplace that had been built on spec and was up for sale, and most likely to appeal to newcomers to the Napa Valley, who wanted to impress their new neighbors and get their house in a magazine. She already knew she was going to invite him to dinner, she just didn't know when. And she was going to invite Sam Marshall too. He was someone she'd like to know better as well.

Christophe saw the light on in Camille's bedroom when he got home, knocked, and opened the door to say good night to her. She was blowing her nose and smiled when she saw him.

"Did you have fun?" she asked hopefully.

"Not really," he said honestly. He'd been lonely going out on his own, but at least he had made the effort and even wore his new tie. "But I met some new people. A French countess who just moved here from Paris."

"How fancy," Camille commented with a smile and he nodded agreement.

"She probably won't stay here long. She's a little too glamorous for the Valley, but she has two sons coming to visit this summer. Maybe they'd be fun for you to meet." Camille nodded and blew her nose again. But at least her father had gone to the dinner. It was a first step back into the world, and she was proud of him. She somehow imagined the countess as very grand and very old, and was glad her father had good company for the evening. He blew her a kiss and closed the door after telling her he hoped her cold would be better in the morning.

"Thank you. I love you, Papa. I'm glad you went tonight."

He smiled, thinking of the very elegant countess. "Me too." He wondered if she really would ask him to dinner, but he didn't care either way. He was thinking of Joy as he went back to his room, and how much fun it had always been, talking to her about the evening when they got home from dinner parties. But all of that was history now. He smiled at her photograph on his night table as he got into bed a few minutes later, and whispered to her as he turned off the light. "Good night, my love." And he knew there wasn't another woman like her in the world.

Chapter Four

Christophe forgot about meeting the countess, and was busy in the vineyards. They had a late frost two days after he'd gone to the vintners' dinner, and he was up all night making sure there were heaters working in all the vineyards, and the cold snap didn't damage their grapes. The heaters were old-fashioned, but effective. A severe frost could have hurt their crop for the entire year. But fortunately it didn't last long, and he and Cesare were up till dawn, doing everything they could to protect the vines. Cesare was tireless in situations like that, which was part of Christophe's deep respect for him, which Joy had never fully understood.

Cesare had been trained in all the European traditions, as Christophe had been, and both men had added modern American techniques to their repertoire. Cesare fully grasped and was proud of his responsibilities as vineyard manager, which made him a kind of "farmer in chief" for the winery, overseeing the ongoing health and safety of the vines, from frost, pests, and other damages. And planting new vines, when they did. He could sense a problem almost before it happened. He saw to it that their crews were always organized and ready to work, their equipment sound. And he made sure that the leaves were pulled, the clusters trimmed, and the grapes picked at exactly the right time. Cesare communicated constantly with Christophe and consulted with him, deferring to his employer, and he was willing to be on call twenty-four hours a day. Every aspect of Château Joy's wine production and their grapes was his priority, and his intuition was flawless, far more than Joy gave him credit for. She thought he was a crusty, cantankerous, dishonest old man, despite his meticulous attention to their wine. To Christophe, it was worth putting up with Cesare cheating them of a few dollars on his expense account, but to Joy it was a capital offense.

Camille found Cesare's constant haggling over a few pennies, and his lies when it suited him, character flaws she had a hard time ignoring, and didn't want to. She knew how important he was to her father and the winery, but she wanted to protect their finances too. And Cesare had begun to carry his grievances with Joy over to her daughter, and disliked her almost as much as he had her mother. He and Camille argued constantly now, mostly about petty things.

Cesare had never married and had no children. He had been a charmer and a womanizer in his youth, although he had calmed down somewhat in middle age, and his looks had faded with time. He wasn't unaware of Camille's beauty, and readily admitted that she was an exquisite girl, but he thought the harshness of character she had inherited from her mother, as he saw it, made her unattractive as a woman, and he wasn't afraid to tell her so, which didn't endear him to her either. They were constantly at odds with each other, unreasonably so, Christophe thought.

"You'll wind up an old maid if you're not careful," Cesare warned her, when she had just challenged his latest accounts. He thought any insult was fair revenge. "Men don't like women who argue over money," he informed her. "I thought you were going back to university for business school," he added hopefully. He had already mentioned it several times since her mother's death. He couldn't wait for her to leave. Christophe never gave him the problems Joy and Camille had, and he put it down to their being American. He had always preferred European women, even though he had left Italy thirty years before.

"I'm not going back to school for another two or three years," Camille reminded him again. "Besides, my father needs me here," she said with determination.

"He can hire another secretary to replace you," he said dismissively, pushing his battered straw hat down on his unruly mane of gray hair that went in all directions in crazy corkscrew curls. He had turned into a cranky old man, particularly with her, since neither she nor her mother had ever been vulnerable to his alleged charm. And he had grown heavier with all the pasta he ate. He was a wonderful cook, but Joy had turned down all his dinner invitations. Christophe occasionally dined with him alone, and Cesare prepared fabulous pasta meals for him, while they sat talking late into the night about the vineyards and what they could do to improve their wine.

Christophe enjoyed his company, but the women in his family did not. Cesare was opinionated and querulous and had only one use for women. He didn't think they belonged in business, and surely not running a winery, which he insisted only a man could truly understand. His lack of respect for Camille showed in his eyes and his manner when he spoke to her. He hadn't been quite as bold with her mother, since Joy didn't hesitate to get fierce with him, and occasionally they shouted at each other. Camille was gentler and respectful of his age, she had grown up with him as a fixture in her life, but she agreed with her mother about his loose relationship with the truth and money. He was a constant headache. But Christophe was kind and fair to his employees, and valued each of them for what they had to offer, despite their failings. He always saw both sides of the coin, as he did in Cesare's case.

"You'll wind up alone," Cesare warned Camille again as he strode out of her office, muttering to himself in Italian as he always did when he'd been caught at something, had no defense, and was angry about it. Just shy of twenty-three, she wasn't worried. And the last thing she heard from him as he disappeared was some derogatory comment about American women. Her father passed him in the hall, Cesare rolled his eyes at him, and Christophe walked into Camille's office with a questioning look. She got along with everyone else.

"Problem with Cesare?" He wasn't upset about it, but saw that his daughter was annoyed, in just the way her mother used to be whenever she had to deal with him.

"The usual, he added twenty-seven dollars to his expense account. I don't know why he bothers."

"You should just let it go. He makes up for it in other ways. He was up with me all night twice this week when the weather turned cold." It had warmed up again, and no harm had been done to their crops. "If we paid him overtime, we'd owe him a lot more than the twenty-seven dollars he adds to his expenses. He can't help himself. It's cultural, it's a game to him to try and get something extra for free. It used to drive your mother crazy, and it wasn't worth the energy she spent on it." But Joy had been a precise woman, she balanced their books down to the penny, and she believed that honesty was a black or white quality, you had it or you didn't. And she often quoted a French proverb to Christophe that he had taught her when they first met, "Who steals an egg would steal a cow." She believed it, and applied it to their vineyard manager regularly. She was always convinced he was hiding greater dishonesty and was capable of stealing more, and devoted herself to making sure he didn't.

"Mom never trusted him," Camille reminded her father and he smiled ruefully.

"Believe me, I know."

They chatted for a few minutes, and Camille went back to work on her computer. Everything in their big leather-bound vineyard ledgers was on the computer, but Christophe loved the old-fashioned traditions and wanted the ledgers kept up to date too, which had been double the work for Joy, and now Camille. He believed in modernization, but only to a point. And Camille had a marketing idea she wanted to discuss with him, which involved using social media to a greater degree to promote their wines, but she was waiting for the right moment to bring it up. And she knew Cesare would be hostile to it. He thought all things modern were dangerous and a waste of time, and he often swayed Christophe in that direction. It was Joy who had kept Christophe moving forward with the times, with her innovative ideas and excellent business plans to grow their business and keep it solid, and now it would fall to Camille to carry on where she left off, with even younger ideas.

Camille could already see a dozen ways to modernize their business and was excited to talk to her father about it, at the right time. She wanted to put some new concepts in place by summer, and she hoped her father would be open to it. Christophe was unpredictable that way. Joy had always been able to convince him, and he had enormous respect for her financial acumen and sound ideas. Camille knew she still had to prove herself to him, and in some ways, he still saw her as a little girl, and she looked like one. Camille had always appeared younger than her years. She had her mother's fine features, but her long blond hair and the big blue eyes she had inherited from her father reminded everyone of Alice in Wonderland at times, which she knew made it hard for men like Cesare to take her seriously. But he hadn't respected Joy either, and in fact was somewhat scared of her since she didn't hesitate to go toe to toe with him. Camille had a gentler style, and she was younger, but Christophe knew she was every bit as smart as her mother, and would be more than capable of stepping into her mother's shoes, and even running their winery one day. Just not yet, and he didn't want to be overrun with modern ideas that were too high tech. He wanted to keep the traditional European aura to their label, it had worked well for them so far, no matter how modern Joy got things behind the scenes. The combination of their personalities and ideas had been a huge success.

When he got back to his office after his brief visit to Camille, Christophe was surprised when his young assistant said that there was a Countess de Pantin on the phone for him. At first, the name meant nothing to him, and his mind went blank, and then he remembered the Frenchwoman he had sat next to at the vintners' dinner. He didn't expect to see her again, despite her allusion to a future invitation, which he hadn't taken seriously and didn't care about. It was one of those social things people said politely, like "Let's have lunch sometime." In most cases, sometime never came. And she was far grander than he was, in her elegant black Parisian suit and fashionable accessories. She had said she was only planning to stay in the Valley for six months for a change of scene. The chance that they'd meet again wasn't great, especially staying home with his daughter at night, which was his preference, now that Joy was gone and he was a widower. It was a role he hadn't adjusted to yet.

He picked up the phone, and the elegant countess greeted him in French, and then switched to English. "Bonjour, Christophe!" she said, sounding almost as though they were old friends, and he could hear laughter in her voice. She had a light tone that was an instant upper, unlike some of the noble Frenchwomen he remembered from his youth, who took themselves very seriously, depending on their rank and title. He could tell she didn't, and liked that about her. She seemed like a happy person, although she was recently widowed too. But her husband had been much older, and sick for several years, she had said, so maybe losing him had been less of a shock than losing Joy at forty-nine, while she was still strong and beautiful and they had been so happy together, and thought they had long years ahead of them. He was still bereft and felt robbed to have lost her.

"I'm so sorry to bother you at the office," the countess apologized. "Is this a bad time?"

"Not at all." He smiled as he listened to her. She had a lovely voice.

"I won't keep you long. I've just organized a little dinner party, on short notice, for next Saturday. Just a dozen people at my rented house. I might as well enjoy it, and I've been meeting so many interesting new people. I hope you can come." He didn't need to look at a calendar. He had no social engagements, although he was leaving for his trip to Holland soon, but he would be home on the date she mentioned. He just wasn't sure if he was ready for a social life as a single man, in fact he was certain he wasn't, but he didn't want to be rude to her, and she was in the same boat he was. She was trying to make the best of it, which made him feel obligated to make the effort too. He couldn't play the recently widowed card with her, and thought it might make him sound pathetic. And Sam Marshall had survived it, so could he.

"It will be very informal," she added, "just jeans and a blazer for the men, you needn't wear a tie, although your pink tie the other night was divine. I'll have to give another dinner so you can wear it again," she teased him, and he was surprised she had remembered it.

"I'd love to come," he responded, flattered to be asked, although he had no idea if he'd be facing a room full of strangers, or people he knew. He dreaded running into people he knew slightly who hadn't heard of Joy's death, whom he had to explain it to, and tell them the bad news. It had happened to him several times at meetings, and while doing errands around St. Helena and Yountville, and the explanations were painful. But it couldn't be avoided at first, unless he stayed home and became a recluse, which was tempting at times, but he knew that wasn't healthy either, or good for Camille. For her sake, he had to at least pretend to be doing better, although he didn't think he was. He still shed a few tears for Joy every day, mostly when he went to bed at night, or woke up in the half-empty bed. During the day, he was busy. "Thank you for inviting me, Countess," he said politely and she laughed.

"Please. Call me Maxine, unless you expect me to address you as Monsieur Lammenais, and call you *vous* in French," she said referring to the formal case used between strangers and very formal people. She was more informal than that, and sounded relaxed talking to him.

"Thank you, Maxine." She told him the time and date and gave him her address. It was appropriately on a road called "Money Lane," which suited some of the extravagant houses that had been recently built there, and some old ones. And from the look of her, and her style, he doubted that the house she had rented for six months would be modest.

"I'm bringing a French chef up from the city, from Gary Danko's, I hope you'll approve." He was impressed again. She was apparently going all out for her small dinner party, which didn't surprise him. Gary Danko was the fanciest restaurant in San Francisco, and the meal would be elaborate. He thanked her again and they hung up, and he got busy at his desk, planning his next trip to Europe and emailing the people he was hoping to meet with, and forgot about her dinner by that afternoon. He had other things on his mind, and he was startled the next day when a delivery boy arrived with a thick creamy white envelope addressed to him in an elegant handwriting in dark brown ink with the initials "B.H." written in the lower left-hand corner of the envelope, indicating it had been delivered by hand to him, and not by mail. And when he opened the envelope, he saw a matching cream-colored card with a gold crest engraved on it, and in Maxine's elegant handwriting the words *Pour Memoire,* which meant "reminder" in French, with the details of the dinner. In the style of a true countess, she was following formal French traditions. His other friends in the Valley would have sent him an email or a text to remind him of the dinner, not a card with her crest engraved on it. And she had added in parentheses at the bottom, "So glad you can come. *À bientôt!* M." Until soon.

He left the card on his desk and forgot about it again, after wondering briefly who would be there, and which of the local groups she was courting. She was much more European and traditional than the people he knew in the Napa Valley, even the most important ones,

like Sam and several others. He didn't know what her own back-
ground was, and it didn't matter. She had been married to a count,
which explained her doing things formally.

He remembered the dinner the night before, when he saw a nota-
tion on his calendar and mentioned it to Camille, as they ate the
chicken Raquel had left for them in their kitchen. They hadn't used
the dining room since Joy died, and Christophe didn't want to. He
was happy eating in the kitchen with his daughter.

"I forgot to tell you, I'm going out tomorrow night. I hope you
don't mind." He looked apologetic and Camille was surprised.

"Of course I don't mind. It's good for you to go out. Are you going
to Sam's?" He was the only friend her father was seeing these days,
because he understood best how Christophe felt after losing Joy. But
he was good company for Christophe, and they had gone out for
Mexican dinners a few times, which they both enjoyed. It gave them
a chance to talk about business and the problems they had in common, although Sam's operation was far larger than Christophe's.

"I was invited to a dinner party," Christophe said, as they finished
dinner. "It sounds a little grand to me, but I felt awkward turning it
down." Camille was glad he hadn't. He needed to see people, and
Camille knew her mother would have wanted him to, and had said
as much to Camille before she died. She didn't want him to lock himself up and mourn her forever. He needed a life, and even a woman
one day, although Camille couldn't think of that without tears coming to her eyes. She wasn't ready for that yet but neither was he.

"Who's giving it?" Camille asked as she rinsed their dishes.

"A Frenchwoman I sat next to at the vintners' dinner I went to a
few weeks ago. She's here for six months. She just lost her husband.
The one with the two sons I mentioned to you." Camille had as-

sumed that they were much older than she, and the countess an old dowager.

"That sounds nice, Papa." She had an old college friend coming to the Napa Valley for the weekend with his girlfriend, and he had invited her to dinner at Bouchon. She had turned him down so as not to abandon her father for the weekend, and now she could go. She looked pleased. "I'll have dinner with friends tomorrow." He was someone she knew from Stanford who had taken a job in Palo Alto, and she hadn't seen him since they graduated. It would be fun to catch up.

"I should have asked to take you with me," he offered generously, "but I didn't think of it, and to be honest, I think you'd be bored." Camille nodded and agreed.

Camille spent the following day with her friends at Meadowood, where they were staying. It was a hotel and a club, and they were going straight from there for a casual dinner in Yountville, at Bouchon, which she liked. She hadn't previously met her Stanford friend's girlfriend, and she found her lively and fun. She didn't have a date to make it a foursome, but they didn't care, and it was fun for Camille to spend some time with people her own age. She hadn't done that since her mother got sick a year before. Working at the winery and keeping her father company now precluded having anything or anyone else in her life.

Christophe dressed as Maxine had suggested, in pressed jeans, with a white shirt and dark blue blazer Joy had bought him at Hermès in San Francisco, and no tie. She had always kept him properly dressed. Shopping wasn't a pastime that interested him, and he was much happier on a tractor, or in his heavy work boots, walking through his vineyards, but he looked more than respectable and very handsome, when he got into the Aston Martin, and drove to the address the countess had given him. He had her reminder card on the front seat of his car, with her phone number on it too, in case he had a problem or couldn't find the house. But he knew the area well, and was there in fifteen minutes, driving fast from Château Joy.

He rang the buzzer at the gate, a man answered on the intercom, and the gate opened automatically after Christophe said his name. The house was even grander than he had expected. It was a large, sprawling one story house with modern architectural details, manicured gardens, a huge pool, and a pavilion at the end of it where the guests were gathering, drinking mojitos, martinis, and cosmopolitans before dinner, served by a waiter in a starched white jacket. And there was a long dinner table covered with flowers and candles, and gleaming crystal and china on a white tablecloth in the garden next to the house. It looked like a magazine spread, as Maxine drifted toward him in a diaphanous pale pink chiffon dress to the floor, with high-heeled gold sandals, and her long dark hair loose down her back. For an instant, Christophe had an acute pang of missing Joy, although Joy had never owned a dress like this one, and had never entertained as formally.

Joy loved having dinner parties at the château, but they were always cozy and informal, with lively discussions and good music on the stereo. The atmosphere Joy inspired was congenial and warm. Maxine's style was entirely different, elegant and formal, and sophisticated in the extreme. Her clothes were French haute couture, and she was thinner than Joy and taller, and strangely intimate and subtly sexy when she kissed Christophe on both cheeks, French style, as though they were old friends. There was something faintly bold about her, whereas Joy was courageous and strong, but she wasn't as outgoing or effusive as Maxine. Joy was like an acrobat of great skill in everything she did, whereas Maxine was more like a ringmaster, with an eye on everything and every detail as she introduced her guests to each other, most of whom had never met before and all of whom were strangers to Christophe, which was rare for him in the Napa Valley, where he knew almost everyone.

There were two couples from LA who were in movie production and had recently bought sizable vineyards they were planning to run from a distance. Christophe could tell they knew nothing about the wine business, and it was a status symbol for them more than a passion. A Mexican couple whom Christophe had read about but never met—he was one of the richest men in Mexico—and their two bodyguards were standing by at a discreet distance. A couple from Dallas who had made a fortune in oil, and a Saudi couple who had houses all over the world, and had fallen in love with the Napa Valley and were thinking of buying a house there. He had recently bought a hotel and a department store in San Francisco, and thought it would be fun to own a home in the Valley and bring their children over in the summer, when they weren't in the South of France, at their home in Sardinia, or on their yacht in the Mediterranean. The one thing they all had in common was a great deal of money. They were the kind of visitors to the Napa Valley whom Christophe usually avoided. These were a wealthy international set, and the couples from LA and Dallas were blatantly nouveaux riches and anxious to flaunt their new fortunes. They were interesting and pleasant but far more exotic than the kind of people he was normally drawn to. He preferred the serious local vintners, with whom he had a great deal more in common. For him, this was a very racy crowd. His own ancestry in France was dignified, noble, and respectable, but these people all existed in a rarefied world he knew nothing about, and didn't really want to. He noticed that he and Maxine were the only single people among them, but at least they were all strangers and none of them asked him where Joy was or what had happened to her. He found himself seated to Maxine's right at dinner, at the head of the table, which was polite and generous of her, but he was slightly embarrassed to find he was treated like the guest of honor. But despite his initial reservations, the conversation at the dinner table was lively and interesting. They all traveled a great deal, and had discovered the charm of the Napa Valley only recently. The dinner was predictably delicious, with many courses, and he was surprised and touched when he realized that all the red wines that were served at dinner were from the Château Joy label, and everyone complimented him on how excellent they were. She had chosen his best and oldest vintages, and he was proud to see how well they held up in a crowd like this one. The Saudi couple said they preferred it to Château Margaux, and Maxine smiled at him, and he thanked her for serving his wines at dinner, while the others were talking.

"You should have told me, I'd have sent them to you," he said politely as she gently touched his hand, which felt like a butterfly landing on it, and then she moved it away again.

"Of course not, Christophe. You can't just give away your wines. And the man at the wine shop gave me very good advice about which ones to buy." He had selected the most expensive ones, and Christophe knew instantly how extravagant she had been. Some of his wines were more costly than their distinguished French competitors.

Maxine put music on after dinner and some of the couples danced, but Christophe didn't. He couldn't imagine dancing with anyone but Joy, but he enjoyed talking to Maxine and the others by then, and had relaxed. She served strong French fruit liqueurs after dinner, and brandy. And it was one-thirty in the morning when the group began to disband. Much to his surprise, it had been an exceptionally lovely evening, with an excellent meal and a very elite group he would never have met otherwise. Maxine had orchestrated it all with elegance and style, to perfection. This had been no "little dinner party." It was a world class rarity even in the Napa Valley, which was known nowadays for its snobbishness, and newcomers with big money. When he got up to leave after the first guests, she whispered to him, and asked him to stay for a few minutes after the others left.

"It's always so much fun to gossip a little," she said, with a twinkle in her eye, and he laughed. It was the sort of thing he and Joy always did in the car on the ride home from a party, and he nodded, and then realized as the guests left that it made it look as though he was Maxine's date and he was spending the night with her, which made him feel awkward again. But she wasn't inappropriate once they were gone. She took off her very high-heeled gold sandals with the red soles of Christian Louboutin, and sat in one of the lounge chairs next to the pool in her filmy dress and bare feet, and suddenly looked very young, as they chatted about the people at dinner. She told him everything she knew about them, other than the fact that they were very rich. She said that the Mexican man had a sexy young mistress who was a movie star, the woman from Dallas was having an affair with an important vintner, which startled Christophe to hear, and the Saudi had three other wives in Riyadh, whom he didn't travel with or take to dinner parties, but he bought fabulous jewelry at Graff in London for all four of them, and the one who had come to dinner with him was his most important wife and related to the king of

Saudi Arabia. She knew the dirt on all of them, and loved sharing it with Christophe.

"How do you know them?" he asked, both amused and fascinated by her. He had never met a woman like her, and there was something very sensual and enticing about her. And he could clearly sense that she liked him, although he was not in the same league as the others by any means. He had done extremely well, and his family ties were illustrious and successful in France, but he didn't come close to the billions of dollars represented by the fortunes at the table that night.

"I've just met them here and there," she said vaguely. "I tried to get your friend Sam Marshall to come, but he was busy." His secretary had emailed her immediately, he hadn't taken her call.

"To be honest, this wasn't his kind of evening. He wouldn't have enjoyed it. Sam stays in his own world." He was as successful and af-fluent as they were, but lived it differently. He wasn't interested in yachts and fancy houses, although he had a beautiful home, but mostly he engaged in his business, and his life in the Valley, among more down-to-earth people. Christophe came from a more worldly back-ground, and the Saudi knew two of his uncles, who did lead a grand life and summered in the South of France, but Christophe had never been attracted by it. But at least it was familiar to him. Sam would have been like a fish out of water, and hated every minute of it.

"My husband was so much older, and sick for several years, and we lived such a reclusive life once we moved from our house in Paris to his château in Périgord, that even though I miss him terribly, I have been starving to meet people, and there are so many interesting people here. The Napa Valley seems to draw people from all over the world," she said happily, as she smiled at Christophe.

"It does," he agreed, "not always the right people. I have to admit, I prefer spending my time with the people in my business, who own the wineries. But tonight was a rare opportunity for me. I never meet people like them," he said honestly. "You must miss Paris, though, this is a backwater compared to the life you could live there." She was so stylish and elegant, and so worldly that he couldn't imagine her among the more ordinary people in the Valley, even the big vintners like Sam.

She was quiet for a moment, and then looked at him. "You know how complicated French inheritance laws are. My husband had five children, and three-quarters of any estate must go to the children. The division of his property has been incredibly complicated, with them owning three-quarters of everything, and my owning the other quarter. It blocked everything, and they wanted to move back into the house in Paris, and the estate in Périgord. We had no children together, and it was all so unpleasant. I couldn't bear it, it just made me too sad. They were always jealous of me because I was kind to their father. He has four sons who are monsters and a daughter who detests me. My friends told me I was very foolish and much too honorable. But I loved Charles, and I didn't want to see everything he loved torn apart. I took a very small amount and sold my share in everything to them, and I left. I wanted to get as far away from them as possible. I don't even want to see the house in Paris again, it would break my heart. It was my home with him for five years, the happiest years of my life. The château in Périgord was a bit dreary and badly in need of repairs, no one had touched it since his grandparents. And I thought the Napa Valley would be a wonderful change. I have no memories here. It's a fresh start for me. I don't know if I'll stay. I might go to Los Angeles for a while, probably in the fall. Or Dallas, where people are so welcoming, which is how I met the couple who were here tonight. I spent a month there before I came here, and I have an old friend in Houston, who married a Texan from a big oil family. She introduced me to lots of people. But for now, I'm happy here, in Napa. I've had a double loss really, my husband, and our whole way of life. My stepchildren ruined everything for me. They were very unkind to my sons too. They lost their own father last year, who was also very old, and now they've lost their stepfather too. It's been a hard year for us.

"I'm looking for a new home, to start all over again. My boys are happier in France, but I'd like them to spend time here with me. And I have an eighty-seven-year-old mother, I want to bring her over once I settle down. I don't want to move her until I decide where I want to stay."

Christophe hoped she had gotten a handsome settlement from them, for ruining her life, as she described. She was certainly living well in Napa in the rented house, and entertaining lavishly, but it sounded like she had gotten screwed over and severely abused by her stepchildren. And she didn't seem confrontational, she hadn't wanted a legal battle with them, and had given up her share in her husband's estate for a relatively small amount, rather than go to court and fight them. He respected her for that.

"Well, I hope you find the home you're looking for, Maxine," he said sincerely. "You deserve peace of mind, among kind people. The Napa Valley is a wonderful place. There are some very good people here, among the real locals, though they're not as glamorous as your guests tonight," he said kindly, and she looked at him with a grateful smile.

"Thank you, Christophe," she said warmly. He set his glass down then and stood up. It had gotten very late and was almost three in the morning. He had stopped drinking a while earlier and switched to water so he could drive home. He was exhilarated after the evening with her friends, but not drunk.

"I had a wonderful time. Thank you for including me," he said as she walked to his car in her bare feet as the filmy dress floated around her. It was by Nina Ricci in Paris, but he wouldn't have known it, even if she'd told him. All he knew was that she looked beautiful, was intelligent and charming, and had gotten a bad deal from her stepchildren in France. Beyond that, he knew nothing about her, except that she was good company and fun to be with, but he didn't need to know more than that. He wondered if they would become friends, or if she would move on to somewhere else, and was too fancy for the Napa Valley. She probably thought that his life was ridiculously simple, and she wasn't wrong. But he loved his life as it was. And she was a rare butterfly from another world, with jeweled wings and brilliant colors, lovely to watch, but not of his world.

She kissed him on both cheeks again when he left, and then floated into the house, as he drove home in his Aston Martin feeling as though he had spent the evening on a UFO, filled with remarkable, fascinating aliens, and now he had been deposited back to earth. And as always, it was a lonely feeling as he drove home, wishing he could tell Joy all about it. But those days were gone.

Chapter Five

Christophe had breakfast in the kitchen with Camille the morning after Maxine's dinner party. She was wearing tennis clothes, and meeting her friends at Meadowood again, to play tennis with them. It felt good to be with people her age, and who were not in the wine business. Most of the time now it was all she thought about and the people she talked to were her father's age. Her contemporaries had exited her life when she left college and her mother died a few months later.

"What time did you come home last night?" she asked with interest, as she set down a cup of coffee next to him. "I came home at one o'clock, and you weren't back yet. Did you have a good time?" She hoped he had, although he looked serious that morning. He had been thinking of the night before when he woke up. It all had an unreal quality to it now, but he had enjoyed it as a one-of-a-kind evening. He knew he'd never see any of those people again, maybe even Maxine.

"It was amazing and crazy, and fabulous and somewhat weird. It was like being in a film. Movie producers and oilmen, a Saudi couple with houses all over the world, and he has three other wives at home. It was a totally different life. I know it exists here, and more and more in recent years, but your mother and I were never interested in that kind of crowd. But they were surprisingly nice, all of them. I enjoyed the evening." He didn't tell her he had come home at three, which didn't sound respectable.

"What's the countess like? Is she very old?" Camille asked, smiling at him.

"No, not really. By your standards maybe, not by mine. I think she's about forty-five." Camille looked shocked.

"She is? I somehow thought all countesses were old," she said, and he laughed.

"Maybe in the movies. Some countesses have that title at birth. She was married to a very old man, and she's younger than his children. It sounds like they gave her a bad time, with the inheritance laws in France, so she left. She's thinking of settling down here, but I doubt she will. She's a bit too jet set for the Valley, it sounds like she'll move on to LA or Dallas. She's here for another four months."

"Does she work?" Camille was curious about her, especially if she was forty-five.

"Not that I know of, I didn't ask. She was a model when she was younger. She's been a wife to her late husband for the last ten years. He was ninety when he died."

"Wow, that is old. Am I going to meet her? Are you seeing her again?" Camille looked faintly nervous, and he smiled.

"If you're asking if I'm going to date her, no, I'm not. First of all, I'm in love with your mother, and probably always will be. I don't want to get married again, or date for now. And a woman like Maxine would never look twice at someone like me. I'm not showy or fancy enough, I don't have a yacht or a house in the South of France. I live in the Napa Valley and make wine," he said humbly.

"She was married to a ninety-year-old man. How racy could that have been?"

Christophe laughed. "You have a point. But he was probably a lot fancier than I am, or ever want to be. So to answer your question, no, you probably won't ever meet her, although I should make an effort to introduce you to her two sons when they come here. You might like them." There were boys Camille's age in the Valley, among the vintners' families, but she knew them all, like Phillip, and she had no romantic interest in any of them, and she never went to the city, although it was close. He worried about Camille not having a boy-friend or dating, she spent all her spare time working, as he did, but she was young and deserved more of a life. Joy hadn't worried about it, but he did. Joy always said she'd meet someone. And he didn't want some dashing man to sweep her off her feet and take her away somewhere, like London or Australia or France, or Chile or South Africa, anywhere they grew wine. He couldn't bear the thought of losing her one day, but he didn't want her to be lonely or unhappy either, so a nice local boy, heir to one of the wineries would have suited him fine as a son-in-law, but Camille found all the boys she'd grown up with in Napa boring.

Christophe was happy when she went off to meet her friends later that morning, and Camille seemed happy too.

But the following week Maxine made a liar of him, when she showed up at the winery unannounced. She asked to see him, and he came out of his office with a look of surprise, in jeans, cowboy boots, and a plaid shirt. She was wearing skintight faded jeans that showed off her slim figure and long legs, a crisp white shirt that was perfectly tailored, and black alligator Hermès riding boots that looked worn in, and she smiled broadly the moment she saw him, and kissed him on both cheeks, as his secretary watched.

"What are you doing here?" he asked, and she laughed.

"I apologize for the intrusion, but I was in the neighborhood and thought I'd drop by. Your note was so sweet." He had written her a thank-you note for dinner, and thought that Joy would have been proud of him. He had never been good about things like that, and she did them for him. But he had to do it himself now, and the dinner warranted at least a thank-you note. He had thought about sending flowers, but decided it would have sent the wrong message. He wasn't trying to woo her, he had just had a very good time.

"The winery is beautiful," Maxine said admiringly. "It's much bigger than I thought, and what is the château up on the hill? I felt like I was in Bordeaux for a minute."

"That's where we live, I built it when we bought the land. I had every stone brought over from France. It's a smaller version of my family's château in Bordeaux, much smaller, it's very human scale when you see it up close. Would you like a tour of the winery?" he offered, and she nodded enthusiastically.

"Is your daughter here?" Maxine asked, smiling. "I'd love to meet her."

"Of course." Christophe was touched that she had asked, and led her down two long halls to Camille's office. She was sitting at her desk, frowning at her computer when they walked in, and she looked up in surprise when she saw her father, and the woman at his side. She had no idea who she was.

"Hi. Someone made a wrong entry about the last two tons of

grapes we sold, from last year's crop." She wondered if her mother had done it when she was sick and perhaps in pain or distracted, but Camille was trying to correct it now. "Sorry." She stood up with a smile, came around her desk, and waited for her father to introduce her to the woman with him. She wondered if she was a new client, or an old friend. Camille had never seen her before.

Christophe made the introduction. "Maxine de Pantin, my daughter Camille," he said easily as the two women shook hands. For an instant, Camille appeared shocked and then recovered herself quickly. But she wasn't anything that Camille had imagined. And this was the woman he had said she'd never meet and now here she was.

Camille felt like a mess next to the impeccably groomed woman who was wearing a faint but distinctive perfume, and looked smashing in the alligator riding boots and tight jeans, with her long black hair pulled back in a ponytail. Camille thought she seemed very young, as well as very chic. Camille felt uncomfortable in an old faded Stanford sweatshirt, jeans with holes in them, and sneakers, but Maxine gazed at her warmly, and didn't seem to notice what she wore.

"I couldn't wait to meet you, so I dropped by. I'm sorry to be so rude," she apologized. "Your father says such wonderful things about you." Maxine beamed at her, which made Camille feel suddenly shy. She didn't know this woman, and she acted as though she and Camille's father were good friends. She had a very open, casual style about her that implied intimacy, even with Camille.

"I say wonderful things about him too," Camille said quietly and smiled at her father, who put an arm around his daughter's shoulders. They chatted for a few minutes and then he said he was going to give Maxine a tour of the winery, and they left. Camille stood watching them from the window, and saw her father laughing as they walked toward the winery buildings. She hadn't seen him laugh in months, and his body language said that he liked her, maybe more than even he knew, as he walked close to her and leaned toward her when they spoke. It gave Camille a little shiver down her spine. She didn't know why, the Frenchwoman had been very friendly to Camille, but something about her made Camille wonder if she was sincere. Her smile would have lit up the world, but her eyes looked dark and cold to Camille, and then she scolded herself for being so stupid about her. She was just someone her father had met. He had said he didn't want to date her. And turning away from the window, Camille went back to work, feeling foolish for having been upset. It was just odd to see her father with a woman. But one day, she'd have to get used to it, even if it wasn't now.

"What a lovely young woman!" Maxine exclaimed to him as soon as they walked outside. "She's beautiful, and obviously very smart if she's working with you."

"She's planning to go to business school in a few years," he said proudly, "but to be honest, I'm not sure she needs it. She's getting experience here she'd never get in school. Especially now, with her mother gone, she's taking on a lot of responsibilities that my wife handled before." It was obvious how much he loved both of his women, and Maxine nodded and looked touched.

"Your wife was a very lucky woman," she said quietly, as they walked into the part of the winery where the barrels were kept.

The facilities were huge, much more than you could see from the road. It was an important winery, even if it wasn't as vast as Sam's. But Christophe made up in quality for what he didn't produce in quantity, and didn't want to. And he was impressed by the questions

Maxine asked. She seemed genuinely interested in the wine business, and what he did. She knew a number of important wineries in
France, and was interested in how he did things differently, and what
was the same. He spent two hours with her, and he enjoyed the time.
She didn't seem as glamorous in his own familiar setting. Other than
the fancy alligator riding boots, she behaved like a regular person,
and he enjoyed talking to her and explaining his business in some
detail. The time flew by, and it was nearly five o'clock when he
walked her to her car in their parking lot, and then he thought of
something.

"Do you want to come up to the house for a glass of wine?" He
was almost ready to leave work by then anyway, and it was too late
to start any new projects on his desk.

"I'd love that," she said, looking pleased, as they lapsed back into
French. "Are you sure it won't be an intrusion?" she asked and he
shook his head.

"Of course not. If you don't mind, I'll ride up the hill with you. I
walked to work today." He and Camille did that often, to get a little
exercise before they started work, and it gave them a chance to chat
before the day began.

He got into the Mercedes she drove, and directed her up the hill
to the château. They could see it peeking out behind the big trees
which surrounded it, and the road up the hill was winding. They
couldn't see how big the château really was until they drove up to it,
and could appreciate its elegant proportions. It was small for a château, but a very large house by local standards, and Maxine looked
startled as she got out of the car and stared up at it.

"It's like being at home, back in France," she said, sounding nos-
talgic, and he thought of the château she had lost to her stepchildren

in Périgord, and felt sorry for her. She had had her share of tragedies and disappointments too, and there was a vulnerable side of her that peeked through her confident demeanor, which touched him.

He led her into the front hall, where he had hung portraits of his family in France, and his parents. And there were photographs of him and Joy in silver frames on the tables, and many with Camille as she grew up. Everything about the house was very personal, and she admired the delicate frescoes Joy had painted when they built it. The château was beautiful, and entirely different from the house she had rented, where it was all new. The home he had built looked as though it had been there for hundreds of years instead of just twenty-three.

He poured Maxine a glass of wine and they sat outside in the garden, where he used to sit with Joy on quiet evenings, and Camille found them there, with a look of surprise an hour later when she came home from work. Her father hadn't sat in the garden since her mother died, and it gave Camille a shock to see Maxine ensconced in her mother's favorite chair.

"Oh . . . I'm sorry . . . I didn't know you were out here, Papa," she said when she found him in the garden, after she followed their voices there, and saw the open wine bottle in the kitchen, of his favorite vintage, from the year Camille was born. He thought it was his best wine.

"I should really go," Maxine said, switching back to English as she stood up and smiled at Camille. She had heard them speaking French as she approached, which bothered her. Her father had always regretted that Joy didn't speak French. She had tried to master it when they were first married, but languages weren't her strong suit and she had given up. He seemed so comfortable speaking to Maxine in his own language, and they looked as though they'd had a nice time together.

They left their glasses in the kitchen, and he walked her out to her car, as Camille heard him say, "I'll give you the full tour next time," which made Camille wonder what he was going to show her. Their bedrooms? His private library, where her parents had spent nights reading by the fire? Joy's office at home? Everything about the house was personal and seemed intimate to her, and not to be shared with strangers, particularly a woman he'd only seen twice in his life, and hadn't planned to see again, and said he didn't want to. But she had shown up at the office, and now she'd had a drink with him, sitting in her mother's chair, in their private garden. And something about it felt creepy to Camille, as though Maxine had invaded their space, and had intended to do it.

"I'll call you when I get back from Holland," he said as she got into her car and smiled up at him.

"I'm sorry I took up so much of your time today," she said apologetically. "The winery tour was fascinating, and your home is spectacular," she said, admiring it again as she turned the key in the ignition.

"I thoroughly enjoyed it," he assured her. "We'll have dinner at The French Laundry when I come back." It was said to be the best restaurant in the Napa Valley.

"I'd love that," she said happily, waved, and drove back down the winding driveway, and he walked slowly back into the house thinking about her. It had been pleasant spending time with her that afternoon, more so than he would have expected. She was easy to be with and to talk to, in spite of the fancy people she knew, she was very unassuming and unpretentious. He thought she'd make a good friend, and he was looking forward to taking her to dinner, to reciprocate for the evening he had spent at her home.

Camille had dinner on the table when he walked back in, and she was quiet as they sat down to Raquel's tamales and enchiladas she had put in the microwave, and a big salad. They both loved Mexican food, and especially Raquel's. Camille didn't say a word as they started eating, and her father could see that she was troubled by something.

"Anything wrong?" he asked her and she shook her head, and smiled at him, but he could see a sad look in her eyes and wondered what had happened. She didn't speak until she cleared their plates, and then she told him about the new ideas she had for social media, to bring their lower priced wines to the attention of younger people. He liked the idea, and she said she was researching companies to handle Twitter and Facebook for them. She had been doing it herself, and had for some time, but she thought they could outsource it and hire a firm to do it, who might do it better. "You do a great job with it," he praised her, but she still seemed upset, and he reached out and touched her arm with a tender expression. He hated it when she was unhappy and she looked so sad, and had all through dinner. "What is it? What's bothering you, Camille?"

"I'm just being stupid. It was weird coming home to see you in the garden with that woman. She was sitting in Mom's chair, as though she belonged there. I guess I'll have to get used to that at some point," she said, with tears bulging in her eyes, and he put his arms around her.

"Not yet," he said quietly, stroking her long blond hair that still gave her the appearance of a child at times, especially when it hung straight down her back or she wore it in braids on days when she was busy. "No one is ever going to take your mother's place. I thought of it when she sat in that chair too, but I didn't want to be impolite and tell her she couldn't sit there. I guess we'll both have to get used to that when people come here. But I hardly know her, I'm not pursuing her. She's an interesting woman who has had some hard breaks too. She's probably very lonely. She doesn't know anyone here, and it's a small community. It doesn't hurt to be nice to people. That doesn't mean I'm falling in love with her," but Camille sensed something about her that she didn't know how to explain to him. It was an undercurrent which was much less innocent than he was describing, and he could be naive about people. Her mother had always said so. Camille thought Maxine de Pantin was a woman on a mission.

"What if she's after you, Papa?" Camille said looking up at him. He was a handsome man with a successful business, and a lot of women would have liked to catch him now that he was widowed.

"She's not after me, Camille." He smiled at his daughter. "She knows lots more important men than me. I'm just a little fish in a small pond to her. She can go back to Paris, or anywhere else, and catch a much bigger one. Besides, I'm sure she doesn't need me. Those boots she had on today must cost the price of a vineyard," he said, laughing, and Camille smiled, thinking about them. She had never seen alligator riding boots before, and had no idea what they might cost.

"I promise you, she has no interest in me, nor I in her, except as friends. You have nothing to worry about. And I won't let anyone sit in your mother's chair next time," he said, and she smiled at him, and hoped he was right about Maxine. Camille didn't know why, but she didn't trust her, and she had an odd feeling that her mother wouldn't have either. She always knew when women were after him, and warned Christophe about it. He always brushed it off and had trouble believing that women wanted him. He was totally happy with his wife, and had never looked at another woman. But Joy was gone now, and Camille knew how lonely he was, and how empty the house was without her. There was a hole in their lives as big as the sky now, and all she knew was that she didn't want Maxine de Pantin to try to fill it. The thought of that made a chill run down her spine.

Chapter Six

Christophe's trip to the Lowlands was shorter than his trip to Italy, and he was back in two weeks, satisfied with how it had gone. He had stopped in New York on the way back, and saw two of their most important distributors, and Camille brought him up-to-date on everything as soon as he got home. She had had another run-in with Cesare, but didn't bother to tell him about it. He always defended him anyway, and she was more interested in telling him about the social media group she had hired. In a single week, they had increased their followers on both Facebook and Twitter, and she was pleased. Her father was ecstatic to see her. He took her out to dinner the following night, at Don Giovanni's, one of their favorite restaurants, and they both ate enormous plates of pasta, until they could barely move.

That weekend, true to his word, he took Maxine to dinner at The French Laundry, for a sumptuous meal, and they sampled three different local wines at dinner. He was trying to educate her since she said she wanted to learn all about the Napa Valley wines while she was living there, and at the end of the meal, she commented that his wines were still the best of all of them that she had tasted so far. They sampled a Sauterne for dessert, which they both loved, although they both agreed that nothing equaled Château d'Yquem, which she said was a favorite of hers.

He told her about his trip to Holland and Belgium, with a quick stop in Berlin on the way back, and she described a dinner party she'd been to, and who had been there. She said that all of them were snobs, and he laughed. He knew all the people she had mentioned. They were the Old Guard socialites, and not likely to extend a warm welcome to her.

"There is a lot of that up here. My wife and I made a pact early in our marriage to stay away from the seriously social group. They think they own the Valley, should be the only ones here, and give parties for each other all the time. It's a very closed group." He was surprised that they had invited Maxine at all. They hated outsiders, and rarely invited newcomers to the Valley. "They don't ask me anymore," he said, looking pleased. "I don't miss it." But Maxine seemed much more social than he was. She had worn a pink Chanel jacket and jeans to dinner with high heels, and managed to look very chic with whatever she wore.

"That reminds me," Maxine said casually, as they walked to his car after dinner, "I don't know how you feel about it, but I have tickets to the ballet next week, and I wondered if you'd want to go with me. It's *Swan Lake,* with a wonderful new young Chinese dancer recently arrived from Beijing. I don't have anyone to go with me, and I was hoping I could take you to it." She tried not to sound pathetic about it, and he grinned at her sheepishly.

"My wife loved the ballet too, and I never went with her. She always took our daughter, or a friend."

"Is that a no?" she asked him, with a pleading expression and he laughed.

"It would be if you'd allow it to be. But how can I say no when you look at me like that?" The poor woman had no friends here. At least he had Camille to keep him company, Maxine didn't even have a close friend to go to a movie with.

"Then you'll come with me?" He nodded, and she was elated. "I hate going to the ballet alone. It just makes one feel lonelier. That's the hard part about not being married, although Charles really couldn't leave home for the last two years. We tried a couple of times but it was too much for him." Christophe had already understood that for the last two or three years of her marriage, she had essentially been a nurse. And although she missed Charles, she felt liberated now, and wanted to live again, which was understandable. She'd been a prisoner for years.

"Why don't we have dinner in the city after the ballet?" he suggested, and he could see that she loved the idea. He already knew she liked Gary Danko, but he had several other suggestions, and they could make a festive evening of it. And although he wasn't a big ballet fan, it sounded like fun to spend an evening with Maxine. It made him feel faintly guilty, since he had always refused to go to the ballet with Joy.

Camille had the same reaction to it when he told her he was going with Maxine to see *Swan Lake*.

"You *never* went with Mom," she said angrily, "you always refused. How can you go with someone else?"

"She already had the tickets, and she didn't have anyone else to go with. I felt sorry for her," he said, looking embarrassed as Camille stormed around the kitchen, in her mother's defense.

"Papa, that woman is playing you. She's acting pathetic, and there's nothing pathetic about her. She knows exactly what she's doing. I can feel it. She's after you." She sounded exactly like Joy when she said it, and he laughed at her.

"You sound just like your mother. I really don't think that's the case this time," he insisted, seeming absurdly naive to his daughter. It was as plain as the nose on his face and he didn't want to see it. He thought Maxine was an innocent, but she reminded Camille of a spider weaving her web.

"I do," Camille insisted. "I think you're wrong about her. She's trying to trap you."

"The only thing she's trapped me into is an evening at the ballet. That seems pretty harmless to me," but his daughter didn't agree with him, and she looked glum the next day when he left the office early, to go home and change, in time to pick Maxine up and drive her into the city at five-thirty, so they didn't get delayed by traffic. And he had made dinner reservations for them at Quince, since the food was comparable to Gary Danko's.

They made easy conversation on the way into the city, and she mentioned her stepchildren again and how evil and unfair they were.

"They would have left me penniless if they could, and starving by the side of the road," but she didn't appear to be penniless, from the way she dressed and was living, and how lavishly she entertained, so he assumed she must have come to a satisfactory agreement with them. But he was sure it had been unpleasant, and it had left her bitter about them, and the laws in France governing inheritances and estates. "We had ten wonderful years together, nearly eleven, and they gave me twenty-four hours to leave the château after he died, and forty-eight to get my things out of the house in Paris. It's amazing how cruel some people can be. People talk about wicked step-mothers, but I think stepchildren are far worse, particularly if there are several of them. They really ganged up on me." She seemed deeply hurt by them as she said it.

He turned to more pleasant subjects then, and asked her about her two sons in France. She missed them and couldn't wait for them to come during the summer. He was surprised to discover how knowl-edgeable she was about modern art, which he enjoyed as well. He and Joy had bought a number of paintings at auction at Sotheby's and Christie's, to hang in the winery.

They arrived at the opera house in plenty of time, put his car in the parking lot, and had a glass of champagne at the bar, before they took their seats in the box where she had bought tickets. They were dead center and the best seats in the house, and he was surprised to find that he enjoyed it, which made him feel even guiltier about all the times he hadn't gone with Joy. And dinner at Quince was exactly what they'd hoped for, an excellent meal in a pleasant setting, with superb service. They were back on the road to Napa at midnight, and sat in comfortable silence in the car. It had been a lovely evening, and he thanked her for inviting him to the ballet as they got on the Golden Gate Bridge, and admired the lights of the city. It was nice being with her, and he was feeling relaxed.

"Have you forgiven me for dragging you to the ballet?" she asked, smiling at him. She was wearing a very sexy black cocktail dress under a black satin evening coat, and had been the best dressed woman at the ballet and the restaurant, which seemed to be her style. Every time he saw her, she looked beautiful. He could tell that she took excellent care of herself, and was meticulous about the way she dressed.

"I'm surprised how much I enjoyed it," he admitted to her.

"Does that mean you'll come with me again?" she asked pointedly and he laughed.

"I might. My daughter reminded me of all the times I refused to go with her mother, and made me feel very guilty about it," he confessed, "but I had fun anyway." He liked her, and it seemed odd to him after so many years, but he felt comfortable being with someone French, and speaking his own language. He was still sorry he hadn't spoken exclusively in French to Camille when she was a child, so she'd be bilingual. She spoke it, but hesitantly, and like an American. He would have loved it if she were fluent, but neither he nor Joy had pushed it when she was small, since Joy didn't speak it at all, and he didn't want her to feel left out.

The drive back to Napa went quickly, and took them barely over an hour to get to her house. She invited him in casually for a drink, but he admitted he was tired and had early meetings the next day.

"I'll call you for dinner soon," he promised as she got out of the car, and she looked lonely to him, as she walked up her front steps, turned off the alarm, stepped into her house, and stood in the doorway and waved. He knew just how she felt. He felt the same way going to his room at night, and climbing into the empty bed. It was hard adjusting to life alone after you'd been married. Maxine seemed so solitary as she walked in and closed the door behind her. And he didn't agree with his daughter. Maxine wasn't "after him," as Camille had said, she was just a woman on her own, trying to fill her time, without the husband she had lost. They had their widowhood in

common. Even Camille couldn't understand how profound that soli-
tude was, and sense of loss, at her age. But he and Maxine knew it
only too well.

Christophe didn't see Maxine for several weeks after that. He made
some domestic trips to Boston, Chicago, Atlanta, and Denver. He had
vintners' meetings on some collaborative projects, and Camille was
very excited about the results of their new social media program.
They had tripled their followers in as many weeks, which was a big
jump. And he and Camille were walking down the street in St. Helena to go to the drugstore, when they saw Maxine coming out of the
fancier of the two local shoe stores, with two big bags. Christophe
stopped to talk to her, and after saying hello, Camille went ahead to
the drugstore with their list.

"Shopping in St. Helena?" he teased her. After what he'd seen of
her wardrobe, that was a major step down for her.

"I was too lazy to go into the city, and they have cute shoes here,"
she said, smiling at him, happy to see him again. "I was afraid I had
driven you away with our evening at the ballet."

"No, I've been traveling a lot for the last few weeks. I'm sorry I
haven't called." And then he had an idea. "If you like Mexican food,
you're welcome to join us for dinner tonight and a movie." Maxine
hesitated and looked tempted for a minute, and then decided to decline.

"I don't want to intrude on your time with your daughter," she
said sensibly. "She might not like it," and he suspected she was right.

"Dinner this week then, I'll call you," he promised, walked Maxine
to her car, and carried the bags for her. He was happy they had run

into her, it reminded him of the pleasant evening they'd had. And her recent silence proved Camille wrong again. If she'd been pursuing him, she'd have called him and she hadn't. They were just casual friends, who happened to be in the same situation at the same time, which was their only bond, other than that they were both French. Camille was pleased to see that Maxine had disappeared when she found her father sitting on a bench and eating an ice cream cone after she came out of the drugstore.

"Where's your friend?" she asked him, trying to sound casual about it.

"She went home to pick up some things. I invited her to spend the night tonight. I hope you don't mind." He looked totally bland as he said it and Camille stared at him in horror.

"You did *what*?" she nearly shrieked at him and he laughed.

"I thought that would get your attention. I have no idea where she is, she went home."

"That isn't funny, Papa. I thought you were serious for a minute."

"You must think I've lost my mind. I hardly know the woman. I've seen her three times in my life." But Camille still believed what she had told him in the first place, that the countess was a conniving woman, was after him, and had a plan of some kind that involved him. Christophe didn't believe it for a minute, and there was no evidence of it whatsoever. But as he had promised her, he called Maxine the next day, and invited her out to dinner the following week. He didn't tell Camille, because he didn't want to hear her theories again, since he knew she was mistaken. She thought everyone was after him because he was her father, but so far none of the local women were pounding on his front door or falling at his feet, nor was Maxine. And he didn't want them to. He needed time to heal, and he had no interest in another woman for now. He had promised to let Camille know when he did.

His dinner with Maxine that week was nothing out of the ordinary. They went out for a simple Italian dinner, and she said she was going to Dallas to visit friends for a few weeks, and to LA on the way back. She seemed excited about her trip, and he told her about an event they were planning at the winery. They held a big Memorial Day barbecue every year, with families invited. It marked the beginning of summer, and was always a happy event. It had originally been Joy's idea, and they had been doing it for fifteen years. It was always a great success.

"I don't think it's your kind of thing," he said to Maxine over dinner, "but you're welcome to come. A lot of locals show up, and some visitors to the Valley. It's from five in the afternoon until ten o'clock at night. It's very informal, ribs and steaks and hamburgers."

"It sounds like fun," she said easily, and she'd be back from Dallas by then.

"I'll send you an email to remind you," and then he laughed. "I don't have any engraved 'pour mémoire' cards with my crest on them," he said apologetically, teasing her, "just an email."

"That will be fine." She smiled. He dropped her off at her house early that night, and other than a brief email exchange to thank him for dinner, and to invite her to the Memorial Day barbecue, they had no contact for a month. He hadn't even thought about her, and was suddenly reminded when she walked into the party on Memorial Day weekend, wearing white jeans, a turquoise silk T-shirt, and sandals, and she had on turquoise jewelry to go with it. She always looked striking. She was dressed more for the South of France than a Memorial Day barbecue in the Napa Valley, and Camille was surprised to see her but didn't comment. Maxine and her father didn't seem to be dating, so she had stopped worrying about it.

By nine o'clock, after he'd circulated among the guests for four hours, and done his duty as a host, Christophe sat on a bench with Maxine in the winery garden, and they had a glass of wine, and talked about what they'd been doing over the past month. It sounded like she'd had fun in Dallas and LA, but she said she was happy to be back. And he was glad to see her. He was surprised to realize he had missed her, and they chatted animatedly in French until the end of the party. The country music band they'd hired was just finishing their last set when they stood up.

"Let's have dinner this week," he suggested, she agreed, and then he told her about the big wine auction that happened in the Valley every year in the first week of June, and asked her if she'd like to go with him.

"I'd love that," she said, with a look of pleasure.

"I'll email you the info," he said simply. It was nice having another human to do things with. He was so lonely without Joy. And he couldn't rely on Camille all the time. She needed time to herself too.

The wine auction was held in a tent at Meadowood, just under a thousand people attended, and they raised approximately fifteen million dollars every year, for community health care and children's education. It was a well-run event, for the good of the community, and he was glad that Maxine wanted to attend with him. She said she'd heard about it, and was excited to go.

Maxine reciprocated for the wine auction by inviting him to a party she was going to on the Fourth of July weekend. It was being given by a group of Swiss vintners who had a relatively new winery that Christophe hadn't seen yet, and was curious about. The Swiss vintners had just moved to the Valley. Christophe accepted her invitation with pleasure, and they both chatted and were animated about upcoming events. It was going to make the beginning of summer more interesting and fun for both of them.

Maxine was fascinated by the wine auction when they attended it. Christophe asked Camille to join them, but she'd been many times and didn't want to go this year. He introduced Maxine to many of the important vintners, and members of the social Old Guard, and the auction made a record-breaking sixteen million dollars. Maxine bid successfully on six cases of Christophe's wines, and he thanked her for her support.

After the wine auction, which was livelier than they'd expected, and got them off to a great start, they had dinner together once a week. And they'd been invited to two other parties on the holiday weekend, one each, and they agreed to go together. It sounded like a busy weekend. This was going to be his first Fourth of July without Joy, and he wanted to keep moving and be occupied so he didn't get depressed about it.

In the past, they had always given a dinner for their friends at the château, and Camille thought he should still do it, but she wouldn't be there since she was going to Lake Tahoe to stay with an old school friend, and Christophe didn't want to entertain by himself, his heart wasn't in it. He had decided that this year he'd rather go to other people's parties with Maxine. There was no history there of a social gathering he and his wife had given for years. It was simpler and less emotional to do something new.

The dinner they went to together at the Swiss winery was very elegant, and Maxine knew a number of people there, as did Christophe, mostly Europeans, Italian, Swiss, and French. They had a pleasant evening, and enjoyed talking to the people at their table. Everyone spoke French all through dinner, the group was sophisticated and the dinner went late. Maxine had worn a white lace dress with a flesh colored bodysuit under it, and she had caused a sensation when they walked in. Christophe wasn't used to being the center of attention with the woman he was with. Several people assumed that they were married, and referred to Maxine as his wife. He gently corrected them each time and said that he and Maxine were friends, and the other men looked at him with envy. He didn't see it that way, but she was a very desirable woman, and other men responded to it immediately.

The second party they went to was a big Fourth of July picnic at the Marshalls'. There were a hundred and fifty people there, with a band, and Christophe noticed that Sam's congresswoman was there. He had invited Christophe, and looked surprised when he showed up with Maxine, although he'd called the winery office to say he was bringing her. Sam never seemed enthusiastic about seeing her, but he was happy to see his friend. And Christophe got the chance to have a long conversation with Sam's date, Elizabeth Townsend, the congresswoman from LA, and found that he liked her immensely. She was a real person, and he could tell that she was fond of Sam, but she admitted readily that politics was her life and the main event for her. She had never married or had children, and said she had no regrets about it. She loved the time she spent with Sam, but she knew that sooner or later he would get tired of how busy and unavailable she was, and she spent a lot of time in Washington when Congress was in session.

In a moment of confidence, she told Christophe that her relationships always had expiration dates, and at some point, the men got tired of waiting around for her, and the romance would inevitably end. She was happy that Sam hadn't gotten to that stage yet, but she was sure that he would. It was why she never invested herself too deeply, or made any long-term commitments, but Sam looked happy with her while Christophe watched them dance. She was a warm, positive, extremely bright woman, and she was good for him, even though she didn't come to Napa often. But she'd said he visited her in LA and DC occasionally when they both had free time.

Christophe took Maxine out on the dance floor then, and they stayed there for a long time. It was a very different evening from the more formal night before at the Swiss winery, but the contrast kept the weekend interesting for both of them, and on Sunday night, they went to a very chic dinner at the home of a couple Maxine had met recently. They had just bought a beautiful Victorian house, and were looking to buy a winery. They were another of what Christophe referred to as the "accidental vintners," who treated it more like a hobby than a business, and all they needed were good people to run it. But the house was very pretty, and it was a pleasant evening, though not as exciting as the two evenings before. It was the kind of dinner party Christophe usually avoided, with hours of small talk, while people bragged about their houses, planes, and boats.

Maxine could see that he wasn't having fun, and they went back to her place to sit by the pool and have a drink. It was a beautiful warm night beneath a starry sky, with a full moon, as Maxine sipped champagne, and he smiled at her in the moonlight. She was wearing a pale green silk jumpsuit, and looked long and lean as she lay on the deck chair chatting with him. The scene reminded him of an Italian movie.

"Well, we certainly had a busy weekend," he commented, as she nodded.

"You're not tired of me by now?" she asked him. Three nights with the same man or woman, when you weren't dating or married, seemed like a lot, but Christophe had appeared to enjoy himself. He liked being with Maxine, and sitting quietly at her pool with her at the end of the evening. She looked at him with a slow smile after he told her how much he'd enjoyed the weekend. He didn't want to say that he was getting comfortable with her, but that was the case. "Do you want to go for a swim?" she asked him. "I have some spare bathing suits in the pavilion, if you want one, or we don't need to bother if you don't care." She seemed very relaxed about her body, and she was beautiful, so she had nothing to hide or be ashamed of, but he was modest enough to want to wear a bathing suit, and headed to the pavilion at the end of the pool to change. He liked the idea of a swim before he went home. It sounded like a great idea to him.

He left his clothes in the changing room, took off his watch, and left it in his shoe, and he was back a few minutes later in a pair of navy blue swimming trunks that still had the ticket on, so he knew they were new. He didn't see her at first. She had turned the lights off around them, and then he saw her at the far end of the pool, with her dark hair streaming behind her, swimming underwater. He dove in at the deep end and swam toward her, keeping an eye on where she was, so he didn't bump into her, and when she sliced through the water next to him, he realized that the bathing suit he thought he'd seen was the tan lines from her bikini. She was naked next to him in the water, came to the surface gracefully, and treaded water near him. He didn't comment on her nudity, and tried to look nonchalant about it, but his body betrayed him almost instantly. It had been nine months since he'd seen a naked woman, and years since he'd seen one as enticing as she was, when things were still exciting between him and Joy, and she wasn't sick. And there was something forbidden and almost wicked about Maxine as she wound herself gracefully around him without a word and kissed him, while his body pounded for her, and he couldn't stop himself. She did nothing to stop him, on the contrary, she guided him into her, and moaned softly, as they moved as one toward the steps, and lay on them as he made love to her, with every ounce of desire he had repressed for months and denied himself.

All he wanted now was Maxine, and he couldn't get enough of her. He made love to her again and again, in the moonlight, and then they scampered naked to her bedroom, still dripping wet, and made love again on her bed. He felt as though he had been hit by a tidal wave, as she walked across her bedroom afterward and lit a cigarette, in all her naked beauty while he watched her, and she stood smiling at him as she exhaled the smoke.

"Oh my God . . . what happened . . . I'm sorry . . ." he said, wondering what had come over him. He couldn't even say he was drunk, because he wasn't. He was drunk on her and looked dazed.

"What are you sorry about?" she asked, as she sauntered slowly back to him, teasing him with her body. Just looking at her aroused him again, he felt as though she had cast a spell on him. He had never known any woman like her, not even Joy. Sex with her had been loving and tender and sensual, even erotic at times. Sex with Maxine was insane, and only made him want more. "Isn't that what you wanted to happen, Christophe? I did. I could hardly keep my hands off you this weekend. You're a beautiful man, and a wonderful lover." It was the physical that attracted her, not his heart or his soul, but that was exciting too.

She came back to bed then, after she put out the cigarette, and her lips found every inch of his body in all the ways he wanted. She read his mind, and knew exactly what he needed from her, and she needed the same from him. The forces between them were so powerful, he couldn't speak for several minutes when they were finished. She had bitten his lip the last time she came, and he didn't feel it, as she licked the blood off with her tongue. She was much more than elegant and experienced, she was a demon in a woman's body and she knew what men wanted, what *he* wanted from her. They hadn't slept all night when the sun came up, and then she rolled gently away from him, purred for an instant, and fell asleep while he watched her. She looked totally sated, content, and he thought of going home while she slept, but he didn't want to leave her, ever again. He knew that as he lay next to her and fell asleep at last. It had been the most exotic night of his life.

She was up and dressed when he woke up in her bed, with the sheets tangled around him, and she handed him a cup of coffee with a tender expression. He smiled as he took it from her, still looking dazed. He had been tantalized by her all night. She was like a drug.

"Interesting dreams, my darling?" she asked him and sat down on the edge of the bed, while he sat up and sipped the coffee. He didn't know what to say.

"That was quite a night," he said, still in awe of her, seeing her naked in the water had aroused him as nothing else ever had, and their lovemaking all night had been alternately violent and gentle. He felt confused as he gazed at her. "Maxine, I'm not sure I'm ready for this," he said, thinking of Joy, but Maxine was the more powerful memory now, and the woman he wanted, not his wife.

"You were ready last night," she said in a husky voice, and he couldn't deny it.

"It's true, but having said that, it's too soon to be involved with anyone else, out of respect for Joy and our marriage."

"She's gone, Christophe . . . just like Charles. I can understand that you don't want anyone to know until the year mark, and especially your daughter. But why deprive us?" She made it sound so simple and so sensible that it even sounded reasonable to him. "No one needs to know what we're doing. We don't have to tell anyone. This is just between us." As she said it, she took the cup from him and set it down on the table next to the bed, ran her hands the length of his body, and then gently put her lips around him, and within seconds, he wanted her again, and without saying a word he took her, and plunged into her, making sure not to be too rough with her, but she sat astride him and rode him hard, and then teased him until he grabbed her again, and they both came. He felt as though he couldn't stop, and he lay on the bed drained afterward and knew that whatever this was that had been born between them the night before, he needed it with every ounce of his being, and he couldn't give her up. And she was right. Joy was gone. They weren't hurting anyone, and no one needed to know. The secret was theirs to share now, like a gift.

Chapter Seven

Christophe felt like he was in a haze for the entire month of August. He drove to Maxine's house on Money Lane several times a day to make love to her. He was late for meetings, he left work earlier than usual. He rearranged plans. She dropped by his office at the winery and he made love to her in a storeroom, and told her they couldn't do that again. He avoided the château because Raquel was there and Camille could come home at any moment, but he made love to her everywhere else, even once in a bathroom at a respectable restaurant. He felt crazed. He thought he was in love with her, but more than that, he was addicted to her, and he was terrified she'd leave the Napa Valley and move away, which she hinted at, at times. She had extended her lease for the house on Money Lane until September, but after that, she said she wasn't sure where she would go. Dallas, LA, Miami, Palm Beach, New York, or back to Paris. She had no anchor anymore, except Christophe. And he desperately needed her. Need had replaced guilt about Joy, but he didn't care. Maxine was the most exciting thing that had ever happened to him, and he didn't want to lose her now.

It was a relief when Camille left to spend two weeks at Lake Tahoe again, with her old friends from school. Christophe had encouraged her to go. She rarely got to see friends anymore, she had too many responsibilities at the winery, so it was a rare treat for her to have some time away to be carefree and young. She never even went to the city now, and her friends were busy too, with new jobs and lives and relationships. So he encouraged her to take the time off, with the ulterior motive of his having more time to spend with Maxine.

With Camille gone, Christophe didn't have to make excuses to her or hide, and Maxine could spend the night at the château as long as they left before Raquel arrived. He would take Maxine home in the morning, make love to her again, and then leave for work. And by lunchtime, he was starving for her again. By the end of August, he knew what he had to do and more important, what he wanted. And he knew when. It was all clear in his mind.

At the last minute, Camille decided to extend her stay in Tahoe, with her friends, over the Labor Day weekend. She didn't know when she'd see them again, since several of them were leaving for graduate school in the East. Most of her friendships were kept alive on Skype now, and they teased her about being a "virtual friend." No one ever saw her now that she was so busy working for her father, so the two weeks in Tahoe had been like old times when they were kids in school. She had promised her father that she'd come home for the weekend, and apologized profusely for staying until Monday night, but he encouraged her to do so. He wanted every moment he could get alone with Maxine.

*   *   *

Christophe was going to Sam Marshall's Harvest Ball and had invited Maxine to join him, and she had been working on her costume for weeks. She had something sent from Paris and was making adjustments to it. Christophe was going to wear the same costume he wore every year, and when he saw Joy's costume in the storeroom in the attic, which Camille had worn the year before when she went with him, a month before Joy died, he was sad for a moment. But he was proud to go with Maxine this year. He knew she would be spectacular, and he had everything planned for her. He made a quick trip to the city before the weekend. He picked Maxine up at her house in time for the ball. She was going to stay at the château with him until Camille came home. Raquel was off for the weekend and the holiday on Monday. It would be their last time together at the château for a while, since Maxine couldn't stay there once Camille returned. And the anniversary of Joy's death was looming, which would be painful for Camille and Christophe, but after that he would be free to see Maxine openly, and he was going to explain it to Camille when she was back from the lake.

When he arrived at Maxine's house, she looked incredible in a costume that molded to her figure and small waist, with her breasts pouring luxuriously from the décolletage, and the huge skirt of the gown rested on wire hoops, and the skirt swayed as she walked. She had even had replicas of antique shoes made, and the wig was perfect, from a theatrical wig maker in Paris, and the mask concealed the lower part of her face. She looked ravishing as she got into Christophe's car, and they drove to the Marshalls' vast estate, where hundreds of people were getting out of horse-drawn carriages and cars, in costumes and masks. It looked like the final days of Versailles, as they made their way to the main house, while liveried footmen held out trays of champagne. Maxine's gown was white, as were her evening slippers, and she held it carefully, so the hem didn't get soiled on the path. She glanced at Christophe from time to time, and she could sense that he was happy even behind the mask.

The evening was even more grandiose than Maxine had expected. Everyone had gone all out, as they did every year. It was in celebration of the harvest, which wouldn't happen for a few more weeks, but it combined the Labor Day holiday with the anticipated success of the harvest, and the vintners were expecting a good crop this year.

They were assigned to a table near the dance floor, and Christophe danced with her all night. He saw Sam in the distance, and went to chat with him for a few minutes, while Maxine waited at their table. Phillip was with his father, and asked Christophe if Camille was there, and he said she wasn't, and had stayed at the lake with friends. He seemed disappointed and said he wanted to tell her he was engaged. He introduced his fiancée, who looked to Christophe like another one of his models or spoiled girls. She was very pretty but was complaining about how hot her wig was, her corset was too tight, her shoes hurt, and the mask made it hard to breathe. Both fathers laughed as Phillip and his fiancée walked away so she could sit down and take off her shoes.

"That's going to be a long road, if he marries her," Christophe commented.

"I tried to tell him that," Sam said with a sigh. "Kids never listen. He thinks she'll be beautiful forever, but the sound track is pretty tough," he said and Christophe laughed. "Who are you here with tonight?" He had heard him say that Camille was at the lake, and wondered if he had come alone.

"Maxine de Pantin," he said easily.

"Ah, the countess," Sam said and hesitated for a minute, but they were always honest with each other and he had to be again. "Be careful, Chris. She's great looking and very charming, but something scares me about her. I don't know what. There's something very calculating about her. I don't know why she's here in the Valley, I thought she was after me at first, but I can't stand her, and I let her know it right away. Just be cautious, don't make any fast moves, and see what happens." Christophe nodded, but he wasn't worried. Sam wasn't used to Frenchwomen and how flirtatious and artful they could be, or seem, at times with no ill intentions. He knew her well now, and he wasn't afraid. She was sincere, he was sure of it. He was sure she had just been playful with Sam and he had misread it.

"Don't worry, I'll be fine," Christophe reassured him.

"Is Elizabeth here?" Christophe asked him. The crowd was so huge, it was hard to tell who was there.

"No," Sam said matter-of-factly, "she's in Washington for a committee meeting. This isn't her kind of thing anyway." He wasn't disturbed about it, and seemed to accept that they had separate lives. He was too busy hosting the event to spend any real time with a date anyway.

Christophe went back to the table then where he'd left Maxine, and she was starting to look anxious by the time he returned.

"What took you so long?" she said plaintively.

"I was talking to Sam. His son just got engaged." Maxine was unimpressed by the news, and her own sons had disappointed her that summer. They were supposed to come to visit her, but her older son, Alexandre, had gone to Greece with friends instead and was still there, and her younger son, Gabriel, had flunked his exams at the university he attended, and had to spend the summer taking classes to try and pass them in September. But in the end, it had left Christophe and Maxine with more time to spend together in their hidden romance, so she wasn't sorry.

They walked in the gardens, and danced a lot that night, although Maxine was hot in the dress she had worn. Christophe introduced her to the friends he recognized in their masks and costumes. And at the end of the evening, they watched the fireworks that Sam had for them every year, in spectacular colors and displays, a rose, a flag, fireworks in every shape and color. Someone said he spent half a million dollars on them, which Christophe knew was possible. And after the fireworks, the guests began to drift away. It was always an impressive evening, but Christophe was glad to leave with Maxine. He had a bottle of Cristal on ice waiting for them at the château. They wanted to get out of their costumes, and talk about the evening while they unwound. Christophe took off his wig as soon as they came through the front door of the château, and Maxine did the same, and let her almost jet black hair fall down her back freely. She took off her shoes and loosened the corset that had constricted her all night. It felt good to be home, while Christophe poured the champagne into two glasses, and smiled at her.

"You looked beautiful tonight," he said in a gentle voice.

"That's good, because I couldn't breathe," she said, laughing. She took a long sip of the champagne, and then looked at him in surprise as he dropped to one knee in front of her, in the château kitchen.

"Darling Maxine, will you marry me? We can't get married until October, and we can't announce it until then. But I want to marry you as soon as we can after the anniversary date. Will you be my wife?" As he said it, he pulled a small red leather box out of his pocket. He had felt for it a thousand times that night, waiting to give it to her at the right moment. It was the ring he had bought in the city at Cartier two days before, and Maxine looked at it in wonder as he slipped the ring on her finger and stood up and kissed her. This was what she had been hoping for, but she didn't think he would make a move until after the anniversary of his wife's death in October. "You haven't answered me," he said gently after he kissed her again.

"I was too stunned." She clung to him as though they were both drowning, and in some ways they were. "Of course I'll marry you." She looked at the ring he had put on her finger. It fit perfectly, and it was beautiful and worthy of her.

"Let's get married in mid-October. I'll tell Camille after her mother's anniversary date." He had been thinking of it constantly ever since he decided he wanted to marry Maxine, and there was no point waiting. She could give up her rented house on Money Lane, and move into the château. He didn't want to live with her unmarried, with his daughter.

"Do you think Camille will be shocked?" she asked, looking concerned, but they both knew she would be, and he didn't answer her for a long moment.

"She'll adjust, this is sooner than any of us expected, but she wants me to be happy." He thought of what Sam had said to him that night about Maxine, but Sam didn't know her. She was a wonderful woman who had been through hard times, and now he would protect her, and nothing like it would happen to her again. She wouldn't be driven from her home, and Camille was a good, loving person and would come to respect her, and maybe even love her. He wanted to be sure he made provision for both of them in his will, so Maxine would feel secure. He said as much to her when they went to bed that night, in the room and the bed that he had shared with Joy. This had all happened very quickly, but he was convinced it was the right thing to do. He wasn't going to continue having a clandestine affair with Maxine. If he wanted her that badly, then it was right for him to honor her and marry her. The last two months had been too crazy. They all needed to share a peaceful, normal life together, and marrying her was the only way to do that. He wasn't Sam, dating a congresswoman who put her career first, didn't want a commitment to any man, and kept their love affair a secret. Christophe wanted to be out in the open with Maxine. She deserved to be his wife and not just his mistress.

"We have a lot to plan in the next six weeks," he said to her quietly as they lay in bed in the dark, and Maxine felt the ring on her finger. She was silent, making plans of her own. She wanted her sons to come over and meet Christophe, and she hoped he would find jobs at the winery for them, even if they couldn't be paid legally. And she had to find a place for her mother. She couldn't leave her where she was in Paris forever.

"I was thinking about my mother and my two boys," she said to Christophe as she rolled over and kissed him.

"We'll talk about all of it tomorrow," he said in a deep sexy voice as she smiled at him in the moonlight. He didn't know it, but he had saved her, and hopefully he would never know the dire straits she'd been in when he met her. She had come to the Napa Valley to find a man like him. She had set her sights on Sam Marshall, but Christophe was so much better, so trusting and so kind. Sam had a sharp edge to him and saw through her.

"Thank you," she said, as she kissed him, and then she worked her magic on him again. It was what she knew how to do best. And all he could think of as he made love to her that night was how much he loved her and that she was going to be his wife. She wasn't Joy, whom he had loved with his whole heart and soul, but he needed Maxine now, as he had never needed any other woman. The last year without Joy had nearly killed him. Maxine had rescued him from his grief and loneliness, and they had a bright future ahead. With Maxine, he knew he would lead a more glamorous, sophisticated life than he had with Joy. But Maxine was the right woman for the next chapter. He could hardly wait.

She lay looking at him after he fell asleep that night. She had lived by her wits all her life, and he was the answer to her prayers. Soon she would be living in the château with him, and she would be the wife of an important vintner. No one could touch her now, and nothing would stop her. And surely not his daughter this time, she was such an innocent. Camille was no match for her. It was all going to be easy now.

Chapter Eight

When Camille came back from Lake Tahoe after Labor Day, fresh from the relaxing weeks with her old pals, she felt young and carefree again. It had been good to get away. But within the hour that she got home, she could sense that something was different. She didn't know what it was, but her father was very quiet. He hardly spoke to her at dinner, went to bed early, and on several mornings, he had left for work before she got up. There was a sudden distance between them that had never been there before, and no explanation for it. He had no reason to be angry at her, and he didn't seem as sad as before. She wondered if he begrudged her the time she took to see her friends at the lake. But it wasn't like him to be resentful, and he'd encouraged her to reconnect with her old classmates and spend time with people her own age. He said that he knew her mother would have wanted her to.

He was acting strange, and she eventually put it down to the anniversary of her mother's death that was looming and upsetting them both. She could think of no other reason for his being so disconnected from her. She kept thinking back to what had been happening a year earlier, as her mother drifted away like a leaf on a stream, carried away from them inexorably. She didn't want to upset her father more by talking about it, but she sensed that it was tormenting him every day, it was distressing her too.

He was busy with the harvest, which was better than ever. Their crop of grapes had exceeded all expectations that year. And on the actual anniversary, they went to church together in the morning, and then to the cemetery to leave flowers for Joy on her grave, and they both cried as they hugged each other, and then went to work.

Camille had been working on marketing ideas that she wanted to share with him, but he was distracted and this didn't seem like the right time. She decided to wait a few weeks until he felt better, and had bounced back a little from the anniversary, which had rocked them both.

Christophe was biding his time too. And Maxine was busy packing up her belongings in order to give up her house and move into the château, after he told Camille their news. They were each playing a waiting game of their own.

Christophe let two days go by after Joy's anniversary date, and then suggested to Camille that they have lunch out of the office. If he took her to a restaurant, it was always for dinner. He either worked through lunch, met with clients or distributors, or had lunch with other vintners. He never took his daughter out in the middle of the day, and she thought it odd when he offered it, but she thought it might be a good time to bring up her new promotional ideas for their wines. She wanted to expand into all the new areas she could and had been working hard on it.

He took her to a deli in Yountville, where they ordered sandwiches and sat in the garden at a small table. Camille saw that he wasn't eating. He kept playing with his sandwich, and finally he looked up at her. There was no point delaying telling her the news. It was happening, and she had to know about it. He couldn't wait any longer. He and Maxine had set the date, they were getting married in less than two weeks. She had extended her rental for as long as she could, and she had to move in with them the following weekend. He had tried to make room in his closets for her, and he had had Raquel move Joy's clothes in boxes to the attic, and asked her not to tell Camille. He knew that the adjustment process would be difficult, but in the end they would all be happier than they were now.

He felt clumsy as he started to tell her, and continued to beat around the bush.

"I'm confused. What are you saying, Papa?" she asked him practically. She was very much like her mother that way, simple, straightforward, uncomplicated, and direct. "You want to make changes in the house? What kind of changes? Like construction? Why? Everything is fine the way it is, and moving things around will make a mess."

He started over, and this time, he mentioned Maxine, and how much he enjoyed her company. He said what a good person she was, and how she'd been victimized after her last marriage, and had been driven out of her home by her stepchildren. Camille wondered if that was true, but she didn't comment, and she didn't like hearing how much he enjoyed being with her. She still thought that there was something sneaky about her, but she didn't see her that often. She had no idea that he had spent every night with her while Camille was in Tahoe, and she had no inkling that several times she had stayed at the château. Even Raquel didn't know.

"I'm glad you like her, Papa," Camille said politely, still wondering where he was going with the conversation. And finally, there was no way to avoid it any longer. He had to force the words out of his mouth.

"Camille, I know this may come as a shock to you. In fact, I'm sure it will, but Maxine and I are getting married." She stared at him, unable to make a sound for a moment, as her eyes filled with tears, and he felt his stomach flip over as he watched his daughter's face. "I'm sorry, sweetheart," he said, as he touched her hand. "It won't change anything between us. Nothing could ever do that. And she doesn't want to come between us either. But I love her, and I don't want to sneak around, or see her in secret. I want her to live with us. I've been so lonely without your mother. I need a wife. I don't want a girlfriend, or to start dating. I want the kind of life we had with your mother. And Maxine deserves a respectable situation too. So we're getting married." He felt stronger after he said it, despite the look on Camille's face.

"When?" she managed to croak out as she stared at him in disbelief. It took courage for him to say the next words.

"Next week. There's no reason to wait any longer. She had to give up the house she's been renting. And I don't want to wait. It's been a year since your mother . . . I didn't want to say anything to you until after the anniversary." She knew now why he had been so strange for the past few weeks. He was waiting to tell her this news, and must have been nervous about it, so he hardly spoke to her, except at work.

"When did you decide this?" Camille asked, as tears rolled down her cheeks and she wiped them away with her napkin. Her sandwich was untouched too. He had stopped her in her tracks with what he said.

"About a month ago. We've been seeing each other over the summer."

"But you hardly know her," Camille tried to reason with him. They had met in March. It had been seven months.

"We're adults, we know what we want. We've both been married before. I hope you try to get to know her. I think you'll come to love her if you do. She's a good woman." Camille didn't believe that about her, but she could see that her father's mind was made up, and she couldn't change it. "She's moving in next weekend. We'll get married sometime next week. You can be my witness if you want to. But I understand if you don't." He had thought of everything, and obviously planned it all with Maxine. And then she thought of something else, with a look of panic.

"What did you do with Mom's things?" Everything had stayed in Joy's closets. Neither of them had had the heart to get rid of anything, and until now they didn't want to.

"I had Raquel put it all away neatly in boxes in the attic. I saved it all for you." It was the only good news she'd heard since she sat down to lunch. At least he hadn't thrown her mother's things away. She wondered if Maxine would have. "We're going to Mexico for two weeks, for a honeymoon, and after that everything will go on just as it is now." But she knew that wasn't true. With Maxine living with them, as his wife, everything would change. It was inevitable, no matter what he promised her.

"What about her two sons? Are they moving in with us too?"

"They're coming for Christmas. One is working, and the other one is in school. They're not moving here. But her mother is," he added. "She's a little old lady, she's eighty-seven years old, and we were thinking about putting her in the cottage we never use." It was the cabin where he had lived with Joy while they built the château. It had been Maxine's suggestion to put her mother there, and if they could decorate it decently, improve the heating system, and put in new insulation, Christophe thought it was a good idea. He was planning to ask Cesare to oversee the renovation. He hadn't told him about it yet either, so Camille didn't inadvertently hear it from someone else.

"You mean the one behind the château?" Camille looked shocked at the idea, but her father nodded. "It's freezing and the place is a mess." It had been used as a storage facility for years. "You can't put an old woman there," she said decisively. "She must really hate her mother to move her into the cottage," Camille added in an acid tone, but she hadn't objected to his plans. She hadn't gotten up and stomped off. She loved him too much to do that. She wanted him to be happy, just not with Maxine. But he had made his choice, and now she had to live with it. "Don't you think you should wait a little longer, Papa?" she asked, pleading with him, and he shook his head. He knew that Maxine wouldn't have waited if he hadn't proposed to her, and would have moved away when her lease was up, or so she said. And waiting to marry for six months more, or a year, wouldn't make any difference. He was sure of what he wanted, and Camille would adjust in time, when she got to know her.

"I'm going to have Cesare work on the heating in the cabin, and put in new insulation and clean it up. We can make it comfortable for her mother," he said, and Camille nodded, speechless with grief.

They sat at the table for a little longer, and both of them gave up the pretense of eating. She threw both their sandwiches away when they left the restaurant. And for the first time since her mother's death, she didn't go back to the office. She just couldn't. She wanted to go home and look around on her own. She felt as though she was losing her home to Maxine. And she was even more afraid that she would lose her father to her. He was totally under her spell. Everything Camille had feared about her had turned out to be true. She was a clever, conniving woman. And Camille could see how naive her father was being. He saw no motive behind Maxine wanting to marry him so quickly, no downside and no risk, although he'd been working on a prenuptial agreement with his lawyer for the past two weeks, and had asked him to draw up a new will. Maxine had said she'd sign whatever he wanted. She wasn't asking him for anything. The only thing she had balked at was giving him her financial statement. She said it was embarrassing. All she had was what was in her bank account, and she had so much less than he did. She had no property and no investments, and had never pretended that she did. She also had no income, and she had offered to work at the winery if he wanted her to, which he had said he didn't. He had all the staff he needed, and Camille, who had been perfectly trained by her mother. Maxine had no experience running a business. She had run their homes for both of her husbands, and done some modeling as a young girl. She had never pretended to have more than she did, and he respected her for it. She said that she had only what was left of the money her stepchildren had paid her to buy out her share of their father's estate, and they had paid her very little. She had been living on it for the past year, and she said she was going to bring her mother and sons over. She didn't expect Christophe to pay for that too, it was enough that he was going to support her. He didn't want her to work, and in fact would prefer it if she didn't. She was an elegant, beautiful, intelligent woman, and a wonderful companion for him. Joy had always been a worker, and had a head for business, but Maxine was an entirely different breed of woman.

When Camille walked into the house after their fateful lunch, she tried not to imagine the house with Maxine in it. She sat in her mother's office for a little while, and her dressing room, all the familiar places that Camille associated with her. And now everything was going to change. She lay on her bed and cried for the rest of the afternoon.

Maxine called Christophe as soon as he got back to the office. "How did it go?" she asked, sounding tense. She had been afraid that Camille would try to influence him, change his mind, or ask him to wait another year, and she couldn't afford to do that. She needed someone to support her and pay her bills, which were mounting up. She had taken a gamble coming to the Napa Valley, and it had paid off. She had been lucky to meet Christophe, and she didn't want his daughter screwing that up now.

"She's a very reasonable girl," Christophe said, sounding somber. And he knew that if he'd had lunch with Sam Marshall instead of his daughter, he would have tried to dissuade him. "This isn't easy for her, and we're not giving her much notice. A week from now she'll have a stepmother, and she hardly knows you, but she wants me to be happy. This is an enormous leap of faith for her." And he knew it was the measure of how much his daughter loved him, that she was willing to accept his decision, whether she agreed with it or not. "Maybe we should have waited a little longer," he said sadly, remembering her face at lunch and the tears running down her cheeks. Maxine's heart nearly stopped as he said it. "But I really don't want to. I want us happily married, and tucked in at the château," he said, smiling, thinking of Maxine and not his daughter. "We're adults. We know what we're doing. We don't need to wait, even if it would have been easier for her. But it will be better for all of us now, living under one roof as a family. She'll get to know you faster that way too." Maxine didn't agree with that, and would have preferred to have him to herself, but she could deal with his daughter if she had to, even if the situation wasn't ideal.

He stopped to see Maxine on his way home that night. The house on Money Lane was full of boxes and suitcases she was filling with her wardrobe. That was all she was bringing with her. The house had been rented furnished. And she had told him she had left everything in France, and had instructed her mother to sell it for her before she left. Christophe was looking forward to meeting his new mother-in-law, he was sure she was as elegant and gracious as her daughter. And he was also looking forward to meeting her boys at Christmas. They were suddenly a whole family now, with three children and a mother-in-law. His family was growing rapidly.

Maxine could see that he was depressed after his conversation with his daughter, and she rapidly took his clothes off, peeled off her own, and lured him to her bed to distract him and cheer him up, and it was eight o'clock before he realized the time, and said he should go home to Camille. He wanted to see if she was adjusting to the startling news she had at lunch. Maxine wanted him to stay, but he felt obligated to see his daughter. When he got home, he found Camille sound asleep in her bed, fully dressed. He could tell from the tissues around her that she'd been crying when she fell asleep, and hadn't woken up since. He gently touched her head and leaned down and kissed her and left her where she was. She smiled in her sleep, and he quietly left the room, hoping that she would soon get used to the idea of having a stepmother, and one so different from her mother. He knew he was doing the right thing for himself. All that remained was to convince Camille.

Christophe hadn't said anything to Sam about his plans, but he felt strange about getting married without telling him. He was one of his oldest friends in the Napa Valley, and Sam had been supportive of him when he lost Joy. He called him at the office the day before they were planning to get married, and Sam was silent for a long moment when he heard the news, and then he let out a sigh.

"I don't know why, but I had a feeling you were going to do something like that, it's why I said what I did that night at the ball." Christophe was just the kind of man who liked being married, and Maxine was an artful woman. Sam was convinced she had preyed on Christophe's loneliness and desire not to be single for long. He would have preferred to see him choose any woman but the one he had. He was convinced she was after money. Sam could smell it, but one of the things he loved about his friend was his naiveté and willingness to believe the best of everyone. He projected his own kindness and trustworthiness onto all those he met. He was a man of honor, and assumed that others were too.

"We have a lot in common," Christophe insisted. "We're both French, we have the same culture, the same upbringing, and she needs someone to protect her. She's alone in the world, except for her mother and two sons in France. She was treated miserably by her stepchildren after her last marriage, when her husband died."

"You're not that French anymore," Sam reminded him. "You've

been here for a long time. Have you had her investigated? Did you run a background check on her?" Sam was above all a practical man, and not as trusting as his friend. He had run into gold diggers before, and she seemed like one to him. Maybe even a pro. She had all the earmarks of it, to Sam. But not to Christophe.

"Of course not." Christophe sounded shocked. "She's not a criminal. She doesn't want anything from me."

"You won't know that till you're married to her. I hope you got a solid prenup." Sam sounded worried.

"Of course I did. We're not going to need it, but I'm not a fool."

"So when are you getting married?" Sam asked him, feeling sad about it. Christophe was a great guy, and deserved to find another woman like Joy, not fall into the clutches of a femme fatale and operator like Maxine. Sam was allergic to women like her and steered a wide berth around them, as he had with Maxine.

"Tomorrow," Christophe said, and at the other end, Sam winced.

"You're not wasting any time."

"She was going to leave Napa otherwise, or go back to France." Not likely, Sam thought to himself, but he didn't say it to Christophe, who believed every word she said.

"How does Camille feel about it?"

"She's not happy," Christophe said honestly, "it's a big change for her, after her mother. And she likes being alone with me. But she'll get used to Maxine once she gets to know her. It may take a while. Her mother is moving in with us after we get back from our honeymoon. It might be nice for Camille having a grandmother around. And her boys are coming for Christmas."

"It sounds like you're going to have a lot on your hands," Sam said and didn't envy him. He much preferred the arrangement he had with Elizabeth, where they had separate lives and came together from time to time, but he knew it wouldn't have been enough for Christophe, who wanted a real home life, and a wife at his side. Sam was sure she had played her cards well. And now they were all going to be living at the château. It seemed idyllic to Christophe, but not to Sam. And he could easily believe it was Camille's worst nightmare come true. He felt sorry for her.

"Well, let me know how it's going. Let's have lunch when you get back." Christophe had told him they were going to Mexico for their honeymoon for two weeks. Maxine had wanted to go to Bali, but Christophe wanted to stay closer to home, so she'd agreed. He had a lot to do when he got back, with all the work they normally did after the harvest, crushing the grapes and making the wine. Sam would be busy too.

"I'll call you," Christophe promised.

"Good luck, my friend," Sam said and they hung up. Sam had a heavy heart all day, when he thought about it.

Maxine had moved in over the weekend and Camille had spent two nights with a friend she called out of the blue, so she didn't have to see it happen. Florence Taylor had been her best friend in high school and they still talked from time to time, or texted. She had lost her mother too and when Camille told her what was happening, Florence was deeply sympathetic and invited her to stay for the weekend. She worked for the Mondavi winery and rented a small house in Yountville. It was almost like old times, as they sat up and talked all night. She tried to reassure Camille, and told her that she and Maxine might become good friends in time. She hadn't liked her father's new wife at first either, and now she loved her. But Florence didn't know Maxine. She was in a class all by herself. Camille couldn't imagine ever loving her, and when she got home on Sunday night, they had a silent and chilly dinner in the kitchen. Camille went to her room immediately afterward. She was polite to her soon-to-be stepmother, but she couldn't bring herself to be more than that. And Maxine was syrupy sweet to her whenever Christophe was around, and ignored her when he wasn't. They retired early to their bedroom that night too.

The next morning, Maxine came down the main staircase while Christophe and Camille waited for her. She was wearing an ivory satin Chanel suit she'd had sent to the château from Neiman Marcus in San Francisco, with ivory satin high-heeled shoes. Christophe looked awestruck when he saw her. Her hair was swept up in a French twist, and she had put white flowers in it. Camille had worn a simple navy blue dress and flat shoes. And they took one of the winery cars for the drive to City Hall in Napa. Camille had agreed to be her father's witness, and he had brought Cesare along as the second witness, for Maxine. She chatted with him in Italian, which she spoke fluently, and he looked as mesmerized by her as the groom did. She had a way with men that seemed to bring all of them under her spell, Camille noticed. But to Camille, everything about her seemed so fake. Her smiles at Christophe were canceled by the cold look in her eyes whenever she talked to Camille when he wasn't around.

The ceremony at City Hall was perfunctory and brief. A judge on duty declared them man and wife, and Maxine beamed, and then Christophe kissed her. She had had one of the gardeners prepare a small bouquet for her, which she handed to Camille during the ceremony, and then carried as they left City Hall, and Camille noticed that she called herself Countess Lammenais now, which she wasn't since Christophe was not a count, and Maxine had acquired the title when she married her last husband and lost it when she remarried. But even in the first few minutes after the ceremony, she made it clear that she intended to hang on to the title. And Cesare continued to address her as "Countess," with a look of reverence. Christophe didn't seem to notice and was floating on a cloud, as he kept kissing Maxine and hugging his daughter, who had a heavy heart thinking of her mother.

Camille had fought back tears all through the ceremony, and felt like she was suffocating in the car on the way to lunch. She had kissed her father, and congratulated the bride, and the final ignominy was having to experience it all with Cesare, while he was visibly impressed by the false countess and used her title in almost every sentence.

The four of them had lunch on the terrace at the Auberge du Soleil in Rutherford, and he was relieved that Cesare and Maxine were so congenial. At least he would not have to referee a war between them, as he had with Joy. Maxine actually liked him.

Christophe had invited Sam to lunch at the last minute, but he said he was busy and couldn't come, which was just as well. When they were together, you could sense Sam's dislike for Maxine coming through his pores. He was never good at concealing what he felt, nor did he try. He had turned the lunch down for that reason. He knew he couldn't hide his distress at his old friend marrying Maxine, whom he considered a clever predator.

Getting through lunch was almost more than Camille could bear. She felt like she was going to be sick on the way back to the château in the car. Mercifully, the bridal couple spent the night in San Francisco, so they could get to their early flight to Mexico on time the next day. It was a relief when she saw them back out of the driveway, in one of the vineyard vans, driven by Cesare, who had become Maxine's lackey overnight. As much as he and Joy had hated each other, he appeared to adore Maxine, which was a relief to Christophe, but felt like a final betrayal to Camille.

Camille waved as the van disappeared, and her last vision of her father was him kissing Maxine again, which he seemed to do constantly. Maxine was always wrapped around him like a snake. It was going to be peaceful to be alone in the house for the next two weeks without them, and she used the time to stay late at work, get a start on new projects, and develop a plan for Internet marketing of wedding events to show her father when he got back. She knew he was going to be busy with the post-harvest work. And Maxine's mother was arriving only a few days after their return.

Camille called Florence Taylor to thank her again for letting her stay, told her about the wedding, and expressed her distrust of Maxine again. Florence told her to stay in touch, and Camille got back to her busy days, which left her no time for anything except work. As a kindness to her father and stepmother, Camille checked on the cottage. The vineyard workers had been working on it at Cesare's direction to get it ready for Maxine's mother. She found several things lacking, and had a comfortable chair moved in, a better couch, more lamps, a rug they were storing and had never used, and some extra space heaters to make sure that it was warm enough for such an old woman. In the end, it looked rustic but inviting, with a big red hooked rug in the kitchen, several small blue ones in the bedroom, which was barely big enough for the bed and headboard, and she had the gardeners clean up the area around the house itself. There was a chicken coop not far from the cabin, a vegetable garden, and a small barn that hadn't been used in years.

The cottage was sweet and had a Hansel and Gretel quality to it, particularly after Camille put the finishing touches on it, but she couldn't understand why Maxine didn't put her elderly mother in the guest room in the main house with them. It seemed dangerous to put someone so old in a tiny house all by herself. What if she fell at night when she went to the bathroom, or stumbled over the tree roots in the garden? Eighty-seven seemed ancient to Camille, who had never known anyone that old, and had never had grandparents of her own, since both her parents had lost theirs before she was born. And she was sure that the hens in the chicken coop would disturb her, unless she was too deaf to hear them. She expected Maxine's mother to be frail, given her age, but she had approved the cottage for her.

Getting the cottage ready gave Camille something to do on weekends, and it looked like a doll house when her father and Maxine got home. They were happy, relaxed, and amorous. They said they had spent two weeks on the beach and at the pool, drinking margaritas, when in fact they had spent most of the two weeks in bed, indulging their insatiable passion for each other, but of that Camille was unaware.

The night they came home, after Cesare drove them from the airport, Camille brought her father up to speed on what had happened at the office. On the whole, everything had gone smoothly despite a minor argument with Cesare, which she told him while Maxine unpacked their suitcases, and Camille showed him the cottage, and he was touched by all that she had done for an old woman she didn't even know, which was typical of Camille. She had her father's kind heart and her mother's head for business. Maxine followed them out to the cottage after a while, and was surprised when she saw the cozy cabin that Camille had transformed. But instead of grateful, she looked annoyed.

"Why did you bother? My mother doesn't need all that, she's used to living in a small Paris apartment." Maxine's financial history was still a mystery to Christophe, and he had assumed that her mother had a little money, which she lived on. "It's very pretty," she conceded, when Christophe thanked Camille for her effort, but Maxine went back to the château after a few minutes, and didn't look pleased about it. As far as she was concerned, having her mother there was going to be an obligation and a headache, not a pleasure. She was an only daughter, her mother was out of money, and Christophe had very generously offered to bring her over and have her live with them, so Maxine didn't have to fly to Paris regularly to check on her, given her age. She said that her mother would prefer to be on her own, was very independent, did her own cooking, and wouldn't be a bother to them. He considered it part of his life with Maxine now, as well as being a good stepfather to her two sons, who were coming for a month at Christmas.

Camille didn't see her stepmother again that night. Maxine had retired to their bedroom before she and her father got back from their walk. He kissed her lovingly on the forehead, and Camille went to her own room, wondering about Maxine's strange reaction to the cottage Camille had gone to so much trouble with, to please her. Her final pronouncement on it was that it was "much too nice for my mother," which seemed very strange to Camille.

*   *   *

In three days, Maxine's mother was due to arrive from Paris. Everything was already starting to change. Strangers were moving in with them. Camille had stepbrothers she'd never even met. And her father had been bewitched by a woman Camille didn't like or trust. But there was nothing she could do about it now. She had never felt so helpless in her life. The tides were coming in so fast she felt like she would drown.

Chapter Nine

The morning after Christophe and Maxine returned from their honeymoon in Mexico, he left early for the office, and Camille was putting her dishes in the sink when Maxine came down to breakfast. She didn't bother to say good morning, or respond to Camille when she did. She poured herself a cup of coffee and sat down at the kitchen table with a surly expression, and fixed her gaze on her step-daughter.

"What was all that about, with your fixing up the cottage for my mother? Trying to impress your father? If it was for me, you needn't bother. My mother is perfectly able to take care of herself, and is a no-frills kind of person, which is why I put her out there. She wouldn't be comfortable in the château in a fancy bedroom." It seemed like an odd description to Camille, but she didn't comment. Maxine's attitude toward her mother was certainly not one of kindness or concern.

"I wanted to be sure she was warm enough out there. It gets cold at night. It might be better for her here, even if she doesn't like 'fancy' bedrooms," Camille finally answered, struggling to be polite.

"She's sturdy for her age. Her apartment in Paris is always freezing, she likes it that way. She grew up in the country." It was the first detail Camille had heard of Maxine's family or childhood. She seemed to have landed full grown, at birth, in haute couture clothes. It was hard to imagine her ever being a child, or even having a mother, particularly the way she spoke about her. It gave Camille the impression that there was no love lost between them. "You know, you can go back to school anytime you want to. Christophe told me you want to go to business school. You might want to think about it for January," Maxine said coldly. It sounded like she was telling Camille to leave.

"It's too late to apply," she said quietly. "I couldn't go till the fall, and I don't want to. I like working with my father," Camille said firmly, with the perfect understanding that Maxine wanted to get rid of her.

Maxine nodded in response to what Camille had said.

"Just so we're clear that I am the mistress of this house now. I'm the chatelaine of Château Joy," she said, using the French term for a woman who owned a château. "You're not. You're welcome to stay here," she said, her eyes boring into Camille's like drills, "but I run the show now. Don't expect to manipulate your father to get what you want, or you'll have me to deal with." It was a shot across Camille's bow, and Maxine hadn't wasted any time delivering it, they hadn't been home a day yet.

"Of course I'm welcome to stay here. This is my home," she reminded Maxine. "And what do you think I want from my father? I don't 'manipulate' him, that's not how we are."

"I see through your little baby doll act, the fairy princess who adores her father. You have him wrapped around your little finger," she said with a bitter expression that Camille hadn't seen on her before.

"Apparently not," Camille commented, referring to their rapid marriage a few weeks before. If she'd had her father wrapped around her little finger, as Maxine said, she would have convinced him not to get married. It was Maxine who had him in her thrall, and controlled him.

"Just know that you will have me to deal with if you work against me," she warned her.

Without a word, Camille left the kitchen, went to her room to regain her composure, and left for work a few minutes later. She wasn't sure whether to tell her father about the exchange or not. The woman was a monster. But Camille also knew that if she told him, he would find some excuse for her behavior, or a gentler interpretation of what she'd said. Her father gave everyone the benefit of the doubt and a fair chance, even cheats and liars, and now manipulators. For the moment, Camille decided, discretion appeared to be the better part of valor. Reporting to him on his wife's behavior, or complaining about it, served no purpose. He wanted to believe that Maxine was perfect, and Camille would only upset him and make him angry if she told him otherwise. She had no one else to talk to about it. She didn't want to call Florence again, since the last time they'd talked Florence had continued to insist that she and Maxine would be best friends one day just as she was now with her own stepmother. She didn't understand Camille's situation or women like Maxine. And thinking about Maxine's warning that morning, Camille walked to work at a rapid pace down the hill to get her anger out of her system. It had gotten her day off to a bad start.

And when she got to work, she found Cesare in her office. He didn't even look embarrassed when Camille walked in. He was sitting in her chair, at her desk, and digging around in the drawer.

"What are you doing?" Camille asked sharply. Her mother would have fired him for less, if Christophe had allowed it.

"I'm looking for your petty cash envelope," he said smugly.

"It's in the safe. Why do you want it?" Her tone was suspicious and harsh, as she felt he deserved.

"The countess said I should be getting more money for expenses, she said she'd discuss it with your father."

"She doesn't work here. I do, and I handle the petty cash. And she's not a countess. She just calls herself that now."

"She was married to a count. That makes her a countess."

"She's married to my father now, and he's not a count," Camille persisted. "And she has no business promising you more money. She doesn't work for the winery, she has no say here. And don't come back here again, and dare to go through my desk." She stood and watched him leave, as he glared angrily at her. After he had left, she took a key from a hiding place and locked her desk drawers. This was definitely the beginning of a new era if he felt comfortable enough to go through her desk, with the purpose of helping himself to more petty cash, and not even apologize for it. She told her father about it that night when they walked home together. They had both been busy all day and hadn't seen each other.

"I'll say something to her," Christophe promised. "She was probably just trying to be nice to him. She said she'd like to help you with some promotions for the label, though. And she wants us to start entertaining at the winery, she thinks it would be good PR." He had already told her she wouldn't be accepted in principle by the aristocratic Old Guard of social types in the Napa Valley, but she could reach out to some of the wealthy new vintners, who were buying wineries as investments or to show off, or both. And she wanted to start inviting some of the new billionaire high-tech investors and the international set, many of whom she knew now. And she was well aware that being married to Christophe would give her more importance than before, and entrée everywhere. She said she wanted to entertain in order to help the winery with new connections, but Camille sensed that it was all about her, and was suspicious of her motives.

"Will she be working with us, Papa?" Camille asked with a feeling of dread. Maxine was acting as though that could happen. It would ruin everything for her if she did. Having to see her at home at night would be hard enough. And Camille didn't want her interfering at Château Joy.

"Just on special events," Christophe answered gently. "She's awfully good at giving parties, and getting people with money together. People always find her enchanting. She adds a huge dose of glamour to everything she touches. We might have something to learn from her," he said, and Camille was careful not to make a negative comment about Maxine, knowing that her father wouldn't like it. "She's not going to work on the things you and I do, but we could make her director of PR and special events if we want to. She wants to learn more about the business. It's a family run business and she's family now." Camille cringed at what he said. The idea that Maxine was part of her family made her ill, but by marriage, she was.

"Just tell her not to make Cesare any promises. I have a hard enough time keeping track of his expenses as it is. Whatever he takes in petty cash, I get no change back, and he always claims we owe him more." Her father knew it too, and Joy had said it about him for years. "He actually gets too much, although he'll never admit it."

"The amounts he gets won't kill us," Christophe said, smiling, as they reached the château. Maxine had seen them coming, and opened the door, wearing a magnificent wine colored velvet evening gown. She had dressed for dinner, and to impress her new husband, if not his daughter. She looked like a queen and the setting of the château suited her. She looked totally at home.

"Home from the wars," she said as she kissed Christophe and handed him a glass of wine as they walked in. The day was crisp and the evening had gotten chilly, and she had built a fire. He sank into a chair in front of it, admiring his wife and enjoying his wine, as Camille went to her room to wash her face and hands and comb her hair before dinner. She was not going to put on an evening gown, and didn't own one as grand anyway. And even if she did, she would have felt ridiculous putting on an evening dress for Raquel's tacos in their kitchen. But Maxine looked very much the lady of the manor, as she sat in a chair next to Christophe and leaned over to kiss him, and the lure in her eyes told him that there were delights in store for him that night. They were kissing when Camille came back downstairs half an hour later.

"Are we still having dinner at seven?" Camille asked them from the doorway, and Maxine waved a dismissive hand toward her.

"That's so absurdly early," she said, laughing as she looked at her husband. "And so American. Why don't we start having dinner at eight or eight-thirty? We're French after all."

"I'm not," Camille said clearly. "I'm half American, and my American half is starving by seven."

"Then why don't you go ahead and eat now, and we'll eat later," Maxine suggested and Christophe nodded. He liked the idea of unwinding with Maxine in front of the fire for a while before dinner, and eating later. Camille didn't answer, went out to the kitchen, and heated two of Raquel's tacos in the microwave, ate them alone at the kitchen table, and went back upstairs fifteen minutes later, while her father and stepmother talked in soft voices, and laughed from time to time, as though they had precious secrets to share. She hadn't interrupted them, she just went back to her room, gently closed the door, and sat on her bed. Their family life appeared to be over. Maxine was taking matters in hand, just as she had warned Camille she would that morning. Camille had just seen the proof, and Christophe didn't even realize what had happened. Maxine was making him French again, his ties to the American traditions he had adopted seemed to be vanishing with Maxine in residence. And their family dinners were over.

For the next two nights, Camille ate dinner alone in the kitchen at the usual time, and Christophe and Maxine ate dinner one night at eight-thirty, and the following night at nine, after he worked late at the office. Maxine had Raquel set the table for two, which was a clear message to Camille that she wasn't welcome to join them. To justify it, she told Christophe that Camille had chosen not to eat later than seven, and he liked their new dinner time. Camille decided she didn't mind being excluded, it was less unpleasant than having to make small talk with her stepmother and pretend to like her for her father's benefit. It made dinner quick and easy, and by seven-thirty,

Camille was lying on her bed and watching TV. She missed catching up with her father over dinner, but not having the meal with Maxine. She had won this round, with ease.

The following day, Maxine's mother was due to arrive from Paris. Her father had told her that by the time Maxine's mother collected her bags, cleared customs, and was driven to Napa, they expected her to reach the château at five o'clock, and he asked Camille to be there to greet her. Cesare was picking her up and would warn them when he was five minutes away, and Camille promised that she'd be there as part of the welcoming committee, and her father planned to be too. Maxine grumbled that they didn't need to make a fuss about her, and Camille was surprised that she wasn't going to the airport to meet her. Maxine said it was much too long a drive, and would be too tiresome waiting for her to come out of customs. So they would welcome her in Napa. Camille wondered how hard the trip would be for her, at eighty-seven, and what condition she'd be in when she arrived, and if they'd need a wheelchair for her. She had told Cesare to put one in the car for her, just in case, since they kept them at the winery for older visitors.

Camille had a busy day, and so did Christophe, and Cesare called them as promised, when he was five minutes from the winery. Camille ran all the way up the hill to be there in time, and was standing on the top step of the château as Cesare drove up, with a woman in a hat in the backseat. And for some reason, given her age and relationship to Maxine, Camille was expecting her to wear a face veil, a huge hat, foxes wrapped around her neck, like Maggie Smith on *Downton Abbey,* and instead as they all waited, and Maxine stood stone-faced beside Camille, a tiny woman emerged in a big battered hat with flowers on it, and a haze of bright red hair peeking out from under it. She had on some kind of long shapeless flowered garment with a coat over it, high-top Converse sneakers, she was wearing a backpack and carrying a tiny ball of white fluff that was barking frantically at all of them. She set it down, and looking like a windup toy, it went straight for Maxine, snapped at her ankles, and growled at her.

"For heaven's sake, Mother," Maxine snapped at her in English, pushing the dog away with her shoe, which made the dog growl louder. "Did you have to bring the dog with you?"

"Of course," her mother said calmly, and smiled at Christophe and Camille, as she kissed her daughter on both cheeks. She was totally alert, had a twinkle in her lively green eyes, and the little white dog sniffed at Camille with interest, and wagged its tail as Camille bent to pet it.

"And what are you wearing on your feet?" Maxine asked when she spotted the high-top Converse under her mother's dress. It looked more like a housedress than something one would wear on a trip.

"They're sneakers. My feet get swollen when I fly, and they are very comfortable."

"You look ridiculous," she muttered, as Christophe greeted his mother-in-law politely in French, in the most formal way possible, and bowed as he kissed her hand. Camille had never seen him do that, although it was the proper way in France for him to greet a married or widowed woman of her age. And Maxine's mother was equally polite as they conversed for a moment, she commented on the beauty of the château, and thanked him for allowing her to come.

He introduced Camille, who spoke to her cautiously in English. Maxine's mother spoke very correct English, although with an accent.

"What's the little dog's name?" Camille asked her, stopping to pet her again as the dog frantically wagged her tail, and cast occasional dark looks at Maxine, whom she apparently knew and hated.

"Her name is Choupette," the elderly woman said warmly, "and I'm Simone."

"What is she?"

"She's part Maltese, and something else, my neighbor's Chihuahua perhaps, or Pomeranian." She was all white and very fluffy, and very tiny, like her mistress, whom Camille guessed couldn't be more than five feet tall, unlike her daughter who towered over her. Simone looked like the good fairy in a children's story, particularly in her funny outfit, with the big hat and flowered housedress and high-top sneakers. She didn't seem to care at all how she looked, and was completely oblivious to it. Christophe suggested that they take her to her cottage, that she must be exhausted from her trip, and observed that it was two o'clock in the morning in Paris for her.

"I'm fine. I slept on the flight, and watched two movies," Simone said, looking around, and interested in everything. She didn't look a day over seventy. She smiled at Camille several times and throughout the conversation, Maxine appeared unpleasant and anything but happy to see her. She obviously hated the dog, and disapproved of her mother. The two women couldn't have been more different. "I'd love to take a walk and look around after I drop my bags off," Simone said as she followed Christophe and Camille to the cottage, with Maxine bringing up the rear with a long face. She knew she had to bring her mother here, for economic reasons if nothing else, but she didn't enjoy having her with them, which she made obvious.

Camille had put supplies in the cottage early that morning that she thought she might need and enjoy. Milk and tea and sugar, honey, coffee, jam, some bread and cinnamon rolls for breakfast, and orange juice and a bowl of fruit. She was sure she'd be eating in the château kitchen, but she might get hungry in the night or the early morning. She had added yogurt, a wedge of Brie and a box of crackers, and a chocolate bar at the last minute. And Simone exclaimed with pleasure as Christophe opened the door for her, and she followed him inside.

"How pretty it all is. What a lovely place!" she said, looking gratefully at her daughter, who did not respond. And then she thanked Christophe profusely for making her feel so welcome. She took her hat off and left it in the bedroom as her mane of wild red hair sprang to life, and Choupette ran around the room barking and wagging her tail. Camille stooped to play with her again, and then showed Simone what was in the kitchen, and was startled when she opened the refrigerator and saw that it was full of more food than she had left there earlier.

"My mother prefers her own cooking," Maxine said with a look of disdain. "She won't be eating with us," she said, glancing pointedly in the direction of her mother, who got the message and didn't seem bothered by it, nor surprised. "I had Cesare buy what she'll need to cook her own dinners."

"You'll have to come and visit me for dinner," Simone said to Camille, who nodded. She was fascinated by the little woman who seemed so full of life and joy, and was so totally the opposite of her austere, artificial-seeming daughter, who hadn't smiled once since her mother arrived, nor even hugged her.

Christophe showed her everything she needed to know about the cottage, how to work the new heating system, and that there was wood in the fireplace. And then he and Maxine said their goodbyes and Simone invited Camille to stay with her, and offered her a cup of tea as soon as her daughter and son-in-law had left.

"Your father seems like a very kind man," she said, after she'd poured the tea into the flowered cups Camille had brought there for her from the château, and they sat down at the small kitchen table, where Maxine expected her to take her meals, which seemed shocking to Camille. Out of respect for her, Camille thought they should be taking care of her, instead her daughter wanted her to fend for herself and had made it abundantly clear from the moment she arrived, and before.

"He is a very kind man," Camille confirmed about her father.

"My daughter and I don't get on very well," Simone said bluntly. "I always tell her what I think, which is probably a mistake. And I'm not elegant enough for her. I've never wanted to be. I grew up on a farm, and I never liked living in the city once I was married. Maxine's father died when she was very young, and I went back to the country with her, to live with my sister. There were cows, and chickens, and goats, and horses, which she hated. She never forgave me for it, and couldn't wait to leave. She wanted to be with the fancy people, not peasants like me and my family, as she always said, even as a child. She went to Paris when she was eighteen and never came back. She was a model for a short time and had odd jobs as a salesgirl in a boutique, and then she married. She's always done well with her men. And I see she just has again.

"My sister died a few years ago, and her children sold the farm, so I had to move back to the city, and I didn't know anyone there, except Maxine. So now here I am in California. I'm so excited," she said, sparkling. As she said it, she took a pack of French cigarettes out of her backpack, much to Camille's surprise. She was full of spunk and mischief and acted far younger than her age.

"You'll have to show me the vineyards and the winery and everything you do here," she said, exhaling the pungent cigarette smoke. "I want to learn all about it. It was so lovely driving up here from the city, with all the vineyards and the countryside. It looks so much like Italy. And you, my dear, how old are you?" she asked Camille, who smiled at her. She suddenly felt as though she had acquired a real grandmother, or a friend, she wasn't sure which yet. Simone was nothing like she had expected, and Camille was so relieved. Two Maxines would have been unbearable. One was hard enough.

"I'm twenty-three. I'll be twenty-four in June, and I work at the winery with my father." Camille seemed very young as she said it.

"I'm sorry about your mother," Simone said seriously, and looked as though she meant it. "This must be very hard for you, having Maxine here and your father remarried. When did you lose your mother?" she asked sympathetically in a gentle voice as she finished the cigarette and used the saucer as an ashtray.

"Thirteen months ago." Simone's face registered surprise, as Choupette appeared at her feet and she scooped her up on her lap. The little dog investigated the table and was disappointed not to see food there.

"That's not long at all," Simone commented. "Your father must have been very lonely without her. Men do that. Some men just aren't good at being single if they were happily married." An odd look crossed her face then, as her eyes met Camille's. "I'm not sure Maxine is the woman who'll give him a peaceful home life. She always has big plans. She takes better care of herself than she does of others," she said honestly about her only child. "She's not a caretaker by nature. She left her boys with me when they were young, between husbands. And I'm not sure that was the right thing to do. They're a great deal like her, my oldest grandson anyway. His younger brother loves to play and is a terrible student. I was far too indulgent with them. But then she remarried and they went to live with her when they were ten and twelve." She was filling Camille in on the family history, she was eager to hear it, particularly told by Simone, who was more likely to tell her the truth. She had already painted a portrait very different from the smooth elegance the "countess" portrayed.

"Was that when she married the count with the château in Périgord?" Christophe had told Camille about him, but said he knew nothing about the first one.

"No," Simone answered her question. "Her first husband was some young boy she married when she was a model. He's the boys' father, his family had money but they didn't approve of her. He divorced her very quickly, and she had quite a hard time for a while, which was when she left the boys to me. Her second husband was a very nice man actually, and he was very sweet to the two boys. He was a book editor in Paris, and he had no money. She divorced him when she met Charles, the count, and married him. I don't think she's ever seen her first two husbands again, the boys never see their father and I'm not sure she admits to Stéphane, her second husband, at all. She had a very nice life with the count, although she hated his children and tried to keep him away from them as he got older and sicker. It was her idea to move him to Périgord, so they weren't checking on her constantly, and she could do what she wanted. She did everything she could to alienate them, and poor Charles was completely under her spell, and spoiled her shamelessly. Jewelry, haute couture clothes, he gave her some paintings, which she sold after he died, so she could move out here. His children got even with her the moment he passed away. It ended quite badly. I don't know the details, but they gave her a day or two to move out of both houses, and they took her to court to get some of his things back, particularly some very valuable paintings she claimed he had given her. She burned her bridges in Paris, and came out here. And now she's happily married again, to a kind man, and the chatelaine of a château once more. Maxine is like a cat. She always lands on her feet and has nine lives."

She smiled as she looked at Camille, and the two women knew instantly that they had each found an ally. Camille listened to her, shocked by the stories Simone had told her, and wondered how much her father knew of Maxine's history, probably almost nothing, except what she chose to tell him. Maxine had portrayed herself as the victim of terrible stepchildren, who undoubtedly would have said the same of her, or worse.

"My father is very much in love with her," Camille said quietly, and Simone nodded. It didn't surprise her.

"Most men are. She knows how to play the game and bewitch them. Men love dangerous women like her. Poor Stéphane was heartbroken when she left him. She never let him see the boys again. They weren't his children, but he was devoted to them. And their own father never saw them. He married very quickly after they divorced, and moved to London. His family are in banking there, but they wanted nothing to do with her, or the boys. Maxine always leaves a trail of rubble behind her, but she doesn't seem to care. She reinvents herself quite easily, just as she did here. She's probably the darling of the Napa Valley by now," Simone said, "and I'm sure your father has opened all the right doors for her." It was what Maxine expected and demanded of every man.

"Not exactly," Camille said thoughtfully, digesting what she had just learned about her stepmother, all of which sounded accurate to her. Her own mother would know the truth about her. "My father doesn't like social life as much as she does. She's trying to convince him to give grand parties, and meet important people. My father is happy at home, and he and my mother didn't go out much."

"She won't let him stay that way," Simone said confidently. She knew her daughter. "It doesn't serve her purposes, she's always looking for a better deal, an opening, an opportunity. That's how she works." This time, Camille looked truly worried.

"Do you think she'd leave my father for someone else?" Camille asked her in a whisper, in case someone came back to check on Simone and overheard the conversation. This was fascinating information.

Simone thought about it for a minute. "She could, unless she's more in love with your father than she usually is. She might leave him, if she had a golden opportunity elsewhere she couldn't resist. There must be a lot of rich men here," Simone said wisely. She was nobody's fool. Camille hated Maxine but she didn't want her father to get his heart broken either. "Men who fall in love with her do so at their own risk and peril. They usually know it, or suspect it, but they can't resist the gamble. She brings them to the edge of insanity, which is always a dangerous thing. If any man ever makes you feel crazy and as though you have to have him, run. He won't do you any good. Maxine's not good for the men who love her either, or even her sons. She's only good for herself." Camille was sure that her father didn't know he was her fourth husband, and not her third. She seemed to have dropped the second one off the face of the earth, and dismissed him as unimportant because he was poor. She didn't keep poor men for long. "She always wants a more important man, or a richer one. Your father will have to be very generous to keep her," Simone said practically, and then looked mildly embarrassed and realized she'd said enough for their first meeting, and probably too much, as usual. "I have a habit of rattling on." She smiled at Camille. "Now, shall we go for our walk, before it gets too dark?" Camille nodded, totally intrigued by her, and she had been mesmerized by Simone's revelations about her daughter. Simone put her coat back on and followed Camille out of the house, with her red hair flying.

Simone was enchanted by the garden, and especially the vegetable garden. And she was delighted when she saw the chickens and clapped her hands, as Camille smiled.

"I haven't had chickens since I moved back to Paris. How wonderful! I'll bring you fresh eggs every day."

"My father says we need more hens, I think these are quite old," Camille explained.

"If someone will drive me to a poultry farm, we can buy them. And you have to come and have dinner with me. Do you like cassoulet?"

"I don't know what that is," Camille said hesitantly.

"Of course not, you're American. Why would you? It's a kind of stew, with beans. We'll have confit de canard, and hachis parmentier, pot-au-feu, kidneys, brains, tripe," she listed off a number of things that sounded frightening to Camille, but she was sure her father would know, and might even love. "You can have dinner with me anytime," Simone offered happily with a warm smile.

"I've been eating alone since they got back from Mexico," Camille said quietly. "Maxine likes to eat late."

"I eat fairly early, because I'm old. And I like to get up early. You can come and eat with me," she promised and Camille smiled.

They wandered back to her cottage, and Camille offered to bring her dinner on a tray from the château, but Simone said she was going to have a piece of fruit and yogurt and go to bed. She said she had eaten too much on the long flight, and the food was very good. She said she hadn't been on a plane in years.

"Come and see me tomorrow," she said to Camille and hugged her before she left. "We'll do lots of interesting things together," she said. "I will teach you French country cooking, and you will teach me about the grapes. Do we have an agreement?" she asked with her eyes dancing, and Camille laughed.

"Yes, we do."

"And by the way," Simone said casually, "don't worry if Maxine tells you I'm senile. She must be terrified that I'll say too much to you. She doesn't need to know what we talk about. And I'm not senile yet." She laughed and reminded Camille of a fairy godmother again. She was a funny little woman, and sharp as a tack, for any age. Camille had learned a lot about her stepmother that afternoon and none of it good. It confirmed Camille's initial instincts about her, but she didn't plan to tell her father. It would only hurt him, but it gave Camille a lot to think about.

"I'll tell her we played with Choupette and took a walk, if she asks me anything. Why doesn't Choupette like her, by the way? She growled at her when you arrived." They had all noticed it.

"Maxine kicked her once. Choupette's not senile either. She never forgets anything." They both laughed then and Camille went back to the château with a lighter step than she'd had in weeks.

Camille was getting her dinner ready in the kitchen when a little later Maxine walked in to open a bottle of wine. Maxine didn't say anything to her for a minute, and as Camille sat down at the table, her stepmother spoke to her in a firm tone.

"Don't pay too much attention to my mother, by the way. She has dementia."

Camille nodded as though she agreed with her, and said they had taken a walk near the chicken coop and Simone had liked it.

"She would," Maxine said with a look of contempt. "She's a peasant at heart. Did you see what she was wearing when she got here?" She was disgusted by it, and Camille smiled and ate her dinner without further comment. Simone was a very sharp old woman who knew her daughter well, and Camille had a new friend, an ally against her stepmother. And for the first time since her father had told her he was marrying her, she no longer felt alone or afraid of what would happen. What Camille had learned about Maxine was priceless. Camille knew she would remember every word of their conversation. It might be useful one day.

Chapter Ten

After her somewhat startling arrival, Simone settled into her new home very quickly, and she never complained about not being in the château. She wouldn't have wanted to live in such close proximity to her daughter anyway. In the cottage she had freedom and autonomy. She studied what was planted in the vegetable garden, and wanted to add some things to it. And she had Cesare drive her to buy three new chickens, and was very pleased with them. They were supposedly good layers, and she had a basket of eggs for Camille every day to take back to the château.

Simone went for long walks in the vineyards with Choupette, who ran ahead and back to her, and chased rabbits. Simone told her young friend that she thought the vineyards were beautiful in the country she found fascinating. She had never been to America before, and now she was living in one of the most exquisite places. And unlike her own daughter, living in grandeur only a few feet away, Camille came to visit her after work every day. They shared a cup of tea, while Simone smoked her cigarettes. Camille had brought her several ashtrays which were always half full when Camille came to visit.

"You shouldn't smoke," she scolded her, but had brought her the ashtrays anyway, since Simone needed them and showed no sign of quitting.

"At my age, it doesn't matter," she said cheerfully. "What? Will I live to only ninety-two instead of ninety-eight? And if it's only eighty-eight?" she said, lighting another one, as Camille smiled at her. She was totally endearing. She didn't have a mean bone in her body, unlike her daughter, who was all about calculation, and herself. "I have no idea where she came from," Simone said honestly, with a puzzled look. "Her father was a lovely person. We fell in love as children and he was kind to everyone. I was quite old when I had her, and we were so excited.

"Maxine was born angry and mean. She has always wanted what others have, nothing is ever enough for her, and she doesn't care who she hurts if it gets her what she thinks she needs. No one has ever said anything nice to me about her. It's sad really. She must be a throwback to some terrible ancestor who poisoned all her lovers and relatives perhaps." It was impossible to believe the two women were related, they didn't even look alike, with Maxine's jet black hair and eyes, and the flaming red hair Simone had had all her life, and dyed to keep the same color now, and her brilliant green eyes, almost the color of the Napa hills in spring. A few days after she arrived, Simone set out some paints and small canvases she had brought with her, and explained that she did landscapes and paintings of animals, and Camille told her about her mother being an artist and promised to show her Joy's beautiful frescoes in the château. "I'd love to see them," Simone said warmly.

At Simone's insistent questions, Camille explained to her about viticulture, and many of the things her father had taught her. She saw much less of him now, especially since they no longer ate dinner together, and he spent every moment he wasn't working with Maxine.

"He'll tire of her eventually," Simone said when Camille mentioned it. "She takes a lot of energy." But neither of them were prepared for what Camille found when she came home from work one day. She noticed it immediately. It took her breath away, as she stared at the pale yellow walls Maxine had had painted that day, to cover where Joy's frescoes had been. Camille found her upstairs in her mother's office, intent on the computer, sending emails. There were tears in Camille's eyes as she looked at her.

"How could you?" Camille was shaking with grief and rage.

"How could I what?" Maxine asked, without turning around to face her.

"You painted out my mother's frescoes."

"Your father said he didn't mind. The walls are a much happier color now. The frescoes and murals were depressing, and they were nearly twenty-four years old."

"I know how old they were," she said breathlessly. They were a few months older than Camille, since her mother had painted them when she was pregnant, while they were building the château and the winery. "My father said you could do that?"

"I told him I wanted to add some fresh color to the house, and he said it was fine with him." But obviously he hadn't understood her, because he was as shocked as Camille when he came home. Maxine looked hurt that he didn't like her color changes. She told Christophe not to make such a fuss about them, and was annoyed about it.

"You treat this house like a shrine," she reproached him. "I live here now." He didn't say anything after that.

Later he went to Camille's room and told her he had photographs of them, and they could have them repainted.

"That's not the same," Camille said miserably. Her mother had painted the original ones with her own hands, and Maxine had destroyed them.

Camille told Simone about it when she had breakfast with her the next day, Saturday.

"It's very like Maxine to do something like that. I'm sure she feels your mother around her everywhere, and every time she looks at you. She can be very wicked, you know, be careful of her, Camille." It was hard to believe she was speaking of her own daughter. "She was cruel as a child too, to other children, and she wanted to hurt Choupette that day when she kicked her, in order to upset me. Choupette has never forgotten it, nor have I. She hates animals, and dogs particularly." She changed the subject then so as not to upset Camille more than she already was about the frescoes. "We're having hachis parmentier tonight. You're in for a great treat." Camille had had brain and tripe with her so far, and was not totally convinced about French cuisine yet.

"What part of the guts is it this time?" she asked ruefully, and Simone laughed at her.

"Don't be such a coward. This is duck with mashed potatoes and black truffles." She had found a store in Yountville which carried them. It was the season for them in France too. There had been white truffles imported from Italy recently. Maxine and Christophe had a feast of them at The French Laundry at an immensely expensive dinner, Maxine said she loved them and Christophe had ordered them for her in advance. He couldn't do enough to please her, as Simone had predicted. It took a lot to keep Maxine satisfied, and feeling that she was getting her due. He bought caviar for her frequently and fresh crab from the city. Maxine loved her delicacies, although she stayed fashionably thin.

Camille had errands to do in St. Helena that day, and she ran into Phillip Marshall, whom she hadn't seen since the summer. She knew he was engaged, but his fiancée wasn't with him and she hadn't met her yet. He was going to the hardware store, and she was on her way to get toothpaste and some other things for Simone. Camille had become her willing errand boy, since Maxine never did anything for her, and Christophe had been very busy with the holidays coming, and special events scheduled at the winery.

Camille was happy to see Phillip, and he waved when he saw her from across the street and came over to give her a hug and talk to her.

"How's your new stepmother?" he asked her, and Camille was noncommittal. She didn't want to complain, which seemed disloyal to her father, but he could see the truth in her eyes.

"It takes some adjusting," also to the fact that she and Christophe spoke French all the time, even in front of Camille. Maxine refused to speak English to him now, and got angry when he spoke it at the house. She always said that they were both French, so why was he speaking English? He pointed out that Camille wasn't fluent, and they were in America, but Maxine got angry, wouldn't speak English with him anymore, and stuck to French, so eventually he did the same. "I have a terrific new French grandmother, though," she said, smiling at Phillip. "Maxine's mother. She's a character. You have to come and meet her. She has flaming red hair, she smokes like a chimney, drinks wine, and cooks weird French dishes for me. She's eighty-seven years old, she's an artist, and she has a funny little French dog."

"That's something at least. What are you doing for Christmas? Are you coming to our party?"

"I hope so. My stepbrothers are coming, so that should be interesting." She didn't look enthused about it, and he could see she wasn't happy. She seemed strained.

"Bring your new grandmother," he suggested and Camille was hesitant.

"She and Maxine don't get along, I don't think that would work."

"Just make sure you come. Francesca will be there," his fiancée. "I want you to meet her. Are you dating anyone?" he asked her and she shook her head. He was always so shocked by how grown up she was now. In his head, she was still a little girl, but now when he saw her, he noticed how beautiful she was, and more adult than he remembered.

"I don't have time to date. I'm busy at the winery. I'm trying to get my dad to do more social media, and I want to get more wedding business. It's lucrative but my dad thinks it's a lot of trouble." The Valley was a highly desirable venue for weddings. The Japanese had recently discovered it, and were flying there in droves to get married and loved to play golf at Meadowood.

"It's not a lot of trouble if you set it up right," Phillip said. "We make a fortune on it, and we have a woman who runs the whole thing for us. She's kind of a freak, but she does a great job." Phillip was impressed that Camille was trying to modernize their winery and public face. "Dad and I disagreed on it at first too. But he came around when he saw our profits. I guess the old guys don't like it.

They're purists and think it's cheesy because it's not wine, but it is big business today and an important source of income you can't ignore." She nodded in agreement and liked what he had to say.

"I hope you come to the party," he said, and hurried off to the hardware store a few minutes later. Camille went to the drugstore, wondering what his fiancée was like. Half an hour later, she went back to Château Joy. Her father and Maxine were gone for the day, to a luncheon at a winery in Calistoga. Maxine was still pushing him to do parties at the winery, and dinner parties at the château. They were doing a Christmas party at the winery, a week before Christmas, and Maxine had finally convinced him to do a small dinner at the château, for some of the billionaires who had recently bought houses there. She had hired the most expensive caterers in the Valley, and invited the biggest high-tech guys and their wives. She was excited at the prospect, and Christophe had agreed to it to make her happy, but he didn't really care. He would rather have given a casual dinner for other vintners and his good friends. But Maxine was far more socially ambitious than that. Christophe would have liked to have Sam there too, but knew he wouldn't have come. It was the kind of dinner party he hated, in addition to his aversion to Maxine.

When the night of the dinner party came, the house looked perfect, the dining room table gleamed with their best silver and crystal, and it was set with a lace tablecloth that had belonged to Joy's grandmother, and was an heirloom they only used on Thanksgiving and Christmas, which Maxine said she didn't know when Christophe mentioned it with a look of concern. There were handwritten place cards at every place in her signature brown ink, and when Christophe toured the table admiring the flowers in an array of small vases with small exotic orchids in them, he realized for the first time that Camille wasn't joining them. There was no place card for her. Camille had been aware of it for weeks and assumed that he was too. But she didn't know any of the people, except what she'd read about them online, so she didn't care, and it didn't surprise her that Maxine had excluded her.

"Why isn't Camille with us tonight?" he questioned his wife and she opened her eyes wide and looked startled.

"But, darling, she's so young, I didn't think you'd want her here, and the guests are very important." The founders of some of the biggest tech companies had accepted.

"I always invite Camille to anything we do here," Christophe corrected her, upset that Camille hadn't been included. To him, that was a given, she was such an important part of his life and he hadn't thought to tell Maxine to invite her, so he took responsibility for the oversight, and was sure it wouldn't happen again. "Why don't you set a place for her? I'll go up and tell her," he said, and Maxine instantly placed a hand on his arm to stop him.

"You can't! We'd be thirteen at the table. Someone would be sure to panic, or even leave. We can't do that. We'll invite her next time." He felt terrible about it, and went to explain to Camille that it was his fault for not telling Maxine to invite her.

"She thought you'd be bored with the guests. In fact," he whispered to Camille, "I might be bored with them too." They both laughed at that, and Camille said it didn't matter. She left to join Simone in the cottage a few minutes later, and Choupette did a little happy dance when she saw her. Camille had a treat for her in her pocket and gave it to her.

She told Simone about the dinner party she hadn't been invited to, and Simone wasn't surprised.

"I have something special for you tonight, my dear," she said with a cigarette hanging out of the corner of her mouth, as she stirred a pot of something mysterious looking. Camille had loved the hachis parmentier so her faith in French cooking had been restored. Simone preferred country dishes and what she referred to as "grandmother cooking," *"cuisine à la grand-mère."*

"What are you making?" Camille asked her and Simone served it a few minutes later with a flourish.

"Rognons!" Simone announced gleefully. Camille had been living on French country dishes ever since Simone had arrived, and she loved having dinner with her, mostly for the company, but she was surprised by how delicious the food was. Rognons were kidneys from an old recipe Simone said her mother had taught her.

"I might make pigs' feet for you next week, or frogs' legs," she said, looking pensive as they sat down to dinner.

"I think I'd prefer if you didn't. I had frogs' legs once, I thought they were nasty," Camille said honestly.

"They taste like chicken," Simone said firmly.

"Yeah, but they're not chicken. The Chinese say that about snake too."

"All right, snails then, if you're going to be difficult about it."

"No," Camille said definitively, "next week we're having turkey. And my father cooks it himself. It's Thanksgiving."

"What's that?" Simone asked with interest and her young friend explained it to her. "I quite like that, a holiday to be thankful for your blessings. That's very touching."

"It's an important family holiday here, it's almost as important as Christmas."

"I'm sure Maxine will love it," she commented drily and they both laughed. "She has more to be grateful for than anyone I know. She's very lucky she found your father. She was on her way to the poorhouse before she met him. She was almost out of money. I was three months late with my rent thanks to her. I thought they were going to try and throw me out, but they can't do that with old people in France. Otherwise, they might have. I think she's spent almost everything she blackmailed out of Charles's children."

"How did she blackmail them?" Camille was interested in the story, and Simone seemed willing to tell it. She was a bottomless pool of damning information about Maxine.

"She threatened to take them to court and fight them for the château. She couldn't have won, of course, since they owned three-quarters of it by French law. Children are protected in France. But she could have tied it up for five or ten years, and she knew they didn't want that, and were planning to use it. She threatened to reveal their family secrets to the press as leverage to get what she wanted from them. Maxine will stop at nothing when she's on a mission. They paid her off just to get rid of her, and she sold them back some of their paintings. It was quite disgraceful, and she talked to the press about them anyway. They were furious with her. They were happy to get rid of her, at any price. I must say, it's a very awkward thing having a daughter whom everyone thinks so poorly of. I was always apologizing for her when she was younger. These days, I'm sure I don't know the half of it, and it's probably best I don't. I hope she's behaving here."

She had no reason not to, and Christophe was giving her whatever she wanted. He had handed her charge cards to Neiman Marcus, Barneys, and Saks in the city, so she could go shopping, and a credit card for any other expenses. And he didn't question her about what she charged to his accounts. The catered dinner they were hosting that night was costing a fortune. And she was helping him plan the winery Christmas party, which Camille normally took care of. But Camille's father had given it to Maxine as a project, and she had already tripled the costs. The twenty-foot tree in the courtyard alone was going to cost them ten thousand dollars and another five to decorate it. Luckily, he could afford it, and Camille reminded him they could deduct it for business, but it still went against the grain with Camille to spend so much money when they didn't have to. They had always given a terrific party at the winery, on a much tighter budget. With Maxine, everything had to be extravagant and lavish. She loved to show off. She said she wanted him to give the best parties in the Valley, and become famous for it. He said he was happy to let Sam Marshall have that distinction, but Maxine wasn't, not by any means. She wanted to be the most important hostess in the Napa Valley. None of it surprised her mother.

Camille read about their dinner party online two days later. The person who had written about what an elite, intimate, exclusive event it was raved about it. And as Camille read the mention of it in a blog with news of the Napa Valley, she had the distinct impression that Maxine had written it herself.

Their Thanksgiving meal was much fancier than usual that year, with the caterer Maxine had insisted on hiring. Christophe had told her he liked cooking the turkey himself, but she wouldn't hear of it. She insisted on hiring a French caterer in the Valley, and invited two couples Camille had never seen before, and Christophe didn't know either. One was Italian, and the other French, which seemed odd to Camille, and they spoke both languages during the entire meal and never English. Camille was the only American at the table, and Simone was there as well, anticipating the meal Camille had described to her in detail. Maxine stunned Christophe and Camille by having ordered pheasant instead of turkey, with caviar and blinis for the first course. Camille was fighting back tears by the time they finished dinner. Nothing on the table was the food she had told Simone about, which was traditional. This was just a fancy dinner party among strangers. Camille was crying when she went to her room after Simone left, and Christophe came in to apologize to her, as she lay on her bed sobbing and missing her mother. Nothing in their home was familiar anymore.

"Why did you let her do that?" she accused him this time. "Thanksgiving is special, it's sacred. It's all about traditions. She just bulldozed right over us."

"I didn't know she was going to. She didn't tell me. She said she wanted to surprise us. She doesn't realize that the classic Thanksgiving meal is important to us."

"Why does everything have to be different now? And fancy so she can show off all the time?" She sounded like a little girl as he put his arms around her. His heart ached for her, and he missed Joy too. Maxine was a completely different woman than Joy, and he was sure that she was just trying to please him. There was no malice to it.

"I promise, we'll have turkey on Christmas."

"It was a terrible Thanksgiving," Camille said miserably. It was their second one without her mother, and the ridiculously different, elaborate meal just made the loss more acute. She was tired of Maxine and her constantly changing things, and never for the better. It all seemed worse now and her father was changing too. He was trying to keep Maxine happy, and losing sight of Camille and what she needed. Maxine was always pulling on him, and telling him that Camille had to get used to life without her mother and grow up. But she was doing it all too quickly and he could see that. They had been married for six weeks, and she had already made some radical changes, starting with painting over Joy's frescoes, which had shaken them both. He was going to ask her to slow it down.

"We don't even speak English here anymore," Camille accused him and he didn't deny it. Maxine was more comfortable in French. And she complained constantly about Raquel, who had been with them for thirteen years, and had come to help take care of Camille as a child. Christophe could see the handwriting on the wall with that too. He was going to warn her that Raquel was part of their family by now and he wasn't going to change housekeepers. But he didn't have time to talk to her about any of it.

The Monday after Thanksgiving, Christophe came home to find a stranger cooking dinner, a Frenchwoman Maxine had hired named Arlette, and she informed Christophe that she had caught Raquel stealing a Hermès Birkin bag and fired her without notice. Camille was sobbing in her room and Maxine refused to allow Christophe to hire Raquel back, and turned it into a showdown with him. In the end, he sent Raquel a check for three months' wages and an apology, and Camille was devastated to have lost someone so important to them, whom they loved. Maxine insisted she was a thief and lucky they hadn't called the police. Camille told Maxine she would never forgive her for it, and took refuge at Simone's cottage more than ever.

Maxine's two sons, Alexandre and Gabriel, arrived two days later, and everything was about them from then on. Maxine treated her sons like princes. Alexandre was twenty-six, and Gabriel was twenty-four. They were handsome young men, but extremely spoiled. They helped themselves to whatever they wanted, with total disregard for Christophe or Camille.

Camille nearly fainted when she saw Gabriel drive out in her father's Aston Martin, which he considered sacred, and Maxine had let him take it.

"I don't think you should do that," Camille said to her cautiously as Gabriel sped down the driveway, and an hour later he scraped a fender and the door in the winery parking lot, which Christophe heard about immediately and rushed out of his office to see what had happened. Gabriel was looking annoyed and said someone had parked too close to him, and insisted it wasn't his fault, with no apology offered. It was a tribute to Christophe's love for the young man's mother that he didn't lose his temper or make a scene about it, but Christophe looked like he had smoke coming out of his ears when he went back to his office. Maxine was convinced her boys were saints and could do no wrong.

The two "boys" took over the house, drank Christophe's best wines without asking him, and they went to San Francisco several times looking for nightclubs. Suddenly the house seemed to be exploding with testosterone. Christophe asked Maxine to invite Camille to dinner, where all four of them spoke French, and Alexandre made lewd remarks to her in English and obviously found her attractive, and Gabriel was rude to her and ignored her. And they hadn't bothered to visit their grandmother since they arrived and referred to her openly as *"La Vieille,"* the old one, and Maxine didn't scold them for it. She thought they were charming and very entertaining, which Camille did not, and Christophe tried not to criticize her children and cause a problem. But they were rude and arrogant, disrespectful and badly behaved. They offended people everywhere they went, and Christophe was hard-pressed to hold his temper. Camille took refuge with Simone, who wasn't anxious to see them either, and wasn't blind to their faults. She knew the kind of havoc they could cause, particularly when the two boys were together. And they were planning to stay a month. It turned out Alexandre was "between jobs," and Gabriel had a seven-week holiday from university, so they were in no hurry to return to France. They were talking about skiing in Squaw Valley. And they had apparently come to the States with no money. They were constantly hitting their mother up for dollars, and she asked Christophe for it. As far as Camille was concerned, they were a nightmare. She didn't know what her father thought, and she didn't want to ask him, but he looked stressed when he came home at night and discovered the latest disaster they had caused.

At dinner with Camille one night, Maxine mentioned casually that Alexandre was looking for a job, and maybe Christophe could find something for him at the winery. But that time, Camille spoke up before her father could answer.

"He doesn't have a green card," she said in a strong, clear voice, and Maxine looked daggers at her.

"I'm married to your father now, I'm sure that makes a difference," she said in an unctuous tone, and Camille stopped her dead.

"Not to immigration. He's not a minor. He can only get a green card if you get one and he's a minor. Or as an adult, by lottery, or waiting for it in his country of origin which takes years, or by marrying an American." They dealt with immigration issues all the time with their Mexican vineyard workers, and Camille knew their regulations and policies, and so did her father. "And we don't hire illegal aliens," Camille completed the picture for her, so there was no question of Alexandre getting a job with them.

"I'm afraid she's right," Christophe added. And Alexandre knew nothing about the wine business anyway, nor did he want to. He had shown no interest in how they ran the business, or in having a job at all. He could tell that it was lucrative from the way Christophe lavished gifts on his mother, and their lifestyle, but that was all he knew about it, and wanted to. He liked the cars Christophe drove, but he had no ambition to get a job in the States. He much preferred mooching off his stepfather and had neither shame nor gratitude about it. The way his new stepsons behaved went against the grain of everything Christophe believed in. And Maxine thought her sons were fabulous and charming. All Camille could see was good looks, no integrity, and bad manners.

Their history was dubious too. Christophe knew Alexandre had worked for a bank in Paris, according to his mother. Alexandre said he was tired of it and claimed he had quit before he came to the States, to pursue better opportunities. Simone told Camille he had probably been fired. She knew that he hadn't been able to hold on to a job since he left university, and had been kicked out of every school he'd ever gone to. And as a child, he wanted to be a playboy when he grew up, but needed someone to subsidize it, and so far no one had volunteered. She said that Maxine's late husband had been very generous with them, and gotten Alexandre several jobs, from which he'd been fired. He systematically dated rich girls whose parents invited him on luxurious vacations, and he was never invited back. And he cheated on all his girlfriends. He had a nasty side to him. Simone had warned Camille that he was just like Maxine. Gabriel was the less intelligent, considerably less appealing version although just as good looking. He'd also been kicked out of all the best schools the late count had paid for. He'd been expelled for cheating and using and dealing drugs. They were a true disaster.

"They're a sorry pair," their grandmother said about them, even though they were her grandsons. She wasn't proud of them, or her daughter. But Maxine was a lot smoother, and had been even at their age. She used charm and her wits to get what she wanted. "I hear Gabriel damaged your father's car after Maxine let him use it," Simone said regretfully, sorry for her new son-in-law to have to house them and put up with them.

"How did you hear about that?" Camille was curious, she hadn't told her yet, and it had only recently happened.

"Cesare told me when he dropped off some fruit, and some of your father's wine." She thought his wine was excellent, as good as the best labels in France. "I don't know why," she said, lighting a cigarette and closing one eye to avoid the smoke, "but I don't like Cesare, although he's always very courteous to me." Simone was always candid with Camille, who was intrigued to hear her say it.

"Why not?"

"It probably sounds foolish to you, since I gather he's been here forever, but I don't trust him. There's something sneaky about him, like a snake slithering in the grass." Camille laughed at the description, which seemed apt to her. Simone was very observant and had good instincts.

"I feel the same way about him, and my mother never liked him either. She and my father used to fight about it. My father loves him, says he's a brilliant and talented vineyard manager, so he puts up with him."

"Maxine loves him, and he plays up to her, that's always my first clue that someone is no good." She had a way of cutting through the layers of falsity surrounding some people, and exposing their core, like a scalpel, or as though she had X-ray vision. There was nothing senile or demented about Simone. On the contrary, she was razor sharp, and saw it all, even about her own daughter and grandsons.

The boys continued their shenanigans, creating minor havoc, racing around the Napa Valley in a Ferrari Maxine had rented for them, at Christophe's expense. He didn't think it was a good idea, but he went along with it, not to be critical of her sons to Maxine, since he didn't want her criticizing Camille. But it added a level of stress to life in the château, and Camille was happy to escape to her room, or Simone's cottage whenever she could. The boys had finally gone to have tea with her, once, and hadn't seen her again. They were utterly disrespectful of her and told their mother she looked as crazy as ever with her wild red hair, her dog, and her chickens. Simone had bought tall rubber work boots in St. Helena, to wear in the garden, and they agreed with their stylish mother that she looked a mess. The boys were as expensively dressed as their mother, and everything they owned seemed to be Hermès. They looked totally out of place in the Napa Valley. And they were unimpressed by Christophe. He obviously had money and was successful, but they thought he had no style and said he dressed like a farmer when he went to work, and his daughter was no better, although Alex conceded that she was a pretty girl, and he wouldn't have minded spending a night with her. He said she had a good body under the dreary clothes. It was the only time his mother called him to order and told him to behave. She didn't want trouble with Christophe over something like that, he thought his precious daughter was a saint, and there were other girls Alex could sleep with.

The boys showed up at the winery Christmas party, and they both got drunk and made advances at several women, who thought they were the sexiest French boys they'd ever seen. The party went off well, although Camille was still upset about the budget, but her father told her not to worry about it. Maxine was happy, and all the guests had loved it. The tree was bigger, the decorations more elaborate, and the food was terrific this year, and they could go back to their usual fare and budget next year. Besides, their crop had been huge this year, and they could afford the additional expense, if organizing the party had kept Maxine happy.

When Christmas came, Simone joined them, in a plain black velvet dress with pearl buttons and a lace collar. And she wore patent-leather Mary Janes like a little girl.

"Don't you have something nicer than that to wear, Maman?" Maxine asked her. She was wearing a long red velvet skirt with a black angora sweater, and diamonds at her ears, and as usual she looked like the cover of *Vogue*. The men were all in blazers, and Camille had on a dark green velvet dress of her mother's that fit her perfectly. Joy had worn the dress for Christmas every year. Camille had put it on to remind her father of her mother, and it brought tears to his eyes when he saw it, and nodded at Camille. It was a way of keeping Joy part of the holiday with them, in spite of Maxine's overwhelming presence.

Maxine fooled them with the food again with another "surprise" for their Christmas meal. She had ordered goose instead of turkey, which was traditional in Europe but not the States. It was greasy and badly prepared, because unfamiliar to the chef. Camille couldn't eat it and the others didn't try. She didn't cry about it this time. Christmas was disappointing but she was resigned to having everything different from now on. It was just the way it was.

Camille had expected it to be painful. She had given Maxine a cashmere sweater she had bought in St. Helena, and Maxine made it obvious that she didn't like it and tossed it aside as soon as she opened it, and then gave it to the maid. She had bought her father a fleece-lined jacket to wear in the vineyards, which he loved. And she had gone all out and bought Simone a gold and red enamel lighter that she was crazy about and said was the best gift she'd ever had. And Camille had added a little red sweater for Choupette with a matching leash and collar. And to each of her stepbrothers a bottle of Cristal. They didn't bother to give her anything, and Maxine had given Camille a red sequined evening bag that was one of her own, and she knew Camille would never wear. Christophe took a gold bracelet that had been her mother's out of the safe. He'd been saving it for her, and he found a beautiful black coat for her at Neiman's. He was extremely generous with Maxine, and gave her a diamond bracelet from Cartier that she put on immediately, and was very pleased with, and Simone gave Camille a little painting that she had painted herself of the château. And Camille noticed that Maxine and her mother didn't exchange gifts at all. Maxine had given Christophe a Rolex watch that he loved, and put on in place of his old one, which Joy had given him. Maxine knew that and had been anxious to replace it. Camille's heart sank when she saw him take off the watch from her mother, but he couldn't do otherwise, and he slipped Joy's watch in his pocket.

The evening ended early, everyone was tired, and the two boys were leaving early the next morning for Lake Tahoe to go skiing.

Camille was relieved that the Christmas holiday was over. They had gotten through it, which was all she could hope for these days.

She thought it would be a relief to have the two boys leave for ten days. They were coming back after New Year. They were both excellent skiers and were looking forward to their trip. And it never occurred to them to ask Camille if she wanted to join them. She was happy they didn't. Camille had her own plans for New Year's Eve with three of her old school friends, including Florence Taylor, whom she'd stayed with the weekend that Maxine moved into the château.

Maxine wanted to give a party on New Year's Eve, but with Christophe leaving the next day to France on business, he had told her he preferred a quiet night at home with his wife and insisted on it. She had complained, but he was adamant, he couldn't stay up late the night before his big trip, and he had an early flight. They had missed the Marshalls' Christmas party that year too, which was one of his favorite traditions. Maxine's friends at the Swiss winery had given a black tie party on the same night, and she had insisted they go there and to keep her happy since it was so important to her, Christophe gave in to her and missed Sam's party that he enjoyed every year. Maintaining a social life at the pace Maxine required wasn't easy for Christophe, who had work and travel to juggle too. Maxine had nothing else to do. But he wanted to do all he could to please her.

Living with Maxine dictating everything, and wanting to do it all her way, was depressing for Camille and exhausting for Christophe at times. He had hoped to maintain their old holiday traditions, which Maxine made impossible and Christophe wanted to respect her needs too. He had felt pulled in all directions over Christmas, wanting to welcome her sons, honor his daughter, and satisfy Maxine all at the same time. He looked worn out by Christmas night, and

Maxine was still pouting and arguing with him about the New Year's Eve party he refused to let her give.

He silenced her with a kiss, and took her to bed. It hadn't been the kind of Christmas he had wished it to be, and as he settled into her arms, he realized that living with Maxine was like a roller-coaster ride every day. Exciting, but stressful at times too. She was fabulous, but without a doubt, she was a handful. Loving her was like trying to keep a hurricane on a leash, and not get blown away.

Chapter Eleven

In contrast to their busy holiday, the week between Christmas and New Year was uneventful. The weather was bad, and it rained most of the time. The house was quiet again without Gabriel and Alexandre, who reported to their mother that they were having a fabulous time at Lake Tahoe and meeting lots of women. They wanted to know if they could bring two of them back to the château to stay with them, and Maxine didn't think it was a good idea. Even if Christophe had left on his trip by the time they got back, Camille would tell him. He had treated them to the trip to Tahoe, and she didn't think the boys should push and add women to the mix staying at the château. Christophe had been very welcoming and generous with them so far, and had footed the bill for all their expenses since they left France, including their air tickets. She could see that the frequent incidents created by the boys, the damage to his property and cars, and being constantly surrounded by people in his home was beginning to wear thin. He never lost his temper about it, but he looked exhausted and could no longer get any peace at home, nor could Camille. Maxine and her sons had taken over every inch of their home.

In the end, the weather was so bad on New Year's Eve, and the roads so dangerous from heavy rains, that Camille decided not to go to Florence Taylor's party, and she spent the evening with Simone instead at the cottage. She made her famous cassoulet, which Camille was surprised she liked, and Simone brought out cards and they played poker. They wished each other a happy New Year and drank champagne at midnight that Camille had brought, and she stayed till two in the morning, and then went back to the château in the pouring rain.

According to his wishes, Christophe and Maxine had gone to bed long before that, and had a quiet night. He was leaving at six in the morning, to catch his flight to Paris at ten A.M. It was scheduled to land in Paris at nine P.M. San Francisco time, which would be six A.M. in Paris the next day, which would get him to his hotel at seven-thirty or eight, to shower and change and start his day of meetings. And he was going to Bordeaux at the end of the week. He had thought of taking Maxine with him, but he had too many appointments and people to see to spend time with her, and she didn't want to miss out on being with her sons when they came back from Tahoe. They were staying in the States for another two weeks.

Having woken up early from the heavy rains, Camille heard her father on the stairs as he was leaving. She tiptoed out of her room in her nightgown and bare feet to kiss him goodbye, and he smiled when he saw her, happy to have a last chance to hug her.

"Take care of everything while I'm gone," he said, but didn't need to. He knew she would anyway. She was so conscientious about her job and their home. "I'll see you in two weeks." She hugged him again and he waved at her from the bottom of the stairs and put his hat and raincoat on, and she heard the door of one of the winery SUVs close outside. A vineyard worker was driving him, and as the car rolled down the driveway, she went back to bed, and woke up again at ten o'clock. The rain had stopped but it was a dreary day and she knew her father was in the air by then. He had texted her just before they took off to tell her he loved her.

It was New Year's Day and she had nothing to do. She stayed in bed till noon, and then dressed and went to see Simone, who was in the garden checking on her chickens, in her tall rubber gardening boots. Simone invited her to stay for lunch. They had oeufs en cocotte, eggs baked in ramekins with little bits of sausage and tomatoes, that were delicious. They talked for a while, and Camille helped her build a fire and then went back to the house around three. She lay on her bed for a while and read, and fell asleep. It was a lazy day, and she woke up at six.

She was thinking about going downstairs for something to eat, when she heard the television on in her mother's old office, and assumed Maxine had it on. Camille wandered past, and saw her stepmother watching CNN with the remote in her hand, and she turned to look at Camille with a shocked expression.

"Did something happen?" Camille was relaxed from her easy day, and Maxine spoke in a hollow tone.

"Your father's plane went down over the Atlantic. It disappeared an hour ago." The whole scene had an unreality to it as Camille's heart pounded and she went to sit next to her and stared at the TV. The Air France flight had sent out a distress signal in heavy weather, and twenty minutes later, it vanished from the radar screen. They had no idea what had happened, and there had been no further information from the captain. No one knew if foul play was involved, or just the weather, but there was no sign of the plane. Naval ships and tankers were heading toward the area, but there were none in the immediate vicinity. Camille felt faint as she listened. It wasn't possible. He was just going to Paris and Bordeaux. He had said he would be back in two weeks. He never lied to her. If he said he was coming back in two weeks, he would. The two women sat in silence for the next hour, watching and listening to the reports. The announcer said it was most likely that the plane had gone down in the Atlantic, and there was no land within reasonable distance of where they had been for them to land safely if they had a mechanical failure of some kind.

Simone had seen the report on the TV in her cottage, and let herself into the château. She followed the sound of the television to the upstairs study, and saw them both sitting there. She sat down on the couch next to Camille, and held her hand. Half an hour later, all three of them were crying. It had been confirmed that the plane had gone down. A tanker in the area had finally reported seeing an explosion in midair, and a ball of fire sinking into the sea. Ships were steaming toward the area, but there were no survivors expected given the description from the tanker. The announcer looked grim, and said that two hundred and ninety people were thought to be on the plane, including the crew. They gave the flight number and it was Christophe's. Camille sat rocking back and forth in Simone's arms as she held her fast, and Maxine stared at them as though she didn't understand what had been said or what they were doing, and left the room. She came back half an hour later and looked like she'd been crying too. She said in a hoarse voice that she had called the boys and told them, and they were coming back from Tahoe in the morning. There was too much snow on the road that night. Maxine stared at Camille then, and the two women exchanged a long look.

"Your father's dead," Maxine said to Camille in a quavering voice. "What am I going to do?" Camille had no answer for her. She couldn't speak. She couldn't imagine her world without him. What was going to happen to all of them? And how could this be? Things like this only happened on the news, not to people you knew. Not to her father. He traveled all the time. They still didn't know what had caused the explosion, but it didn't matter now. The plane and everyone on it were gone, without a trace. Divers were already searching for wreckage, bodies, and the black box that would have recorded their last moments.

Simone went down to the kitchen and brought back water and tea for both of them. She didn't know what else to do. It was Camille she was worried about, whose life revolved around her father. Maxine would always be a survivor and find a way to reinvent herself, but not this child. She looked shattered by the news, having lost her only living parent fifteen months after her mother had died.

The phone rang half an hour later. It was Sam looking for her, and Camille held the receiver in her shaking hand. "Was he on that flight?" he asked in a breaking voice. He had seen Christophe two days before and knew he was flying to Paris on New Year's Day. He had been seized by a wave of panic when he heard about the crash on CNN.

"Yes," Camille said in a whisper and Sam burst into sobs, and then offered to come over as soon as he composed himself. But she didn't want to see him, she didn't want to see anybody. She wanted her father, not his friend, although she was grateful for the call. "No, I'm okay," she said, sounding like a child again and she felt like one. He promised to come and see her the next day.

The airline called them after that, to tell them the news but they already knew. They still had no idea if the failure had been mechanical, or an act of terrorism. It sounded like a missile from some of the early reports, but that didn't seem possible or likely. There was no reason for it. They planned to continue searching for the remains of the plane in daylight, and the black box, although the plane had gone down in very deep water. Camille heard what they said, though from a great distance, and then Phillip called. He was in Aspen where he had gone skiing with Francesca and some friends.

"Are you okay?" he asked her, sounding as protective as ever and almost as shocked as she was. He was worried about her. The question was a moot point. How could she be okay now? She had just lost her only surviving parent, and Christophe was such a good man, and a wonderful father. Sam hadn't been able to stop crying himself when he had called Phillip to tell him. Christophe had been like a brother to him.

"I don't know," Camille said honestly, she was dazed.

"I'm coming back tomorrow. Tell me whatever I can do to help you. I'm so sorry, Camille." Neither of them knew what to say, and nothing would change the horror of what had just happened. And she wasn't ready to be on her own at her age. It had never occurred to her that she could lose her father. "You're going to be all right," Phillip tried to convince her as well as himself, "and Dad and I will do anything we can to help." Even at his age, Phillip couldn't imagine losing both parents. He was still deeply affected by his mother's death four years before. "Is Maxine being decent to you?" She would have to be in the circumstances. Even a woman as calculating and manipulative as his father claimed she was would have to be compassionate now, and it was a blow for her too. Phillip promised to come and see Camille as soon as he got back, and they hung up. After that, Simone gently led Camille to her room and put her to bed and offered to stay with her that night.

Camille nodded, and when she finally closed her eyes, Simone went to check on her daughter, who was lying on her bed and staring into space.

"Why are you being so nice to her?" Maxine asked her mother in an accusing tone.

"Someone has to be. She just lost her father. You lost a man you were married to for three months and hardly knew."

"I just lost my future and my security," she said harshly. "What do you think will happen to us now?" She sounded frightened, which was rare for her. Christophe had been the solution to a problem. Now the solution was gone, and the problem was still there. She had a mother, herself, and two unemployed, expensive grown sons to support, and no way to do so. She hadn't had a job in years. She lived by her wits and the men she had married, the last two anyway. Her marriage to Charles and her security had vanished into thin air when he died, and his children got rid of her. And she hadn't been married to Christophe long enough for him to provide for her. They had been off to a good start, and now it was over.

"You'll figure something out," her mother said quietly. "You always do. We have to take care of Camille now."

"She has nothing to worry about," Maxine said coldly. "She has all of this. She's his only heir. I'm sure he left her everything." She sounded angry about it.

"He may have left you something," Simone said, no longer shocked by how her daughter functioned, without compassion for anyone else. It was always all about her.

"I doubt it," Maxine answered her, "and if he did, it won't be enough. He wasn't stupid, and he was crazy about her." She nodded toward Camille's room. "He was still in love with her mother."

"She's only been dead a year, and they were married for a long time."

"And now Camille owns all this. Alex ought to marry her," she said as Simone wondered how she could have spawned someone like her. She had ice in her veins, and a calculator for a heart.

"Do you need anything?" Simone asked her, and Maxine shook her head. Simone went back to Camille's room then, and lay on the bed next to her. She knew that at some point in the night, Camille would wake up, and reality would hit her like a bomb. She wanted to be there for her when that happened. And the coming days would be very hard. This was the least that Simone could do for her. She was sorry to belong to the pack of vultures that had come to prey on Christophe, but at least she could be there for his daughter now.

And as she'd predicted, Camille woke up at six o'clock, and sobbed in Simone's arms as she held her. And then they went back to her mother's office to watch CNN again. Debris from the plane had been found by Navy divers, and the black box had been located. It was still speculation but believed from what they knew that a mechanical failure and a fuel leak in one of the engines had most likely caused the explosion. None of the aviation experts thought it was terrorism. And it seemed that it was an act of fate that Christophe had been on the plane when the explosion happened.

Camille was still in her nightgown looking shell-shocked when

Sam Marshall arrived at nine o'clock. He sat and cried with her for a long time. There was nothing for them to do, no body to reclaim. There were people they would have to notify, the winery, his attorney. Sam offered to help her with it. Maxine looked stunned to see him at the breakfast table with Camille and her mother when she came downstairs, and immediately offered him breakfast and coffee with a smile, and talked inanely about what a terrible thing the crash was and how shocked they all were, as Sam looked at her in disgust.

"Please. Don't. I just lost my best friend. And Camille lost her father. I don't need coffee or breakfast. And I don't want to make chitchat about it." She looked as though he'd slapped her, and he wished he had.

Sam left Camille around noon, and promised to come back later, if she wanted him to. He stopped at the Château Joy winery when he left and spoke to the department heads and Cesare. They had all heard about it, and most of them knew Christophe was on that plane. The entire building was in mourning, and he gave them all his cell number in case there was anything he could do to help. There would be a memorial service to plan eventually, but not yet.

By late afternoon, after listening to the recordings of the black box they had retrieved, the airline said again that it was unlikely there was foul play involved in the crash, and it seemed increasingly likely that it was mechanical and the explosion had been due to the leak in the engine that the pilot became aware of in the final moments of the flight. And whatever the reason for the crash, Christophe was dead.

Camille had moved around the house like a zombie all day, with Simone following her like a ghost. Maxine had stayed in her own room most of the time. She had nothing to say to them. The boys arrived from Lake Tahoe at eight o'clock. It had taken them eight hours to drive home instead of four, with heavy snows on the road. The two boys greeted Camille briefly, and told her they were sorry about her father. She nodded, and went upstairs with Simone. She had nothing to say to them. They had only known her father for a few weeks and didn't care about him. The boys had dinner in the kitchen with their mother and talked for hours, in low voices about what to do next. Maxine was sure that Camille would ask her to leave once she started to recover from the shock and was more coherent. It was exactly what had happened with Charles's children, although they were older and two of them were lawyers and knew what they were doing. Camille hadn't figured it out yet, but Maxine knew she would. She was a bright girl and would want Maxine to leave.

The boys wanted to know if their mother wanted them to go back to Paris immediately, but on the contrary, she wanted them with her, for support, especially if things got unpleasant. And all four of them could leave together when they did, including her mother. They were a small army of occupation, and Camille had the winning hand now. As far as Maxine could guess, the war was over, but she wasn't ready to surrender yet, and she wanted her sons at her side for a show of strength.

Maxine would stay for the reading of the will, just in case he had left her something they could live on for a while. There was no point leaving before that. They were better off here at the château for now, until Camille threw them out. Maxine already hated her for it, and the thought hadn't even occurred to Camille yet. She was too broken over the loss of her father to even think about Maxine and her sons and what would happen next.

*   *   *

Phillip came to see her that night and they sat in the upstairs study with the door closed and he hugged her as he had when she was a little girl when she got hurt. She already seemed more grown up to him. She was no longer a child, and despite her devastation over losing her father, she was starting to think clearly and worried about the winery, and Phillip vowed to help her in every way he could. He was still the big brother he had always been to her, and he promised that would never change. He left after spending an hour with her and cast a dark look at Maxine and her sons when they walked past them, and told Camille once they were outside, "You need to get rid of that bunch as soon as you can." He was serious about it, and Camille nodded, at least that would be a relief, though it wouldn't bring her father back.

Much to everyone's amazement, Camille dressed and went to the winery the next day. She felt she had to. She owed her father that. She cried every time someone came to offer sympathy. And Cesare was crying every time she saw him. She called Sam to thank him for his visit the day before, and told him she was trying to figure things out, and then she called her father's lawyer. He said he'd been planning to call her, but wanted to give her time to catch her breath. He made an appointment to come and see her the next morning at the winery, and said he would bring the will with him. He asked her to have her stepmother with her, which told Camille that he had left Maxine something, which was typical of her father, who was so generous, responsible, and kind. And he had loved Maxine, even if only for a short time.

She went home at five o'clock and felt as though she had been pummeled all day. Maxine and the boys were in the living room when she got there, and she told Maxine they had an appointment with the lawyer at ten o'clock the next morning in her office at the winery.

"You didn't waste any time, did you?" she said in a scathing tone. They'd been drinking since noon and she looked drunk to Camille, who didn't bother to answer her at first.

"He asked for you to be there," she said finally. Maxine nodded and drained her glass of wine, and Camille walked up the stairs. She hadn't eaten all day and didn't care. She couldn't eat. She just wanted to lie down on her bed and die, like her parents. It dawned on her then that she was twenty-three years old and an orphan. The same thing had happened to her parents, who had lost their parents when they were young, and now it had happened to her. She couldn't imagine anything worse.

Camille walked to the winery the next morning, and was waiting in her office when the lawyer arrived, looking serious and respectful. He had worn a dark suit for the meeting, which was fit for the occasion. Camille hadn't done anything about a memorial service yet, or even the obituary, but she knew she had to. There was so much to think about.

Camille and the lawyer were talking quietly while they waited for Maxine, who arrived ten minutes late and typically had worn a short black dress which showed off her legs. Camille was wearing jeans and an old black sweater and didn't care how she looked. All she wanted was her father. Without him, nothing made any sense. The brightest light in her life was gone.

Her father's attorney handed each of them a copy of the will, and informed them that they were the only heirs. He read from a copy of it himself, and said that he would explain it to them, and some of it was just boilerplate that was standard in all wills for tax purposes. He reminded Camille that the taxes on the estate would be due in nine months, but her father had provided for them, and the money would be readily available at the appropriate time. He said her father had been a very responsible man. And they could see by the date that it was a new will he had written a few days before he married Maxine. He had addressed his bequest to her first.

Christophe had said in the will that since he was about to marry Maxine de Pantin, he wanted to make some provision for her, and if their marriage continued, and proved to be solid, he would write a new will at a later date. But since he wasn't even married to her yet when he wrote it, he was leaving her the sum of a hundred thousand dollars, as a gift to her, in the event of his death. Maxine didn't look pleased when she heard the amount, but tried not to show it. Considering the fact that he wasn't married to her at the time, it had seemed reasonable both to Christophe and his lawyer. He also provided that if the marriage had not taken place for some reason at the time he died, the bequest he had specified for Maxine would be null and void. But since they had gotten married, she had just inherited a hundred thousand dollars.

The remainder of his estate and all his property and belongings, the château and its contents, his art, the winery, his investments, and any money he had at the time of his death, he left to his daughter, Camille. In effect, she inherited everything he had, and he had left a considerable estate. He had disposed of it intelligently so as to minimize the inheritance taxes, as best as he could, and Camille had become a very wealthy woman overnight, and the owner of an important winery, and all of his investments. It hadn't even begun to sink in yet. And Maxine looked at her with open envy.

Christophe and Maxine had signed a prenuptial agreement before they married, so she stood to inherit only what was in the will. They had no community property.

And then the lawyer explained that Christophe had added a provision that he had struggled with, in order to be fair both to his then-future wife and his daughter, and since Camille had no other parent to guide her. Given Camille's youth, in case of his sudden death before she reached the age of twenty-five, which was seventeen months away at the reading of the will, he said that his wife Maxine could continue to reside at the château with Camille until her twenty-fifth birthday, so Camille wouldn't be alone until then. At twenty-five, it would be up to Camille if she wished her stepmother to continue to stay with her or not. If Maxine remarried before Camille reached the age of twenty-five, or wished to live with a man, then she would have to leave the château at that time. Likewise, if Camille should marry before she reached the age of twenty-five, Maxine would leave the château, and her presence would no longer be needed. But he had essentially given Maxine a grace period before she had to leave the château, and protected Camille from finding herself totally alone, which had concerned him. But a new man in Maxine's life, or a marriage for Camille, would terminate the arrangement. He didn't want a strange man in Maxine's life forced on Camille in her own home, and Maxine's presence would have been redundant if Camille married.

He had declared clearly that Camille was the sole owner of the winery and all of his estate and would remain so, but again because of her age, he felt she would need support and guidance at first, and time to adjust to all her responsibilities after his death. So he named Maxine as co-manager of the winery until Camille's twenty-fifth birthday, to share the challenges and burdens with her, and from the age of twenty-five, Camille would manage it solely, and Maxine would have no further involvement in Château Joy, the winery, and all its holdings. Until then, he urged Maxine to help Camille with the business and to make good decisions while managing the winery with her. He said he had every confidence Maxine would be a great help to her.

He also provided that if Camille had issue, a child or children, or were pregnant at the time of his death, her issue would inherit one-third of the winery only, and Camille would retain two-thirds of the winery, and all of his financial holdings, as declared at the time of his death. If she had no children alive or in utero when he died, she would inherit his entire estate. And if Camille predeceased him, having a child, her child would inherit everything. None of those conditions applied since Camille had no children and was not pregnant so she had inherited it all. He stated as well in the event that Camille predeceased him, or died before her twenty-fifth birthday and had no issue, then in that case, he left half of his estate to his wife Maxine, providing their marriage had taken place, and the other half to be divided equally between his relatives in Bordeaux. And if Camille were to die after she turned twenty-five, her own will would take precedence, and Maxine would get nothing. He specified in effect that his widow Maxine Lammenais only stood to inherit if Camille died before her twenty-fifth birthday, and had no children. After that time, it was his assumption and his hope, that Maxine would have moved on to a new life of her own, and their marriage would have been of short duration. And Camille would have her own will in place by then, and he urged her to do so, given the large amount she had inherited from him.

It was an odd way to divide his estate, but Camille's age had influenced him, the attorney explained. And he added that her father had thought her capable of running the winery on her own, but that it would be a heavy burden for her immediately after his death, while his estate was being settled, and Maxine helping her to manage the money for a short time might lighten the load on her until she reached the age of twenty-five, and would take it on solely on her own. He had left Camille everything he owned, but he was allowing Maxine to live with her for the next seventeen months, and help her run the winery. And after that, it was *all* up to Camille, at twenty-five. And he assumed that Maxine didn't need the hundred thousand he left her, but it was a gesture and small token of his love. They had waived financial disclosure in their prenup at Maxine's request, and he assumed that her finances were solid.

The attorney further explained that Christophe had tried to address every possibility and considered setting down the entire arrangement in an irrevocable trust, which would have been a tax advantage, but he wanted the flexibility to change it, given Camille's age, his very new marriage, and the fact that he did not expect to die anytime in the near future, so it was not left in trust, but outright in the will.

The death taxes to the estate would be high, but there were ample funds to cover them. And Camille inheriting everything wasn't a surprise since she was his only child. The one thing that startled both women was his generosity in allowing Maxine to continue living at the château and have a voice at the winery for the next year and a half. It gave Maxine time to figure out what to do with her life, and decide where she wanted to go, and permitted the two women to form a bond or not. And if not, Maxine would be gone in seventeen months, when Camille turned twenty-five and took over the reins fully herself. In the meantime, she had someone to lean on.

Camille thanked the attorney and he left shortly after offering his sympathy again. She put her copy of the will in her bag so she could read it again carefully later, and Maxine stood watching her in the short black dress and still holding her copy in her hand.

"Well, you came out winners, didn't you? I'm not surprised," she said, sounding bitter. She had hoped for better than a mere hundred thousand dollars, maybe more like a million, or half the estate, even if it wouldn't have been reasonable after three months of marriage, and he'd written the will before they were married. As Maxine saw it, she had gotten screwed again in the lottery of life. She was always a day late and a dollar short, in France due to the inheritance laws, and now because she and Christophe hadn't been married for long enough before he died, and he hadn't had time to write another will giving her more of his fortune, but that would have taken years, not weeks or months. Christophe wasn't foolhardy, even if he loved her. She was too new in his life.

Even she realized that three months was nothing, and if he'd lived another year or two, he would have rewritten his will, and she would have gotten more. "You want me out, don't you?" Maxine said, turning overtly nasty, with no one else in the room to observe her.

"I don't know what I want," Camille said, feeling exhausted, and hoping not to get into a war with her quite this soon. The emotions of the last two days had washed over her like a tidal wave. "But yes, it will be easier if you leave now. I can manage the winery on my own, and Sam Marshall can help if I have any problems," Camille said honestly.

"Well, you're stuck with me for the next seventeen months, like it or not," Maxine said with a wicked look. "And I get to manage the winery with you. I'm surprised he did that." She knew how much faith Christophe had in his daughter.

"So am I," Camille said, watching her from across the room. "He trusted you, Maxine, and thought you were interested in his business. I don't think you are, but he did." Camille knew her feigned interest was all for show, but Christophe didn't see it. He had died still believing Maxine was sincere.

"Actually, I'm not. But you own a very successful business. You're a lucky girl. And let me explain something to you. You want me out, and I don't want to be here either. If you want to get rid of me, it's going to cost you. We can make a business arrangement now, if you're willing, and get this over with quickly. And I don't mean a deal for a hundred thousand dollars, which won't do anything for me, I mean millions. I want an appraisal of this whole operation, and I want a nice big chunk of it, if you want me to disappear before your twenty-fifth birthday. And if you don't do that, darling Camille, I can make your life a living hell for the next seventeen months. And trust me, I'll do that. I want a decent amount of money, equal to half the winery, and I'll go away politely. Without that, I'm going to sit here and bleed you dry, and your father isn't here to protect you. So think about it, the evil stepmother will happily go on her way, all you have to do is pay her to do so. And then we'll both be happy." She stared long and hard at Camille, waiting for the words to sink in and they did quickly.

"That's blackmail, it might even be extortion," Camille said coldly.

She had shown her true colors, the ones Maxine's own mother had warned Camille about, and that Camille had always sensed were there. Only her father hadn't believed it. He would have been devastated to hear her now. She was all about money and no longer had to hide it.

"You can't prove it. There is no record of what I just said to you. But you heard me. Give it some thought. I mean it. You know where to find me. I'll be in your father's bedroom. And in your face every moment of every day until you pay me to leave here. I trust I've made myself clear," she said viciously, and with that she turned on her heel, strode to the door of Camille's office, walked out, and slammed the door behind her. Camille wasn't sure what to do next, but she wasn't going to pay her millions in blackmail money to get rid of her. She could put up with Maxine for seventeen months if she had to. And it looked like she did according to her father's will. Maxine had come out of the woodwork with a vengeance and guns blazing. She was a formidable enemy, and all Camille had to fight with was decency and truth on her side. She didn't have her father or anyone else to protect her. All she had now was herself. She was going to stand up to Maxine, whatever it took. Seventeen months was not forever. And then Maxine would be gone at last.

Chapter Twelve

After Maxine left her office, Camille tried to calm down and organize her thoughts for the memorial service she had to plan for her father. She called Sam and asked his advice. She didn't want to turn the memorial service into a circus, with half the Valley there just because he was an important man. Her father had lived his life discreetly and in private, and she wanted the final rites honoring him to be meaningful and respectful, attended by people who loved him, and whom he loved.

She had already exchanged emails with his family in Bordeaux, and due to illness, age, and family problems there, none of them were able to come. She had just inherited her father's remaining share in their winery as well, which was an extremely profitable one. Christophe hadn't participated actively in their business in many years, and was only one of many heirs and he had always given them his proxy when called upon to vote, but he still owned a sizable share of the family winery in Bordeaux. He trusted them to run it as they thought best, and Camille intended to do the same. Her problems were more immediate now and closer to home. She had to run the winery the way her father would have wanted, and as she had learned from him and her mother. And she had to deal with Maxine at close range, and whatever problems she intended to cause her, unless Camille paid her to leave. She wasn't going to squander her father's money to do that. She'd just have to put up with her for the next year and a half.

Sam was torn about the memorial service. On the one hand, he thought she should keep it small, as Christophe would have preferred since he was a discreet person, and on the other he thought Camille needed to pay homage to the important figure he had been in the Napa Valley and the wine industry for many years. She was going to have a headstone made to place next to her mother's. Since there was no body, it would be less painful in some ways than it had been following her mother's casket up the hill to the cemetery where they had buried her.

She didn't tell Sam about the reading of the will at first, not wanting to air their dirty laundry in public, or disclose her father's poor judgment about Maxine, out of respect for him. But as they debated how best to honor her father, Sam made a comment about Maxine.

"I assume she'll be leaving, after the memorial or before," he said with relief for her, and Camille didn't answer for a minute.

"Not exactly. My father made provision for her to stay at the château and manage the winery with me until I turn twenty-five," Camille said, still shocked at the news herself. "She's not going anywhere for now." She didn't tell him Maxine had already tried to blackmail her and wanted to be paid off to leave, and in a very large amount.

"Don't worry about it, she won't stay long. She wants a rich husband, not a winery. She won't want to run it, and she doesn't know how. She'll be gone in no time," he said confidently, underestimating Maxine for the first time.

"That may not stop her, but I hope you're right." They went back to discussing the memorial, and decided that a service by invitation only at their facilities at the winery made the most sense. And she didn't want anyone at the house afterward. They could serve a buffet at the winery that could be set up after the service. He knew Camille had the staff to handle it there, and she knew how to do it. She wanted it to be a dignified affair attended by the people he cared about, and those he had done business with for so many years. They had already had a flood of calls asking when the funeral was, and if there would be one or a memorial service at a later time.

"Let me know if I can do anything to help you," Sam said kindly, "and don't let that woman get to you. She won't stick around. One of the things I loved about your father was his faith in people, and his innocence. It didn't serve him well in this case, but she'll be gone soon." He believed that Camille would be successful running the winery. She had already been taught by a master, and she had a good instinct for business like her mother. She was unusually mature for her age, even though she looked like a teenager at times. Camille was a smart woman, although not as wily as the stepmother her father had saddled her with three months before. He deeply regretted Christophe marrying her, and had tried to warn him to not.

Camille made headway with the arrangements that afternoon. She set the day for the service, called the pastor of one of the local churches whom she knew her father liked, and walked back to the château, thinking about her father with tears in her eyes. She still couldn't believe he had died. She had hugged and kissed him only days before.

She found Maxine and her sons at the kitchen table, drinking wine and talking, and they stopped immediately when Camille walked into the room. She paid no attention to them, and remembered verbatim her conversation with Maxine that morning and her threats. All she did was tell her the date of the memorial service, and leave via the back door to visit Simone.

Their conversation continued the moment Camille left and they heard the door close behind her. Maxine and her sons had been discussing the terms of the will for several hours, and how to make it work to their advantage.

"It's very simple," Maxine spelled it out for them again. "We have seventeen months to make some serious money here, and I don't intend to lose this time. We have until the little witch turns twenty-five. Before that day, you can either marry her or get her pregnant, in which case, you will have a hold on her forever, and your child or children will inherit all of Camille's estate one day. And if you marry her, you can divorce her if you want and get a fabulous settlement. So you have a job to do here, if you want a major share of what she just inherited," she said pointedly to her oldest son. "She's not as naive as her father, but you're a handsome boy, and she's lonely. She has no one now, almost no friends, no boyfriend, no parents. The field is open. Make her want you, you know how to do it. Marry her, get her pregnant, convince her you love her, it won't be hard to do. There is real money in it for you if you do it. You'll be set forever after you divorce her. You'll never have to work again. And I expect you to pay me a portion of it. I'll split it with you," she said coldly as Alexandre looked pensive. "It's not hard work to seduce a girl her age. God knows you do it often enough for a free vacation. We're talking about a life of luxury forever if you do this right. And if you get her pregnant, she'll marry you immediately. She won't want to disgrace her father's name." Maxine had it all figured out. Alexandre grinned evilly as she said it, the prospect of seducing Camille was not unpleasant and had appealed to him since he first saw her and now there was serious money in it, and a golden future.

"What's in it for me?" Gabriel complained, looking petulant. "Why does he get everything? You always favor him. Why can't I marry her?" he said, looking from his mother to his older brother.

"You're the same age she is," Maxine said matter-of-factly. "She's more likely to want a man two or three years older," and she didn't tell him he would screw it up, as he always did. His brother was smarter, and hungrier. Gabriel was a bumbler and more interested in drugs and drinking than women. Alexandre wanted money, which would serve them well, and he was less likely to fail than his younger brother. "We'll cut you in on whatever we get," his mother assured him.

"You didn't after Charles died," Gabriel reminded her.

"There wasn't enough for me from those cheap bastards, let alone for the two of you. But I brought you here, didn't I?" Gabriel nodded and poured himself another glass of wine, as they listened to their mother's plan.

"So our goal is for Alexandre to marry her and get her pregnant, whatever order it happens, we don't care. The alternate plan is that she pays us the value of half the winery to get rid of us immediately. I'm not sure she'll do that. She may think she can outlast us. We will need to make her life miserable to convince her, and I mean *misera-*

ble in every possible way, physically, mentally, and financially. I'll start on that immediately. And, Alex, you know what you have to do. Your part in this is easy, you get the fun job. And then you can divorce her, and live on her money forever."

"What if he stays married to her?" Gabriel asked, and they ignored his question as ridiculous. Why would he stay married if he didn't have to and could get a fortune out of her? They were all three like-minded and cut of the same cloth, motivated by greed.

"You know, you're going about this all wrong," Alexandre said to his mother, squinting as he thought about it. "Why have her pay you off to leave? Her father gave you free rein here for the next seventeen months. That winery is a gold mine. Stay and get everything out of it you can. You'll have access to the accounts, I assume. I think there's money to be made there. Take advantage of what you can, and then see what she's willing to pay you to leave. But get what you're able to out of it first, don't just pack and run." Maxine thought about it for a minute and wondered if he was right. Christophe had named her as co-manager for the next year and a half. That was a lot of time to make some serious money if she was smart about it. Alexandre could help and he was clever enough not to get caught.

"I'll think about it," she conceded. And then Maxine laughed as she poured herself another glass of Christophe's wine. "It's a shame we can't just kill her, but that's too much even for us. If she dies without children before she's twenty-five, half of everything her father left her comes to me. That's a bit over the top, even for me. So, my darling Alexandre, it's up to you to seduce her and marry her, and in the meantime we'll get as much money out of her and the winery as we can. We have time. Let's concentrate on romance, not murder, although I have to admit, I'd love to strangle her for what she just inherited. She doesn't deserve it. She's a lucky girl to have had a father like that. Now we just have to get her to share it with us." Maxine laughed again and both boys smiled. "And if she does agree to pay me half the value of the winery, then we will graciously leave. For any less, we'll stay and Alexandre can use his charms on her."

"I should go back to France for my exams," Gabriel complained.

"You'll flunk them anyway. We have more important things to do here," his brother said.

Maxine looked pleased. Camille was bright and brave, but she was no match for them and easy prey. And Alexandre was grinning. The fun was about to start for him.

When Camille walked into the cottage, Simone was quietly reading, with a cigarette in her hand.

"How did it go today?" Simone asked her, concerned, she knew that she and Maxine had met with the lawyer. "Any bad surprises?" She knew from her long years that you never knew what would turn up in a will, hidden mistresses, illegitimate children, long lost relatives the deceased had forgotten to write out years before. But Christophe didn't seem like a man of secrets to her, too trusting and sentimental perhaps, and she doubted that he had hidden lives.

"Some," Camille said as she collapsed in the battered leather chair next to her, and Choupette jumped onto her lap, wagging her tail. They had become fast friends since Simone had arrived. "My father said that Maxine can stay here at the château for seventeen months, until I turn twenty-five, and he wants her to manage the winery with me, to 'lend me her support and help me make good decisions.' She offered to have me buy her out and she'd leave now. She wants a lot of money to do that. Millions. She said she wants half the value of the winery. I'm not going to give it to her. I don't see why I should, to get rid of her a year and a half early." Simone looked pensive as Camille said it. She had heard it all before, when Maxine's last husband died.

"That's what she did with her stepchildren in France. She threatened to sue them and try to overturn the will, but she was married to Charles for ten years. I don't think she'd have much power here after three months. You are your father's heir, but she may be a considerable nuisance in order to induce you to pay." She knew her daughter well. "Did he leave her anything?" Although she didn't see why Christophe should after only a few months, but he was a generous man.

"A hundred thousand dollars," Camille confided to her. "It's not much, compared to what the winery is worth. She knows that. He wrote her into the will right before they were married, and he didn't think she needed money, so it was just a token gift."

"He was wrong," Simone said, and stubbed her cigarette out. There were ashes down the front of her dress. She hadn't combed her hair since she got up that morning, and she hadn't bothered to take off her gardening boots. Camille had come to love the way she looked, and even the familiar smell of smoke around her.

"Maxine always created the impression with my father that she had a great deal of money behind her, and had done all right in the settlement with her stepchildren, although she thought she deserved more."

"Don't believe everything you hear. I told you. She could hardly pay rent. I was three months behind when I left. And the boys are no better. I heard something the other day from Gabriel that Alexandre is deep in debt. I'm not surprised. Make no mistake, she'll go after you for everything she can, if she has a leg to stand on legally, and if not, she'll try to bully it out of you. That's more her style. You'll have to be strong," Simone said firmly and went to check a pot on the stove. When she lifted the lid a wonderful aroma filled the room. It was coq au vin made with Christophe's wine. "It's a sin to cook with wine like that, but it makes the cooking very good," she said and smiled at Camille who was too tired to even want to eat. But Simone ladled two portions into big bowls and told Camille to sit down at the table. "You'll need your strength to deal with Maxine," she reminded her and Camille knew it was all too true. Maxine would stop at nothing to get what she wanted. No one knew that better than her own mother, and now Camille.

"The other thing my father put in the will," Camille explained to Simone as they ate, "is that if I die before my twenty-fifth birthday, with no children, half of everything my father left goes to her. If I have a child or children, it all goes to them. But if I die without children in the next seventeen months, half the estate is hers, the rest goes to his family in France. After I turn twenty-five, if I die, Maxine gets nothing and is out of the picture. Until then, she can live here, run the winery with me, drive me crazy, I can pay her blackmail to leave, or she can inherit half of everything if I die." Camille said it all matter-of-factly, having thought about it all day, and Simone frowned as she listened. She didn't like any of the possibilities for her young friend, and at the very worst, Christophe could have signed his daughter's death warrant without realizing it. But Simone believed that even Maxine wasn't bold or evil enough to kill her. She was a blackmailer and a crook, but not a murderess. She was greedy, but she wasn't crazy. Knowing that reassured Simone as Camille snuck Choupette a little piece of bread.

"And if she marries, can she still stay?" Simone asked curious.

"No," Camille answered. "If she marries, or wants to live with a man, she has to leave immediately."

"Your father was smart to put that in," Simone approved. "She'll start looking for a husband soon." She knew her daughter well. But she still didn't like the idea that if Camille died without children in the next seventeen months, Maxine would inherit half of everything. It was a powerful temptation for someone like her, and her sons. The thought of that worried Simone all through dinner and late into the night, long after Camille had gone back to the château to sleep. She didn't think Maxine would kill her, but you could never know how far greed would push someone desperate for money. And Maxine's long-term future had vanished with the plane. She had seventeen months of comfort ahead of her, and nothing after that, unless she could badger or blackmail Camille out of enough money to be secure.

Simone sat up almost all night, stroking Choupette, and thinking about her daughter, wondering what she was capable of, and how far she would dare to go to achieve her goals.

The next morning, Camille was surprised to hear from one of her father's assistants that Maxine was in an office down the hall, and Camille noticed that one of their big ledgers was missing from the table behind her desk where they were kept.

She went down the hall to see what Maxine was up to and why she was there. She found her sitting at a desk with Cesare and Alexandre on either side of her as Cesare explained the system of the ledger to them.

"What are you doing here?" Camille asked Maxine in a firm tone, and she glanced at Cesare with disdain. He had become a traitor so soon. Her father hadn't even been dead for a week.

"I came to work, as your father intended, to co-manage the winery with you," Maxine said innocently. She was wearing a navy skirt, a white silk blouse, and high heels, and looked official sitting behind the desk. "Cesare is explaining to me how the ledger system works."

"It's all on computer. The ledgers were just to indulge my father, to memorialize the way it used to be done in France. You don't need to spend time on them," Camille said evenly, as she approached them. "And what is Alex doing here?"

"I just hired him to work with me. He worked at a bank and has a very good head for figures."

"I'm sure he does," Camille said coldly. She knew she couldn't show weakness for a moment. Maxine was doing what she had promised, turning Camille's life into a living hell. "You can't hire anyone, except personally out of your own pocket. You're here to 'support' me and help me make good decisions, not to run the winery. I can do that myself." It was an awesome job, but she had been trained for it since birth. "And you can't hire him. He's an illegal alien. He doesn't have a visa to work in the States. And I told you, we don't hire illegals here."

"I'm getting him a student visa," Maxine said smugly. "He's going to sign up for oenology classes at Sonoma State." Camille looked startled by that. It had been Cesare's suggestion to them a few minutes before, which seemed the best way to bring Alexandre into the business. He could be hired as an intern for the next year and a half, possibly even for credit for his class. Maxine had loved the idea. It was open warfare between Cesare and Camille now that Christophe was gone. His loyalty had been to her father, never to Camille or Joy, who gave him a hard time over the expense accounts he padded and small amounts of money he stole. And his new champion was Maxine, who had plans on a much grander scale.

Camille made no further comment and asked Cesare to come to her office immediately. But they had won the first round. Getting him a student visa and signing him up for classes was a brilliant idea. Cesare sauntered into Camille's office half an hour later and sat down across from her desk. He'd been in no hurry to get there, and his attitude was one of defiance as he gazed at her with contempt.

"It didn't take you long to betray my father, did it?" she said bluntly with fury in her eyes. "What are you doing with those people? If you help them screw me over, or cheat me, it will hurt the winery you love. Think of that."

"I loved your father. She's his wife, and he's gone," he said stubbornly.

"They'll be gone soon too. If you double-cross me in some way, it won't go well with us. I own the winery, she doesn't."

"That's not true," he said, shouting at Camille. "He left half of it to her," he said staunchly, and he had obviously cast his lot with the wrong team, but wouldn't admit it, and Maxine had apparently lied to him about being half owner of the winery now.

"Is that what she told you?" Camille said, looking shocked. "She has a temporary position here until I turn twenty-five in a year and a half, and then she's gone. Do you want her to destroy everything my father built? And her son has no role here at all. You're making a big mistake, Cesare." But Maxine had promised him a huge amount of money if he helped her take control. And she had handed him a check for $25,000 from her personal account that morning, from the money she would inherit from Christophe. It was worth it to her, if Cesare would become her secret agent, and her mole. And he had believed everything she said. She was very convincing, when she chose to be, just as she had convinced Christophe, who was a lot smarter than Cesare.

"I don't believe you," he said to Camille as he walked to the door. "You and your mother have accused me falsely for years. Your father never believed you. His new wife is a smart woman, she knows what she's doing."

"She knows nothing about the business." Camille was horrified by what he'd said, and that Maxine and Alex had successfully seduced him. He was in bed with them now.

"Neither do you," he said viciously, walked out, and went back down the hall to Maxine's office. He went to lunch with her and Alexandre that day at Don Giovanni's, while Camille ate a yogurt and a banana at her desk. She had no time to eat. She had work to do, while Maxine and her minions plotted against her. Camille had no patience with their machinations, she had a winery to run. And at least now she knew that Cesare had to be watched even more carefully with Maxine around. He had gone over to the dark side openly against her. She knew her father would have been crushed.

The memorial service Camille organized was exactly as her father would have wanted it to be. People he had cared about, old friends, winemakers he respected, employees and associates, and even some long-term clients he had worked with and loved. There were so many people who admired him that almost everyone had accepted, and six hundred came to honor him, two hundred more than she had wanted, but so many had called and begged to come.

She put together a beautiful brochure for the service, with photographs of what he and her mother had accomplished at the winery since the beginning, the château they had built. There were photographs of her parents in it, and Camille with them as a child, and many of her father as a young boy and man in France at his family's vineyards and château. There was a list of his awards since he had established Château Joy, and a beautiful photograph of him on the cover, looking very dashing on his tractor during the harvest, which were the moments he most enjoyed. There were no photographs of Maxine, Camille considered that she had been in his life for too short a time, and there were several of him with Joy. They were together again now, and had loved each other deeply. Maxine had been an aberration, a terrible mistake. She was livid when she saw the brochure with no photos of her, which was a narcissistic injury for her, to be ignored and excluded was a greater blow to her than his death. Her name had been mentioned in the obituary Camille had written for the newspapers, but nowhere else.

The pastor Camille had chosen made a moving speech about what an honorable person he was, a man of strong morals and outstanding integrity, greatly loved and admired by his peers, and above all a family man, and a wonderful father.

They played the classical music he had preferred. Sam Marshall made a moving speech about him, and broke down several times. He sat next to Camille in the front row of seats during the service, as did Maxine and her sons. Phillip was farther back with Francesca, his fiancée. And Simone had worn her black velvet dress with the lace collar and was sitting in the back row, which even her daughter didn't notice. Raquel had come too, with her children, and Camille cried when she saw her.

Afterward people gathered around the buffet set up at the winery for a long time, telling stories about him, and sharing memories, many of which included Joy. Maxine was a stranger in their midst, flanked by her two sons, and many of the people there didn't know who she was or even that he'd remarried. She had worn a dignified black Chanel suit, but looked overdressed in a black hat with a veil. She played the grieving widow to the hilt and no one seemed to know or care. She was irrelevant now that he was gone.

Camille moved through the crowd looking dazed. She stopped and spoke to Phillip and Francesca for a minute, and later she had no memory of who she'd talked to. Simone had stayed discreetly in a corner, watching her, in case Camille needed her, and she walked back up the hill to the château with her when it was over. Neither of them wanted to ride back in a car. And instead of going home, Camille walked around the château on the narrow path through the trees, and went home with Simone. She felt like the only relative Camille had now. Camille dropped into one of the two big leather chairs, and sat stroking Choupette when she jumped on her lap.

"You put together a beautiful service for your father," Simone said gently, and handed her a cup of chamomile tea to soothe her. Camille took a sip and closed her eyes. The whole thing was so unthinkable. Only days ago, he had been alive and she had kissed him the morning he left, and was grateful she had done so, and now he was gone. And she was stuck with Maxine and her sons. The prospect of living through the next seventeen months with them seemed like a nightmare of epic proportions.

* * *

The following day, Camille saw Cesare drive down from the château in one of the winery trucks, as she walked home after work. She waved but didn't smile at him. She wasn't happy with him, and his sudden allegiance to Maxine and Alexandre. She wondered what he'd been doing up at the house, but then forgot about it when she went to visit Simone, and stayed for dinner. Each night was a surprise eating with her, as she prepared all her favorite dishes from France. Camille always said to her it was like eating at the best country-style French restaurant every night.

The next day, as she walked home, Camille saw Cesare driving down again. She wondered if he'd been visiting Maxine at the château for another reason. Sometimes he oversaw repairs on the property, but she didn't know of any at the moment, and none at the château.

It was a full two weeks later before she discovered Maxine's latest project, when Camille saw a truckload of old furniture driven past the château in a truck. They kept a lot of simple used furniture in the main barn at the winery. They had summer quarters for their migrant workers, and used it at times to furnish a bunkhouse or cabins. It was useful to have. But they had no use for it up at the château. She asked Cesare about it the next day and he was vague, but he looked guilty when he responded to her, and then finally had to confess when Camille grilled him about it. She was his boss after all.

"She's fixing up the little barn behind the château. I think she wants it as a studio or something, for one of the boys," he said and then left her office. What he had said made no sense. Her sons were sharing the best guest bedroom in the château, and seemed happy there. The little barn served as a storage space and hadn't been used for horses in years.

She asked Maxine about it that night. "What are you doing with the little barn? Are you using it for storage? You should have asked me if you are." She didn't want her filling it with junk.

"I thought it would make a nice guest house," Maxine said pouring herself a glass of wine. Camille had noticed that she drank a lot of it these days, and had Cesare bring their best vintages to her by the case. She and the boys went through it pretty fast, and she always had a glass in her hand when Camille saw her at night. But she was coherent.

"You can't use it as a guest house with the stalls," Camille explained to her. "And I don't want the migrant workers up here. We have quarters for them on the valley floor." Camille suspected she was bored at the office and probably had nothing to do there. So she was decorating now. But that was an odd place to do it. Camille couldn't imagine spending a night there, and the simple shower stall, toilet, and washbasin were rudimentary.

"It's too drafty for anyone to live in, except in summer, and you can't air-condition it with all the open spaces in the walls. We use it as a shed, but it's pretty rickety. We should probably tear it down," Camille said sensibly.

"I really think it's a sweet little house," Maxine insisted and Camille didn't want to argue with her. If she wanted to decorate a shed, at least she wasn't doing something worse.

But just to be sure, Camille walked out to look at it the next day, before she visited Simone. It was a little farther in the clearing beyond the vegetable garden and the chicken coop, and Camille was surprised to see it had been freshly painted, and the broken windows she remembered and kept forgetting to have fixed had been replaced. They hadn't used it in years, so it was one of those things they all forgot about. They hadn't kept horses in it in a long time, not since Camille was a child and had a pony there because it was close to the house.

She walked to the front door and found it open, as she cautiously stepped inside, not sure what she would find, if the place was solid, or a bat would fly at her from the place being deserted for so long. But instead she found the walls freshly painted white, and their battered old furniture for the workers haphazardly arranged around the room. The floors were bare and there were no curtains at the windows. The small bathroom was clean but ancient and basic, and there was a sink area with a small counter and a microwave in lieu of a kitchen. It gave Camille the feeling that someone was going to camp there. But she couldn't imagine who. It was almost like the kind of refuge, or fort, or treehouse that teenagers would put together to escape their parents. A kind of clubhouse for lost boys. And there were still little tufts of hay on the floor, which made her sneeze. It would have been suitable for their migrant workers but it was too far from the vineyards, and her father didn't like them close to the château. It was very close to Simone's cottage and one of her chickens walked by as Camille closed the door. She asked Simone about it when she went to the cottage after her inspection of the little barn.

"Have you seen people up here working on it?" she asked, and Simone nodded in response.

"They've been in and out for a couple of weeks, with furniture and stuff. They painted it last week. I thought you knew." But Camille shook her head.

"It must be some project of Maxine's," Camille said, and Simone agreed.

"She was there telling them where to put the furniture. Is it nice?

I tried to look in the windows, but I'm not tall enough." Simone grinned.

"The door is open, if you want to go in. It's just a lot of old furniture we keep in the barn for the migrant workers. It would take real work to fix it up, but we don't use it. It would make a nice art studio. It's very bright. You could paint in there," she suggested, since Simone painted on her small canvases in her kitchen, but she didn't need an entire barn, even a small one.

"I'll take a look at it when I go out to the chicken coop," she said, and they forgot about it. It was a mystery they didn't need to solve, until the following weekend when Maxine told Camille she had a surprise for her. She was uncharacteristically pleasant and offered to drive her, and Camille cautiously agreed. She got into Maxine's car, and within a minute, they stopped in front of the small barn; it had access from the road too.

"I saw it the other day," Camille said, as they got out. "You had it painted. What are you going to do with it?" she asked as Maxine stepped through the door and Camille followed. A worn couch and a desk had been added in the past two days, and battered bed tables with mismatched lamps on them next to the bed.

"I thought you might like having some space to yourself," Maxine said grandly with a false smile. "You must be so tired of sharing the château with us," she said mock-sympathetically as Camille looked at her with a puzzled expression.

"What does that mean?" It made no sense to Camille at all.

"The poor boys are so cramped in their room. They're driving each other crazy and argue all the time. They're too old to share a room and Gabriel is dying for your room, just until he leaves. They really need the floor to themselves, you don't want to share it with two men." And Maxine had turned their other guest room into her office when she moved in, and had no intention of giving that up. "I thought it would be fun for you to be out here for a while. We'll put space heaters in for you, of course. You'll be warm as toast." She looked delighted as she grinned and Camille stared.

"You can't be serious. Why doesn't Gabriel sleep out here?" He came home so drunk at night, they could have parked him anywhere.

"He's allergic to everything that grows. He'd be in the hospital with asthma after an hour. There's too much shrubbery out here. He'd get sick immediately."

"So will I. Maxine, my father said that you could stay at the château with me, which was generous of him. He could have had you leave immediately if he died. But he didn't say you could push me out, give my room to your sons, and move me to a horse barn behind the château."

"Just for a little while," Maxine said soothingly. "They won't be here forever." Neither would she fortunately, Camille thought. But seventeen months in the drafty horse barn was a long time, with space heaters or not. "My mother sleeps in a cottage right next door. Why can't you make do with this one?" She made it sound so sensible when in fact it was an outrage.

"Because the three of you are living in my house. I own it. And this is not what my father intended," Camille said with a look of determination as Maxine's eyes turned to steel.

"Your father isn't here now, is he? And I am. My sons are big men. You don't need a room the size of yours, they do. The least you could do is be hospitable to your stepbrothers, they're your guests."

"They're not my stepbrothers anymore. And you're not my stepmother. My father is gone."

"Yes, he is. Precisely. That's my point. He's gone, and I'm here. And for now, you will be sleeping out here. Since you seem to be so fond of my mother, you can spend more time with her. Now go and pack your things, and clear out your room. I want you sleeping here by tomorrow." Camille could see that she meant it. She was literally throwing Camille out of her own home. And as the realization hit her, tears sprang to her eyes, and she felt young and vulnerable again, and completely at the mercy of this evil, conniving woman, who wanted to do everything she could to break her down. And once again, Cesare had known about it, and played into her hand. He had colluded with her to throw Camille out of her home.

"Maxine, be reasonable," Camille tried to get her to give up the ridiculous idea of moving her into a horse barn. She couldn't be serious about it, and yet Camille could see that she was. And Maxine had power and age on her side, and her willingness to go to extremes to achieve her goals.

"I am reasonable," she said with a vicious look. "And if you would be sensible and make a deal with me, I would be more than happy to leave, with my sons. And until you are, you can sleep out here. I hope you enjoy it. The fresh air will do you good." And with that, before Camille could say another word, she got in her car and drove off. Camille stared after her, and then stumbled to Simone's cottage, blinded by tears. She felt like a child again. She found Simone with the cigarette in the corner of her mouth, winking one eye to avoid the smoke, painting a vase of wildflowers. Simone saw that she was crying, and stopped what she was doing to comfort her.

"She's putting me out of the house!" Camille said with a combination of despair and outrage. She felt helpless and devastated. "Until I pay her what she wants to get out of here, she's making me sleep in the horse barn." Simone looked shocked. There seemed to be no limit to what her daughter was willing to do, or capable of. Camille looked embarrassed admitting it to her. She had no recourse and no ally against Maxine.

"That is ludicrous! You own the whole place, for Heaven's sake," Simone said, frustrated. But legalities and ownership meant nothing to Maxine, as she had proved before.

"I told her that myself, but apparently she won't let me sleep there. She claims the boys are too 'squashed' in the guest room, which isn't true, and Gabriel wants my room. She's using the other guest room as an office, which she won't give up either. So she's giving Gabriel my room, to make him 'comfortable.' She says he needs more space."

"I doubt that. He's so drunk by the time he goes to bed, he would sleep in a phone booth with a moose." Camille laughed at what she said, but the situation wasn't funny. She was effectively being put out of her own home by the monster her father had foolishly married, and Camille had no idea how to stop her. She had the feeling that if she refused to move out of the château, Maxine would have her physically removed to the barn, and in another way, Camille wondered if she was safer out of the house, and away from the drunken boys. That was something to consider too. "She just wants you out of the house to punish you," Simone said with a look of fury. "It's another way to torture you. And she's so good at it!" Simone said, wanting to defend Camille and protect her from Maxine, but not sure how.

"I feel like I'm in a nightmare or some terrible fairytale. I feel like Cinderella being forced out of my own home by the wicked stepmother, so the ugly stepbrothers can have my room. All that's missing are the pumpkin and the mice," Camille said glumly as Simone smiled at her.

"Don't forget the handsome prince and the fairy godmother," she said, joking with her to lighten the moment, since Camille had brought it up. "And we'll need a pair of glass slippers."

"We need to get rid of the wicked stepmother," Camille countered. "What happened to her anyway, at the end of the story?"

"I'm not sure. I think she vanished. Someone threw her in the river or something and she melted."

"I think that's the witch in *The Wizard of Oz*, the one with the ruby slippers and the green face."

"Perhaps I'll have to put a spell on her for the green face," Simone said and hugged her. "I suppose you could refuse to move into the barn," Simone added with a sigh.

"And then what will she do? Lock me out of the house at night? I don't want to buy her off, Simone. She doesn't deserve it. My father worked so hard for what he had. I don't want to squander it paying a fortune to get rid of her. And she wants half the value of the business. I can't do that." Camille was firm in her resolve.

"No, she doesn't deserve it," Simone agreed. "It's exactly what happened with Charles's family in France. She drove them crazy till they paid her, not what she wanted, but something. But seventeen months until you turn twenty-five is a long time to have her torment you."

"I'm stronger than that," Camille said with determination. "I owe it to my father not to give in to her. He wouldn't want me to. We'll win in the end. But I hate to give that bastard my room now. I think she'll put me out physically if I don't."

"The only reason for you to move is that you may be safer away from my rotten grandsons. I'll help you move into the barn tomorrow, if you're really going to do it," Simone said sadly, upset for her. But she didn't see how Camille could force the issue to stay in the house either. The boys were bigger and stronger than she was, if Maxine had them remove her physically. And there was no one to stop them, surely not Simone.

"I'll move for now. But we have to figure out a way to turn this around," Camille said as she stroked Choupette, and Simone watched her, hating her own daughter for the kind of cruelty she was capable of.

Feeling angry and helpless, Camille packed her bags in her room that night, locked her closets with the things she didn't want them going through, took her favorite books and photographs, mostly of her parents, and the next morning she moved into the little horse barn with Simone helping her. Camille was determined to make the best of it. They drove into St. Helena to buy some flowers, and she found a rug at the antique store, and by the afternoon, Camille was settled in her new lodging, living in a horse barn on her own property, while her stepmother and stepbrothers were ensconced in her château. No one would have believed it, as Simone opened the door with one of the chickens following her, and Choupette bounded into the room. The place actually looked pretty with the things Camille had brought with her, but it was crazy nonetheless. And Maxine had won again. For now. The good guys were not doing well at the moment. But Maxine's days in power were numbered. It was Camille's only consolation as she looked around the horse barn that was now her home. She couldn't even begin to imagine what her father would have said. He wouldn't have believed it.

Chapter Thirteen

Having been driven from her home, and living in a horse barn, Camille got tougher on everyone at the office, and here she knew she was in control. Whatever Maxine's title or the conditions of her father's will, Maxine knew nothing about running the winery, and Camille did. She kept a tight eye on everything, and was watching Cesare's accounts closely. She saw an irregularity in them, and a considerable amount of money she couldn't account for, and Camille went to his office to discuss it with him. The door was closed when she got there, and she knocked and opened it immediately, and stood stunned by what she was seeing. Cesare had stacks of cash on his desk, and was dividing it between Maxine, Alexandre, and himself. All three of them looked up like guilty children, and he rapidly slid the money into a drawer, as Camille saw Alex shove a thick roll of bills in his pocket and Maxine closed her purse with a haughty expression.

"You won't get away with this for long," Camille told them in a fierce tone, and asked Cesare to come to her office, as Maxine and

Alex left the room without a word. It was clear what was happening. Cesare was stealing money from the winery, and sharing it with them. And even if it wasn't huge amounts, even the idea that he was clearly stealing from her made her sick, not just for her, but for her father who had defended him for years. And Maxine and Alex sharing it with him was icing on a very bitter cake. She was living and working among thieves. The three of them were no better than common criminals.

Looking angry, Cesare followed her to her office and exploded immediately. "What right do you have to come into my office, and act like the police? You think you own the world now, because your father left you this winery. You don't know what you're doing and you're going to run it into the ground," he ranted at her and she looked at him with icy eyes.

"You're fired." She hurled the two words at him like rocks.

"You can't do that. You need Maxine's permission to do anything now," he said confidently.

"No, I don't. I can take her advice if I want. And in this case, I don't. You're fired. You're a thief and a liar. My father would be disgusted if he could see you now." No matter how talented Cesare was with the wines, Christophe wouldn't have tolerated blatant stealing to this degree either.

"I'll go to work for her," he threatened. "She's going to own this place one day."

"She's going to be out of here in sixteen months. And you'd better be out of here in sixteen minutes, or I'm calling the police. I'm going to have an accounting firm audit our books for embezzled funds now, and if they find anything, Cesare, I'm pressing charges against you. If I were you, I'd run." He hesitated for a long moment and she watched the wind go out of him. He knew when he'd been caught, and she shuddered to think how much he had taken in small amounts over the years. He had gotten bolder since her father's death, with Maxine to protect him. The three of them were thick as thieves and had been stealing from her. Cesare had been a perfect source of petty cash for her and her son, without getting her own hands dirty. Camille looked at her watch. "If you're not out of here in five minutes, I'm calling security. In ten I'm calling the police. You overplayed your hand, Cesare. You're done. Get your things and leave." Tears welled up in his eyes as she said it, and he decided to play the sympathy card, but it didn't work with her.

"You would do that to me? After I loved your father for so many years? It would break his heart if he knew what you're doing."

"No!" she cut him off. "It would have broken his heart if he knew what a crook you were. You're finished here. And don't go back to Maxine to save you. She doesn't own this winery, I do. I will allow you to quit officially, which is more than you deserve."

He started to say something else, then saw the look on her face and turned around and left her office. She saw his battered Jeep drive away five minutes later. She went to his office, and saw that he had cleared it remarkably quickly, and left all the photos of himself with her father on his desk. So much for sentiment. She pulled open his desk drawers, and in the bottom one, she found the money he'd been dividing up. She sat down and counted it. There was seven thousand dollars in cash there. She took it with her to give to accounting, slammed the door with her foot, and went back to her office, wondering how much he had withdrawn in the first place.

She called their personnel office and told them that Cesare had just quit, and was not welcome back in the building, and a ripple

went through their offices as word went out that the vineyard manager had quit or been fired, and half an hour later, Maxine was in
Camille's office in a rage.

"How *dare* you!" she shouted at Camille.

"How dare *you* steal from me!" Camille fired back at her, but she
didn't shout. She didn't need to. The tides had turned.

"We were just settling some petty cash expenses he made for us."

"Where are the receipts?" Camille said coldly.

"You can't fire an employee without my permission," Maxine raged
at her, which confirmed that Cesare had been a money source for
them. At least that had been stopped. She'd been lucky to walk in on
them when they had the cash in their hands.

"It doesn't say that in the will. It says you're here to help me make
good decisions. I just did. Without your help. And if you or Alex steal
from me again, I'm calling the police. Is that clear?" Maxine was
nearly shaking with rage and frustration, and she stormed out of
Camille's office, and crossed her son in the hall.

"She fired Cesare," she whispered to him.

He didn't look surprised. "I figured she would when she saw the
money." He wasn't nearly as upset as his mother. He thought the
vineyard manager was an old fool. And his mother was a bigger one
for having given him twenty-five thousand dollars to help him cook
the books. They'd only gotten about ten thousand dollars out of him
since. "Don't worry, Mother. There's lots more where that came from.
And you have time."

"He says she watches everything like a hawk."

"I'll bet she does, she's smart, but you have time on your side.
There's no rush. And sooner or later, she might pay you what you
want. Or our other ideas will work." He smiled knowingly, although

his mother evicting her from the château made her a little less accessible than she was before. But the problem wasn't insurmountable, she wasn't far away.

"I'm not going to sit here for almost two years in this backwater," Maxine stormed at him. She needed to find another husband, she thought as she drove back to the château. Christophe hadn't panned out. And even if he hadn't died, maybe he wouldn't have been as generous as she'd hoped. She was thinking about it, and the single men she'd met in the Valley, when Alexandre came home, walked into the kitchen, and poured himself a glass of wine. He drank it without pausing, poured himself a second glass, and smiled at his mother.

"What are you looking so happy about?" She could tell he was up to something.

"You just worry about getting what you can out of the winery, and find me a new stepfather. Leave the rest up to me." And with that, he went upstairs to lie down. The wine had made him sleepy.

Camille had dinner with Simone that night and told her what had happened with Cesare. Nothing surprised her. She said Alexandre had stolen money as a child too. She used to lock her purse up so he didn't get her grocery money when he lived with her, and he was always stealing money from friends and it had caught up with him at the bank where he worked. They had allowed him to quit instead of pressing charges, but word got around and he hadn't had a job since. He was known to be a thief.

Camille had called their accounting firm and asked for an audit. She didn't think Cesare had taken huge amounts or she would have seen it, but a steady flow of relatively small amounts, particularly if he was giving money to Alexandre and Maxine.

She was disgusted with all of them, and wondered if she should talk to Sam, to ask his advice, but she didn't want him to think she was incapable of running the winery or losing control of her employees. She was thinking about it as she walked to her little horse barn after dinner with Simone. It was a chilly night, but the space heaters kept her warm. She was careful to turn them off before she went to sleep so they didn't start a fire in the old wooden building that was barely more than a shack.

The house was dark when she walked in, and she turned on the light and jumped when she saw Alexandre sitting on the couch. He'd been waiting for her in the dark.

"What are you doing here?" she asked him, frightened, but she didn't want to show it. He looked drunk and unsteady when he stood up. He was tall and good looking, but she knew what a slimy character he was. His looks didn't compensate for it any more than his mother's did. The only one who'd been fooled by her was Christophe.

"I was waiting for you," Alex said as he made his way toward her, weaving slightly, and he grabbed for her breast when he got close enough to touch her. She took a step back, afraid he was going to rape her or worse. She was suddenly aware that if he killed her, Maxine would get half of everything. She hadn't understood at first that the clause in her father's will was a potential death sentence for her now, and didn't know how far they'd go.

"Go back to the house," Camille said harshly, hoping to scare him. But he looked undaunted and amused as he tried to kiss her. Alexandre loved seduction scenes, particularly those that involved force used on his victim. He had been planning this all night, had been drinking steadily, and didn't bother to eat dinner, which had been a mistake. The wine hit him harder than he'd planned, but he still knew what he was doing, and what he planned to do to her. He was powerful and nothing was going to deter him. There was too much money riding on it to allow anything to stop him. There were no locks on her doors, so he'd had easy access. Camille tried to push him away, and he dragged her toward the bed with him. He was more powerful than she was, and pinned her down easily once he got her there, and she realized the worst was going to happen. She fought with him, pushed him away from her with every ounce of strength she had, and leapt off the other side of the bed as he leered at her. He had her cornered and victory was in his eyes.

"Come on, Camille, you know you want me. Let's have some fun. I'm so bored here, I can't stand it. We'd make a good couple, you and I." He was inching slowly toward her, trying to convince her, and she jumped onto a chair, and managed to open a loose window, which slid up easily behind her. Without saying a word to him, she jumped out the window, dropped onto the wet grass, and ran as fast as she could to Simone's cottage. It wasn't far, and she could hear Alex shouting at her to come back, and then finally calling her a bitch as she kept running, and exploded through Simone's door without knocking, as the old woman stared at her in amazement, and Choupette barked, happy to see her. Camille was breathless and she'd torn her jeans on the windowsill, and her knee was bleeding.

"Good heavens, what happened to you? Are you all right?"

Camille nodded, she was shaking. "Alex," she said in a single word and sat down. "He was waiting in the barn, in the dark. He was drunk, but he grabbed me and forced me onto the bed. He was going to rape me. I climbed on a chair and jumped out the window, since the windows in the barn are higher than normal."

"These people are savages," Simone said with a look of fierce disapproval. "I'm ashamed to be related to them. You can stay here tonight, or as long as you want. And we're getting locks on your doors and windows tomorrow. Maybe you should have a gun." Simone meant it, and Camille smiled at the suggestion. She didn't want to shoot anyone, although in his case it was tempting.

"I'll be fine without a gun. I'll get a whistle, you can call for help if you hear me." She had thought of calling the police but didn't want to cause a scandal, and in the end, no matter what his intentions, he hadn't hurt her, just scared her.

"It might be too late by the time you whistle and the police come," Simone said, looking worried. "What's wrong with him?" She looked genuinely distressed over what her grandson had done to her young friend, or tried to do if she hadn't been resourceful and faster than he was.

"He said we'd make a good couple," Camille said, calming down, as Simone went to get peroxide and a bandage for her knee.

"And he wanted to prove that by raping you?"

"He was drunk," she said pensively. But he would have raped her if he could. She was certain of it.

"That's no excuse." But she could tell that Maxine and the boys were desperate to get the money Christophe hadn't left them, any way they could. It had been quite a day. Camille had fired Cesare and nearly been raped by her stepbrother.

"Maybe it's a good thing you're not living in the château with them." She took out a flowered nightgown and handed it to Camille. Camille put it on in the bedroom, and Simone made her a cup of chamomile tea, which was her remedy for everything. And then she tucked her into bed, which no one had done for Camille since her mother died. Simone kissed her gently on the forehead and turned off the light. "Now go to sleep," she whispered, and Camille smiled as she drifted off, safe and warm in Simone's bed.

"You are my fairy godmother," she said sleepily, as Simone smiled, and went to sit in the living room with a glass of port and a cigarette, her favorite pleasures, as she stroked Choupette's head, and thought about what a wicked piece of work her grandson was. He was just like his mother, perhaps even worse. And there was no telling what they'd do next.

Chapter Fourteen

The day after Camille had fired Cesare for stealing, Maxine walked into Camille's office and sat down as though nothing had happened. Camille was wondering if Maxine knew Alexandre had tried to rape her the night before, but her face gave nothing away.

"I have an idea," she said blithely, as though she and her step-daughter were best friends, which was hardly the case, after the experiences of recent weeks. "You need a new vineyard manager, and Alex is very excited about the wine business and wants to learn more about it. I know how you feel about hiring illegals, but with his student visa, what about hiring him as an intern as vineyard manager, and he could step into the role officially once we can get him a green card. I hear they're easier to get for agricultural workers," she said and obviously had something up her sleeve. Camille had begun to know her better. She always had an agenda for whatever she did. It was never a simple project, but always a plot with a benefit to her at the end of it. She wasn't sure what this one was.

"I can't hire him as vineyard manager, even as an intern," Camille said, sounding as tired and worn out as she felt. She had so much to learn herself about running the entire business and having all the responsibility, while trying to defend herself from Maxine and her sons. Gabriel was harmless, he was either drunk, driving too fast, or in bed with someone. Alex was far more dangerous and did his mother's bidding. "He doesn't have the experience," she explained, "and I can't put an intern in one of the most important jobs we have. It takes years of experience in the field to manage a vineyard. Cesare was dishonest, but he knew his job, which is why my father kept him for as long as he did. And how are you proposing to get Alex a green card?" Camille inquired, curious about how her stepmother thought she could pull that off. It took years to get a green card, and the only fast way to get one was to marry an American, and he wasn't dating any that she knew of. She shuddered thinking of his drunken advances of the night before. And what if he had trapped her and succeeded? It was a frightening thought.

"You two might become close one day," Maxine suggested. "You're almost the same age, and he's a gorgeous boy. You need a husband to help you run this place, and he needs an American wife to stay in this country to help him get ahead." She had it all worked out except for the fact that he was a crook and a slimeball, and had almost raped Camille. Her knee still hurt, and had been bandaged by Simone again that morning before she left her cottage.

"I don't think that would be a good idea," Camille said quietly, not wanting to provoke her fury, nor to become their victim. "And what do you get out of that?" she asked her directly, since that was clearly part of the deal.

"Oh, I'm sure we'd be able to figure something out, a little gift to your mother-in-law." So Maxine would get money, Alex a green card and a rich wife, and whatever else she would be willing to give him, and Camille would get a crook as a husband, who was marrying her for her father's money, and the mother-in-law from hell. What a deal!

"I don't think mixing family and business is a good idea. That's not going to happen, Maxine. When are the boys going back to France?" And then she added, "I could tell the police about last night." Maxine ignored her and went on.

"They're in no hurry. Alex has his student visa now, and I'm going to be here to help you until June of next year. We have lots of time to figure things out," she said breezily and then informed Camille she was going to start entertaining again, as she had when Christophe was alive, and had wanted to do more of. "Just some little dinners at the château with people I've met in the Valley." If she had loved her father, Camille couldn't imagine her wanting to entertain yet. But in Maxine's world she was out of a job, and she had to move on to the next husband. It was exactly what Sam had said about her. And she wanted a big fish. She had landed a big fish with Christophe, but bad luck had struck again, even though he was half the age of her previous husband.

She didn't say she was going to invite Camille to her dinner parties, just warning her that they were going to happen. "And of course, I'm organizing the Fourth of July party for the winery." Camille could imagine what that would cost them, like the extravagant Christmas party her father had let her do. But if it kept the peace between them, she was willing to sacrifice the money again, although it irked her to spend so much on a party, just so Maxine could show off and say she had. "I've already started on it," she said as she got up. "I think we should have fireworks like the Marshalls have at their masked ball. He comes to all your parties, of course, since he and your father were so close." As she said it, Camille understood her agenda on that one. It was Sam Marshall she wanted, and always had, the biggest, richest, most successful vintner in the Valley, more so than even Christophe. Sam Marshall was the prize. Camille knew it wouldn't get that far. But she could try. It would keep her off Camille's back while she worked on landing a rich husband again. It was a career move for Maxine. Camille was still thinking about it after Maxine left her office. Camille's words about calling the police hadn't been lost on Maxine, although she had appeared unconcerned. She went to Alexandre when she got back to the château and found him tinkering with Christophe's Aston Martin in the garage.

"What happened last night?" she asked him with her eyes blazing. "What did you do to her?" she shrieked at him, since there was no one around to hear her.

"Nothing." He shrugged. "I paid her a visit but I had too much wine before I went." He looked unconcerned. "She ran away."

"Did you rape her?" she asked him bluntly.

"I would have." He grinned at his mother. "I didn't get that far. She runs faster than I do."

"For Christ's sake, can't you seduce her without violence?" He shrugged and got back in the car, and Maxine stormed into the house.

Three weeks later to the day, Maxine gave her first dinner party at the château, for sixteen people, catered by Gary Danko again. Camille saw the valet parkers and the Bentleys, Rollses, and Ferraris arriving, as she walked between Simone's cottage and her little barn. Her father had been dead for less than three months, and everything in Camille's life had changed. She was an outcast from her own home, and her father would have been horrified that she was living in the old horse barn, but she was almost used to it by now. It didn't matter, she knew she'd have the château back in a little more than a year. And she didn't want to live under the same roof with them. She'd had locks put on all her doors and windows and kept a shrill whistle under her pillow and a baseball bat next to her bed ever since Alex had tried to rape her.

The parties continued at the pace of one every two weeks, and Maxine invited her sons to dinner, but never Camille, who wouldn't have gone anyway. The people she invited didn't know her, so they didn't ask where she was. They barely knew Maxine, but she had a talent for rounding rich people up for parties. Most of them always came, out of curiosity if nothing else.

And by May the audit on their books was complete. Cesare had been cheating them of about twenty thousand dollars a year, but it wasn't as bad as Camille had feared, and she hadn't heard from him since he left. She'd been told a rumor that he went back to Italy for a few months, and she hoped he stayed there. She didn't want to see him again. That chapter was finished. The doors of Château Joy were closed to him forever, both professionally and personally.

Camille began working on new promotions again and decided to go after the bridal market, more aggressively than they had before, advertising the winery at Château Joy as the perfect spot for a wedding, with package deals, special rates, and fees that included photographers, videographers, florists, caterers, and transportation. It was a very important market, and she knew it could become a big money maker for them. She was already taking bookings for the following year. They had stepped up their social media dramatically to attract younger clients, and visitors to the Valley from all over the world. Camille was always thinking ahead to what she could do to grow their business. Her father had been more focused on the quality of their grapes, but she knew that was well established, so she concentrated on the business side, as her mother had. And in June she was able to hire a new vineyard manager she recruited in Bordeaux. She'd written to her cousins, and they strongly recommended him. And by some miracle, he'd been married to an American and had a green card. He flew over for an interview and she hired him immediately. He was young and smart and exactly what they needed. It was a relief to be rid of Cesare at last, and to have replaced him.

She was doing everything she could to protect her parents' dream and what they had worked so hard on, to increase their business and move with the times, while maintaining the quality of their wine. The new vineyard manager, Francois Blanchet, was going to help her with that and they worked well together.

She turned twenty-four in June, and spent her birthday quietly with Simone, who made her a soufflé and hachis parmentier, which had become Camille's favorite dinner. She had learned to love blood sausage too and ate it with gusto. Simone had made her a painting and told her she needed to get out more, but Camille said she didn't have time.

And just after her birthday, Phillip dropped by to see her, at the office. He had appointments at a winery nearby that his father was thinking of buying, and he was doing due diligence for him. He said he was getting married in September, but that Francesca hated coming to the Valley, she was allergic to everything that grew there, even the grapes. He laughed when he said it and seemed confident she'd get used to it. He was anxious to know how Camille was doing, and happy to see her.

"Everything going okay here?" he asked her as they walked outside for a few minutes and sat down on a bench. She said she needed a break, and hadn't even stopped for lunch. He knew she worked too hard, but thrived on it. And he admired how responsible she was.

"More or less," she said in answer to his question, not wanting to say too much to him about her problems with Maxine, or sound pathetic. It had been a hard five and a half months since her father died, there was no denying that. "I only have another year of the stepmonster here with me. And the wedding business is speeding up." Phillip nodded, always impressed by her dedication and focus on work.

It was hard for Phillip to believe that she was running the whole place now, without her father's help. He didn't think he could have done it himself at her age. At thirty-one, he wouldn't have felt ready to take over if something happened to his father, let alone at twenty-four. She had grown up, particularly since her father's death.

"Your stepmother's not interfering too much?" he asked her with a look of concern.

"She did in the beginning," Camille said carefully about Maxine, "but the winery bores her. Now she's entertaining a lot, which keeps her busy. I think she's looking for a husband."

"That's what my father says about her," along with worse things. Sam hated her and everything she stood for.

They were talking about Maxine when Camille heard a familiar roar and looked up with a strange expression, as though she'd seen a ghost, and seconds later, Gabriel came racing down their drive in Christophe's Aston Martin. No one had driven the car since he'd died. Gabriel squealed right up to them, put the car in park, and hopped out looking pleased with himself, as Camille stared at him.

"What are you doing driving that car?" He had already damaged it when he'd arrived in December. "And where did you get that jacket?" She looked at him, it was the beige suede fringed cowboy jacket that Christophe had loved and wore all the time.

"I found it in his closet," he said with a supercilious look, since she no longer lived at the château and he did, and had access to her father's clothes, which nearly ripped her heart out. "My mom said I could wear it."

"Well, you can't. Take it off, please," she said, stretching her hand out for him to give it to her. She was so focused on Gabriel, she forgot Phillip was there.

"I'm not giving it back to you now," he said angrily. "It's cool. It'll ruin my look if you take it now. I'll put it back in the closet. What's the big deal? He's not going to wear it," he said with a snide look. Camille nearly choked as she listened to him, and Phillip saw her face go pale.

"Please give it to me," Camille repeated, "out of respect for my father." She said it in a low rumble of a voice. She kept her hand outstretched, and Gabriel didn't move. He just stood there, wearing the jacket that was too big for him anyway.

"I'll give it back later," he said petulantly, and headed toward the car again.

"You need to take the car back to the house, and leave it in his garage," she said in a strong voice. Maxine and her sons had no respect for Christophe's things, or anything that belonged to Camille now. They felt totally entitled to do whatever they wanted.

"Whatever," he said, ignoring her, and as he was about to get into the car, Phillip took one step forward, stretched out a long powerful arm, grabbed him around the neck, and stopped Gabriel dead in his tracks. He looked at Phillip in panic. "Hey, that hurts," he complained to the man who was bigger and older than he was, and had no intention of letting him disrespect Camille.

"You heard what she said, take off the jacket."

"What's the big deal about the jacket? It's just an old suede jacket. We have better ones than this in France," he said, pretending to look unimpressed by Phillip but Camille could see he was scared.

"Good. Then go home and buy one. Meanwhile give her back her father's jacket." Looking like an angry, petulant child, he took off the jacket and threw it at her. She caught it before it could hit the ground and get dirty.

"Thank you," she said politely, visibly shaken by the incident.

"Now take the car back up the driveway and put it away," Phillip added with a menacing look.

"I have to do errands for my mother."

"Take one of the winery cars for that, not this one," Phillip said sternly.

"What is it with you?" Gabriel complained. "Who made you king?"

"Well, he sure didn't make you king." Phillip was within an inch of hauling off and hitting him. Camille could see it in Phillip's eyes and the tension in his jaw. One more word out of Gabriel and Phillip was going to lose his cool. It was stretched to the breaking point already. He hated to see a rude little shit like that bully Camille. "Are you going to take the car back, or am I?" Phillip was totally fed up with him, and in a last show of bravado, Gabriel threw the keys at him, and started to walk away.

"Do it yourself," he said over his shoulder, as he headed for one of the vineyard vehicles, which he helped himself to whenever he wanted, without asking permission to drive them either. Even though he had damaged two of the cars already, Camille hadn't made an issue of it.

Phillip looked at Camille with fury in his eyes. "How do you put up with those people? I was itching to kick his ass." She smiled at the way he said it, but it was better that he didn't. She didn't want another battle with Maxine over her precious son who could do no wrong.

"I have to admit," she said, grinning at him, relieved to have the car and jacket back, "I would have enjoyed it, but they probably would have sued you."

"Let them. It would have been worth the pure pleasure of it, and avenging you. What a little jerk." She couldn't disagree. "Come on, I'll put the car away with you." He had things to do, but he didn't want her to deal with it alone. The car was such a symbol of her father, he knew it was emotional for her. And she was carrying his jacket like the holy grail.

Phillip drove the car into Christophe's garage, which Gabriel had left wide open. And Camille helped him put on the protective cover, which either Alexandre or Gabriel had left on the ground. Everything they did, and the way they did it, was an affront, with the example set them by their mother. But Maxine was subtle and more artful and polished than either of her sons, and more diabolical. Camille knew she ran the show.

"I'll just drop the jacket off at the house," she said apologetically, after they closed the garage door and she locked it with one of her keys. As she said it, Phillip started up the steps to the château. She stopped him with a hand on his arm and he looked at her in surprise.

"I don't live there anymore. At least not for now," she said quietly, with some embarrassment and he looked stunned. He was the only person who knew now, other than Simone.

"What do you mean? Where are you living?" He assumed she was living in their château, where she had lived all her life, and which belonged to her now.

"Maxine fixed up a place for me in the back," Camille said, humiliated to admit it, but it was the reality of her life here now, at Maxine's hands.

"So who's living in the house?" Phillip looked puzzled.

"Maxine and the boys," she said quietly and led the way around the château, to the path in the back that led to the old barn.

"And you're not in the house?" he asked as he followed her. She shook her head and he stopped her with a gentle hand on her arm. "Are you kidding? What's going on here? They put you out of your house, or did you want to move out?"

"No, I didn't. She wanted my room for Gabriel, the one you just saw. She's a force to be reckoned with. She's a woman who's used to getting what she wants." They had reached the little painted barn then, and Phillip looked horrified as he walked into it with her, and she carefully hung her father's suede jacket on a hanger. She was living on battered furniture like one of their vineyard workers, not the daughter of the house.

"Oh my God, Millie," which was what he had called her when she was a little girl and he was a teenager. "How can you live here?" Seen through his eyes, she was embarrassed.

"I didn't really have a choice. It wasn't worth the battle with her, and it's just for another year. To be honest, I feel safer here, away from the two boys." He wasn't sure what she was implying, but it sounded ominous to him.

"You're going to freeze in the winter." He looked furious as he gazed at her and as though he might cry. "You have to get them out of here."

"I'm trying, but my father provided in his will for her to live in the château until I'm twenty-five, in another year. I can't get her out till then, unless she wants to go."

"But he didn't mean for you to live in a shack, and her and her sons in your house. Do you even eat here? There's no kitchen." He was appalled, and worried about her now, more than he had been for the past six months. He had assumed she was all right, and he'd been busy himself. He felt guilty for it now, and wanted to help her, although he wasn't sure how. He had assumed that Maxine was an annoyance, not that they had put her out of her home. He suddenly realized that Camille had no one to defend her from their abuse and disrespect.

"Her mother is wonderful. She put her in the cabin over there. It's nicer than my barn, with a real kitchen. She cooks for me every night. Maxine doesn't like her either."

"Camille, this is insane." He was going to talk to his father about it, but he didn't want to tell her that. "When did she put you out of the house?"

"About three months ago. It was a little chilly then, but it's fine now. They're after money. Or at least Maxine is. She wants me to pay her off to leave. Otherwise she won't go until the end of the term of my father's will. So I'm sitting it out. I'm not going to pay her to go." He was wondering if she should, but he didn't want to ask her how much Maxine wanted for them to clear out. They were total crooks, his father was right, and taking full advantage of Camille. He admired her for dealing with it herself for all these months. It made him realize how strong she was and respect her all the more.

They walked back down the driveway and Phillip was quiet. He was thinking about everything he'd seen and heard, and the look in her eyes when she showed him the barn haunted him. She was his friend and he couldn't bear anyone treating her like that. She had no one to protect her with her father gone. He was sure that his own father had no idea what she was going through. And like him, he had thought that she was fine. Technically, she was, but she was living a nightmare all alone.

"Are you coming to our Fourth of July party?" she asked to change the subject and he shook his head with regret.

"I can't. Francesca's parents have a house in Sun Valley, and I promised her I'd go with her. It's a big deal to her, and she's just not comfortable here yet." Camille wondered how they would work that out when they got married. His whole life was here.

He chatted with her for a few more minutes, and then he had to leave for his appointment for his father. He stayed much longer than he meant to, between the confrontation with Gabriel, putting her father's car away, and walking her to her little barn. He was shaken by his visit, but glad that he had come.

He went to the winery meeting and when he got home two hours later, he went to find his father immediately. He found him working in his office and walked in with a somber expression.

"I saw some really disturbing stuff this afternoon, and I want to tell you about it," he said as he sat down across from his father, and

Sam leaned back in his chair and looked at his son. It was obvious that Phillip was upset.

"At the winery you went to see?" He was hoping to make a deal there so Phillip's comment wasn't good news to him.

"No, I dropped by to visit Camille on the way. I haven't seen her in a while."

"How is she?" Sam asked, with a look of concern.

"I'm worried about her, Dad. She's living in some kind of a shed behind the house. She's not living in the château, they are. That bitch her father married put her out of the house three months ago, and she's living in a drafty little barn." Sam frowned as he listened to him. "They use her father's things. Maxine is trying to extort money from her in exchange for leaving. They treat her like Cinderella." His father smiled at the comparison. "They're taking gross advantage of her. Who are these people, and why are they getting away with it?" It didn't seem right to him, and he couldn't understand it.

"I'm not sure her father even knew who they are. I told him to run a background check on that woman and he was incensed. I would have in a hot minute. She has always seemed like an operator to me."

"So are her sons."

"Can you check up on them now? Maybe they have criminal records or something. I'm afraid they're going to hurt her. There's something very wrong there. I nearly punched one of them today for the way he treated her. He was driving Christophe's car, the Aston Martin, and wearing his jacket, and she was almost in tears, trying to get them back."

"Well, don't go around punching anyone. That's not going to help.

I'll try to make some inquiries. Chris was far too trusting, and he was snowed by her. She made a play for me when I met her before he did. She'd go for any guy with a bank account and a wallet. She's a piece of work. I'll see what I can find out. Maybe we can help Camille get rid of them."

"Thank you, Dad," Phillip said with feeling, and for the rest of the afternoon he thought about her, in the miserable little barn. What had she done to deserve that, just because her father had married the wrong woman? It broke his heart. He found himself thinking about her constantly, worried about her.

He was still bothered by it when he went to meet Francesca in Sun Valley a week later. Sam hadn't heard anything from the international detective service he had hired to investigate Maxine and her sons. They had told him it might take a while. But Phillip called to check on Camille now. She was touched whenever he called her. It was nice to know that the protector of her childhood was still watching over her. And just like when they were growing up, he always made her feel safe, even if she wasn't, with Maxine still around.

Chapter Fifteen

Maxine's preparations for the Fourth of July party at the winery became a full-time job for her by mid-June. She had rented elaborate decorations from a theatrical company in LA that provided movie sets. She insisted on having long tables instead of round ones that she said were in style but twice the price. The flower bill was going to be astronomical, and Camille was wondering if it was really worth indulging her, before the big day arrived.

But when it was all put together it looked incredible, and their fireworks show at the end was supposed to last for half an hour, as long as the big fireworks displays in the city. And this was just a private party in the Napa Valley. Maxine turned it into an event, and the winery tweeted about it daily. Under Camille's supervision their followers on Facebook and Twitter had multiplied exponentially.

Simone had agreed to come to the party, and Camille had promised her a table in the shade before the sun went down. It would be hot at the beginning of the party and cool in the evening.

Maxine had had her outfit sent by a designer in New York. It was a one-piece white jumpsuit that showed off every inch of her body and what spectacular shape she was in. She had hired a photographer and a videographer and she wanted to put it all on the Internet after the party. Camille agreed that it was good publicity, especially for their wedding business, which had really picked up.

"You should make me your marketing director," Maxine said smugly as she and Camille surveyed the scene before the party started. Camille readily agreed that everything looked great, except the bills. The initially excessive cost had tripled in the last two weeks.

"I couldn't afford you," Camille said honestly. But the PR was good. It was by invitation and they were expecting a huge crowd. People had been begging to come. There would be line dancers and lessons after dinner. And square dancers she flew in from Texas, and a band from Vegas. Maxine had gone all out, at Camille's expense. But it was a good showcase for Maxine too.

Alexandre and Gabriel were both wearing white jeans and long sleeved blue shirts, with Hermès alligator loafers without socks, and looked straight out of Palm Beach or Saint Tropez. Camille had worn white jeans too, with a red T-shirt and flat sandals. It was a work night for her. And she was relieved when she saw Sam in the crowd halfway through the party. It touched her to see a familiar face.

"I was looking for you." He smiled warmly and hugged her, which reminded her of her father and she had to fight back tears. "How's everything going?"

"Smoothly so far," she said, surveying the scene.

"I didn't mean the party. How's everything else?" he asked her so no one else could hear.

"Okay," she said and wondered if Phillip had told him about his visit before he left for Sun Valley. She was sorry he wasn't there. But he had texted her several times to say he was thinking of her.

"I'll take you to lunch sometime," Sam promised, "so we can talk." The party wasn't the right place for it, and he wanted to hear more from her, not just his son, who might have been overreacting with what he described. It sounded a little far-fetched to Sam, even if he didn't like Maxine. And Phillip had always been protective of Camille.

Maxine had spotted him as soon as he arrived, and made her way through the crowd to join them a minute later. She glanced coyly at Sam, and there was no way to avoid looking at her remarkable figure. The outfit was meant for that. Sam wasn't impervious to it, but he clearly didn't like the woman who was wearing it. She was flirtatious as she greeted him, and hugged him a little too tight. Elizabeth was at a political rally in LA and couldn't come, which seemed to give Maxine the impression that Sam was fair game, which wasn't how he viewed it, at least not with her. He couldn't stand her and it showed when he talked to her.

"I can't wait for your Harvest Ball," she told him. "You set such an example to us all. No one could top that."

"It's a tradition in the Valley, people expect it now. Sometimes I think it's a bit too much. The wigs and costumes are so damn hot," he said casually, wishing he could get away from her, but she didn't move an inch. He noticed how sensuous her lips were, and couldn't keep his eyes off her breasts, even if he disliked her. He knew exactly what had ensnared Christophe. There was a kind of heady sexuality to her that was impossible to ignore, and he suspected she'd be great in bed. But she reminded him of a praying mantis who would kill her lover when she'd had use of him. There was something dangerous about her. She hadn't killed Christophe certainly, given how he had died, but it was easy to believe that she had skeletons in her closet and all of them male. He hadn't been listening to her and turned back in time to hear her say something about having dinner with him, and he glanced at her in surprise.

"Why would you want to have dinner with me?" he asked her, looking her right in the eye. Her eyes were deep and dark and sucked you into them like magnets.

"You're a very exciting man," she said in a voice just loud enough for him to hear her. Camille had left them by then, and gone to check on Simone, who seemed to be having a good time, and was chatting with everyone around her, with a cigarette and a glass of red wine in her hand. She hadn't brought Choupette because she knew it would be too hot. But Simone was doing fine.

"What makes me exciting?" Sam asked, playing with her, and she looked pleased that he had responded. "Would it be money?" he said, and her eyes narrowed as she watched him. He was one of those men she would never catch and she suspected it at that moment, but was not yet ready to accept defeat. He was on to her, and always had been. She had had her eye on him since before she met Christophe. She had wanted Sam, but Christophe had been easier to pull into her net. She didn't answer Sam's question, and he went on goading her. He couldn't resist. "It's fascinating how some women respond to money, isn't it? It's almost like a drug." One of the things he loved about Elizabeth was that she didn't care how much he had. She liked him for the man he was, regardless of his income or his success. She wasn't impressed by him. Maxine was practically drooling. "I don't like you, Maxine," he told her honestly. "And I don't think you'd like me either, once you got to know me. I'm tougher than you think, and I'm not as polished as Christophe. You're damn lucky you caught him. But some hands fold early in the game, and you have to take your losses and leave. This may be one of those times." He was looking past her in the crowd as he talked to her, as though she didn't even deserve his full attention. "I don't think you've got a winning hand here. The odds are with the house. And I've got my eye on Camille." He looked her dead in the eye then, to let her know that whatever she did to Camille, she would pay for it in the end.

"What did she say to you?" Maxine's eyes sliced through him like a knife.

"Not a thing. But I know what's going on here. I'm watching you and so is my son. She's like a daughter to me. And I'm not going to let anything happen to her. Keep that in mind."

"I've been nothing but kind to her since her father's death. She's a very difficult girl. She's very rude to my sons."

"I doubt that. She's got her father's sweet nature. And does your 'kindness' include having her sleep in a horse barn instead of the château she owns, where you're living with your sons? It may just be time to move on," he said, fixing her with a merciless gaze.

"Her father wanted me to keep an eye on her until she turns twenty-five."

"I don't think she needs that. We'll see how it goes. I don't believe you're going to find what you're looking for here. Christophe was a lucky lottery ticket. There aren't many of those here. Have a nice evening," he said, then, "Nice party," and moved away from her into the crowd. She had done the whole party to impress him, and it didn't mean a damn thing to him. He had only come there to lay down the law. She was sure that Camille had said something to him, or she had played poor little rich girl with his son. There was going to be hell to pay for that. She was getting tired of Camille. And Sam was right, the Napa Valley wasn't for her. The really wealthy ones were married, or boors like Sam. She doubted she'd last another year. What she had to do now was find a way to make Camille pay, so she could move on to better playing fields. She was utterly fed up. "Striking oil, Mother?" Alex asked as he sidled up to her. "I saw you talking to Sam Marshall. Another stepfather in your sights?"

"Actually, no. He's not my style," she said, as she went in pursuit of other fish to fry. But there weren't many there that night. Sam had been her principal target, and her mission had failed. The party was a bust for her. He left before the fireworks, and she watched him go with hatred in her eyes.

The Fourth of July party Francesca's parents gave in Sun Valley was less fun than Phillip had hoped. They had a lot of very conservative friends, and most of the guests were their age, and not their daughter's. The entertainment they had hired was a banjo player and an accordion player that were painful to listen to. All Phillip could think of was what he was missing in the Napa Valley. He knew his father was at the party at Château Joy that night, and he wished he could be there too.

"Fun, isn't it?" Francesca said, smiling at him, happy they weren't in Napa for a change. Sun Valley was much more her cup of tea.

"It's a little quieter than I expected," he told her honestly. And he wondered if the wedding would be that way too. They were getting married in Sun Valley in September at a country club her parents belonged to, and there were going to be two hundred guests, mostly her parents' friends. Phillip had had no say in the wedding. Francesca's mother was planning everything, and it was going to be very traditional. It made him long for the slightly rowdy, more down to earth, even nouveau riche side of Napa, which seemed like a lot more fun to him.

Francesca had an older sister and brother, both of whom were married and lived in Grosse Point, Michigan, like her parents. They spent summers and Christmas vacations in Sun Valley, and Francesca expected them to do the same. Phillip had met Francesca at a wedding in Miami that they were both in, and they'd had a lot of fun, with a salsa band and a boisterous crowd at the wedding.

Since then, they had met for weekends, and she'd come to the Napa Valley, but she didn't like anything about it, and compared to her parents, she thought Phillip's father was a little rough, and he made no pretense of being otherwise. Phillip was more polished and more educated. He had an MBA from Harvard, and she couldn't understand why he wanted to waste it on the wine business in the Napa Valley, even if they made a lot of money. She thought he should work at a bank like her father. Her mother had never worked and was the head of the Junior League. Francesca had been living in San Francisco for the last six months, in order to be closer to him, and she wanted a job at a museum, but she had been a receptionist at an ad agency since she'd arrived and hated it. She missed Michigan, where her family and all her friends lived. She kept complaining that California was so different, and he kept thinking she'd get used to it.

She was talking to him about the flowers at their wedding while the accordion droned on in his ear, and the banjo got on his nerves. He was feeling claustrophobic, and wanted to go away somewhere with her. He had suggested Tahiti for their honeymoon, Bali, or the Dominican Republic, and Francesca wanted to go to Hawaii or Palm Beach.

"Don't you want to go somewhere more exciting?" he asked gently. "What about Paris?" She looked blank for a minute and then shook her head.

"I don't think so. The weather is terrible. My sister went there for her honeymoon and it rained the whole time." She didn't have a spirit of adventure, but he had liked that about her at first. He thought she'd be a good person to settle down with, instead of the girls he'd been dating who wanted to go out all the time and party, but he had started to miss them, and felt guilty that he did. The only time he had ever seen her cut loose was at the wedding in Miami, where she was drunk on margaritas all weekend. She'd been a lot more fun then.

The party seemed to last forever, and finally the guests left. They had dinner at the country club that night, and afterward, he took Francesca out for drinks. He wanted to see something more exciting than the dreary people he'd been with all day. And he was sitting in the bar with her, when suddenly he felt as though he'd been hit by lightning, or had gotten sane. What was he doing with this woman who already bored him before they were married? And she said she wanted four kids in the next five years. He felt trapped thinking about it, and he didn't know what to say to her. He decided to sleep on it that night and not do anything hasty. But by the time they went back to the country club for lunch again the next day, all Phillip wanted to do was bolt and run.

He took her for a long walk afterward and told her the bad news.

"I don't think I can do this. I'm either not ready for marriage, or this isn't right for me. I love the Napa Valley, you hate it. I love the business I'm in, you don't. I love traveling to exotic places, that's your worst nightmare. I don't feel ready for children, I just stopped being one myself. You want four immediately, which terrifies me. I think we need to call this off before we both make a terrible mistake."

"I think you're phobic about marriage," she said and blew her nose on a tissue she had in her pocket. He felt awful doing this to her, but he felt worse doing it to himself. It seemed as though he had to give up his life to marry her. And he didn't want to do that, ever. She was shrinking his life day by day. And he was never going to become a banker in Grosse Pointe like her father. He wanted to be like his father and run the biggest wine business in the Napa Valley, even if his father was rough around the edges. He loved him that way and he was the smartest man he knew.

He booked a seat on the plane to Boise for that night and they told her parents before he left. He hadn't expected it to turn out that way, but he knew it was the right thing for him. She gave him back the ring before he left. And as he got on the plane that night and they took off, he felt liberated, and had never been as relieved in his life. He had done the right thing. He was thirty-one years old and a free man again. He had never been happier in his life.

Chapter Sixteen

Phillip called it his Freedom Summer, after breaking his engagement with Francesca, and was embarrassed to realize he hadn't really been in love with her. He just wanted to be, and had convinced himself that it was time to get married since many of his friends were, at his age. And she seemed like the right kind of woman to marry, but not for him. And the relief he felt after ending it with her was far greater than any emotion he had experienced while they were together, except on the night he met her.

He had dinner with his father when he got back from Sun Valley, and they talked about it, while Phillip tried to figure out what to do next. He had been on a straight career path since college and business school, but he never seemed to be able to get his love life on the right track.

"What are you looking for?" his father asked him, and Phillip didn't know what to answer.

"I don't know, a woman I'm crazy about, who sweeps me off my feet, glamour, excitement." Francesca certainly hadn't been that, and the women he went out with weren't either. In his heart of hearts, he wanted a story like his parents', who had been madly in love with each other until the day she died. And in a way, his father's relationship with Elizabeth had substance too. Neither of them wanted to get married, for their own reasons, but they brought depth and perspective to each other's lives, and even though they lived in different cities and didn't see each other often, they talked for a long time every day. They understood and cared about each other. They were both honest and there was no artifice to what they felt. Phillip didn't want a woman who pretended to be something she wasn't, or wanted him because of who his father was, or was after him for the wrong reasons. It had to be real, and no relationship he'd had so far felt that way to him. His feelings hadn't been real either, but at least they had been distracting and fun. But he couldn't talk about anything serious with any of them. His father assumed he would find what he wanted eventually, and he had plenty of time to figure out what was important to him. Phillip was still young.

He asked his father several times in the course of the summer if he had heard anything from the detective agency he'd called in France with inquiries about Maxine and her sons. But Sam said they hadn't contacted him. They obviously hadn't turned up information on her, or he was sure they would have gotten in touch with him, but their response had been very slow.

Phillip checked on Camille several times, and she insisted that she was all right. He called and texted and dropped by the office once. She said it was hot in the little horse barn and there was no air-conditioning. But she had gotten used to it and didn't seem to mind. In some ways, her life was simpler than it had ever been. She was focusing on her work, and trying to increase their outreach at the winery. Maxine showed up at the office from time to time, but she was more interested in her social life at the moment. She was invited everywhere, and did a fair amount of entertaining too. Alex and Gabriel were talking about going back to Europe. Gabriel wanted to meet up with friends in Italy, and Alex had been invited to go on a boat in Greece. They were tired of the Napa Valley, and hadn't met people they liked. Alex was dating a girl from a wealthy family with an important art collection, but she was young and he told his mother he didn't care about her. And there was no hope of their getting closer to Camille, Alex had blown that prospect to bits and she wasn't willing to pay Maxine a penny to leave.

It was a week before the Harvest Ball Sam gave every year, and Maxine said she wanted them to go with her.

"Why? You don't need us." She was dating two widowers from San Francisco and a divorced man from Dallas who was in Napa for the summer. But none of them were substantial enough for her. She still had her eye on Sam as the big prize. He was the ultimate challenge since he had rejected her. No man had ever done that to her before. She didn't take it lightly, and she had to win him. She had to make him want her. She had only seen him once at a dinner party that summer, and he hadn't spoken to her, but she hadn't given up, and she was working on her costume for the masked ball. It was going to be even more fabulous than the one she'd worn with Christophe the year before.

Camille had told Simone about the ball, and she asked if Camille was going, but she said she didn't want to. The only time she'd been was with her father when her mother was sick and she said it would make her too sad to go without him now.

"Nonsense," Simone said, blowing smoke rings in her direction as she thought about it. They were sitting in her cottage and had eaten a salad from the garden. It was too hot to cook. "At your age, you don't have time to be sad. You have to go and meet a handsome prince." Camille laughed at what she said. Simone always said that she believed in fairytales. And two days later, she was waiting for Camille with a look of excitement, when she got home from work.

"What have you been up to?" Camille asked her. "You look very naughty today." Her hair was wild and she was wearing a bright green summer dress, the color of her eyes.

"I stole something for you," she said, giggling like a young girl.

"What did you steal?" Camille looked mildly shocked, but she was sure it was nothing important, since Simone was an honest woman. And what could she possibly steal?

"I know where Maxine keeps her ball gowns. She told me they're in boxes in the attic. I know the boxes because I packed them myself and shipped them from Paris when she left. She went out this morning to a luncheon, so I went up and looked around, and opened some of the cartons. I found one that's perfect for you!" She went to get it from the bedroom, and it was the palest pink with layers of chiffon over a hoop skirt. "She hasn't worn it in years. She wore it when she was a model, and younger than you are now." Simone's eyes were ablaze with excitement as she held up the exquisite dress.

"Maxine will kill me if she finds out you took it. And where would I ever wear that?" It was the most beautiful dress Camille had ever seen.

"To the Harvest Ball of course, to meet your handsome prince. I found a mask that must have been your mother's, and a powdered wig. You'll look like a young Marie Antoinette."

"I don't want to go to the ball," Camille insisted, although she was touched by Simone's efforts on her behalf.

"Maxine won't even remember the dress," Simon promised. "And all you have to do is come home before she does, so she doesn't see you in it. Camille, you have to go. You told me it's the most important event of the year in the Valley. You need to have some fun. You can't work all the time. That's just not right at your age."

"I have no one to go with, and I don't have shoes anyway." She used every excuse she could think of to get out of it, and Simone went to forage in a trunk in her bedroom where she kept sentimental things and mementoes of the past. She had poetry books and love letters from her husband, and a pair of kid gloves she had worn as a young girl. She pulled out a package wrapped in tissue as Camille watched her, and she carefully revealed a pair of sparkling shoes.

"I wore these to the only ball I ever went to," she said as she held the shoes reverently, remembering a magical night seventy years before, the night her husband had proposed to her. "These shoes deserve to go to a ball again," Simone said seriously as Choupette sniffed them and walked away.

"They look very small," Camille said dubiously, "I don't think they'll fit."

"Try them," Simone said, holding them out to her. Camille took off her ballerina flats and slipped the sparkling shoes on. They fit perfectly, as though they had been made for her. "See, you're meant to wear them and to go to the ball." She had brought everything back from the attic with her, and insisted Camille put it all on. Camille did it to make her happy, but she still didn't intend to go to the ball. How would she get there? Who would she go with? She would feel foolish being all alone.

"Your friend Phillip will take care of you." Simone thought he sounded like a very sweet boy, and he seemed to want to protect Camille like an older brother, from all she said. He was a beloved childhood friend. "Just tell him that you're going, and he'll look for you." It was a thought. But then what? She didn't need to go. But Simone had gone to so much trouble for her, even digging through Maxine's old ball gowns, that she hated to disappoint her. It seemed to mean so much to Simone that she go. "The time to do things like this is when you're young. You'll regret it later if you don't. When you're my age, you need something to dream about. You can't dream about going to work every day. There has to be some magic in your life." What she said made sense, but Camille still wasn't sure as they put the dress and shoes away in Simone's closet where no one would see them. She had hidden a wig and mask there too.

"I'll think about it," Camille said cautiously.

"Call Phillip. Maybe he'll send a car for you."

"That's too much trouble," but everything Simone said made sense. Or would have, if Camille wanted to go. She went back to her own cabin then, and lay on her bed thinking about when she had gone with her father and how handsome he had been. She wished she could go with him again. She closed her eyes and remembered dancing with him. He had been her handsome prince, and she knew there would never be anyone else like him. For a moment, she felt as though he would want her to go to the ball. Maybe Simone was right, and she needed a little magic in her life. It was a thought.

Simone was walking in the garden the next day, after collecting the eggs from her chickens, and she heard voices on the other side of one of the hedges that surrounded them. She recognized Maxine and Alex immediately, and Maxine was complaining about what a nuisance Camille was.

"I'm so tired of her and the winery. She runs it like a shrine to her father." And they both agreed that with Cesare gone, it was impossible to get the small but useful amounts of cash he had provided them. She said the money they had given him had been wasted and the bequest from Christophe was running out. She had spent most of it on parties for the past six months. Entertaining was expensive, and no worthwhile eligible men had turned up, not on the scale she wanted.

"What about Sam Marshall?" Alex asked her.

"I'll see him at the ball in three days," Maxine answered. "We have to do something about Camille, though. We have to scare her into paying me off." Maxine made it sound like an ordinary occurrence. "She's tougher than I thought."

"What about getting rid of her forever?" Alex suggested with an evil tone in his voice. "Don't forget that you inherit half of everything if she dies before she turns twenty-five. Have you forgotten? That would be a nice windfall for all of us."

"Of course I haven't forgotten. But don't be ridiculous. You can't beat her over the head with a chair, for heaven's sake, or shoot her. That's rather obvious. Can't you think of something subtler to frighten her? I'm so fed up with her. She's such an annoying girl. It would have been useful if she'd married you, but you bungled that."

"I didn't 'bungle' it. She wasn't interested."

"Most women aren't if you get drunk and try to rape them." He had admitted it to his mother and blamed it on the wine.

"It was an error of judgment," he said, as they turned back toward the château, and Simone stood rooted to the spot after listening to them. She couldn't believe they would dare try to kill Camille, but she believed that neither of them were above it. Maxine had everything to gain if Camille died in the next nine months. And her opportunity was now while she lived at the château herself. After that, Camille would be harder to get to. Simone didn't trust either of them. What if they poisoned her or did something subtler? Simone went back to her house and smoked a cigarette while staring at Choupette. After she put it out, unable to contain herself a moment longer, she marched up to the château, let herself in the front door, and went to look for her daughter. She found her alone in the kitchen, reading French newspapers on her iPad, and she looked startled when she saw her mother in her high-top Converse and another flowered housedress. Maxine normally went to great lengths to avoid her mother and considered her an embarrassment.

"What do you want?" Maxine said inhospitably.

"I have only one thing to tell you," Simone said. "If anything happens to that girl, no matter how innocent it appears, I will go to the police and report what I heard you say just now, in the garden."

Maxine looked mildly uncomfortable and tried to brush her off. "I have no idea what you're talking about." She narrowed her eyes at her mother then. "But if you ever report me to the police for anything, or your grandsons, I will have you declared incompetent and shut you away in an old age home forever. You're a senile old woman and no one will believe you."

"Don't be so sure. I'm saner than you are. You've done enough to torture her. She lost her parents and has had to put up with you, and you have her living in a horse barn. I promise you, Maxine, if you hurt her, I will see to it that you go to prison."

"And I will see you dead," Maxine said viciously. "Now get out of my house."

"It's not *your* house, it's *her* house. And you don't frighten me. I'm eighty-seven years old. I made my peace with dying a long time ago. If you kill me, it doesn't matter. If you kill her, you'll go to prison, where all three of you belong. You're a terrible person and I'm ashamed that I gave birth to you," and with that, Simone walked out of the château and back to her cottage. She was shaking, and had a cup of chamomile to soothe her nerves. She wondered what Maxine would do now. If they would dare to try and get rid of Camille, or frighten Camille into paying them, or if she would think twice. But Simone meant what she had said, every word of it. And more than ever, she wanted Camille to go to the ball. She needed a better life than this, living in a barn, banished from her rightful home.

When Camille came to see her that afternoon, Simone was still shaken and upset and Camille asked her if anything had happened. She said only that the heat had given her a headache.

"But I wanted to tell you something. It sounds like the rantings of a foolish old woman. Be careful of Maxine and Alex, and even Gabriel. Never trust them."

"Did they say something to you?" Camille looked puzzled. Simone was so vehement, which was so unlike her. She was a gentle person.

"They don't have to say anything. They're terrible people, all three of them. I just want you to be careful, that's all. And I made a decision today. You're going to the ball, whether you like it or not. Call Phillip and tell him that you're coming. I'm your grandmother now, and you have to do what I say. You're going," she said firmly, and Camille smiled at her.

"I kind of decided that myself today. I want to wear the shoes and the dress." She and Simone exchanged a smile then. The decision had been made. Camille was going to the ball.

Chapter Seventeen

The morning of the Harvest Ball, Sam had just watched the sound system being set up, and listened to the sound checks. Everything seemed to be in order, and they'd been working on the lighting for three days. It was going to be, as always, a spectacular event, and invitations to it were the most coveted in the Napa Valley for the entire year. People never forgot it once they'd been there, and begged to be invited again. Doing it as a formal masked ball set it apart from everything else, and gave it an aura of elegance that nothing else compared to. And in spite of all the work, the manpower to set it up and run it, the complaining he did beforehand, and the enormous expense, Sam even enjoyed it himself. And it was always a moment of nostalgia and a tribute to the wife he had loved and lost.

His entire staff and the additional people they hired had been running around troubleshooting and communicating with each other on two-way radios for days, and he had one in his hand as he left the area where five hundred people would be seated for dinner, and he was on his way into the house when one of his assistants called him. She used his code name on the radio and he responded immediately.

"Big Bird here. Go ahead," he said as he walked past two security guards in front of his house.

"You have a call from Paris. They're holding on the line. I'm not sure what it's about, their English is pretty sketchy." He couldn't imagine who it was at first, and then he remembered. "Should I tell them you'll call back, and take a message?"

"Negative. I'll pick it up in my office. I'm almost there. Tell them to hold, please."

He picked the call up in his study two minutes later, and a sexy-sounding French secretary told him to wait "one minute please." The head of the detective agency came on the line and introduced himself. Sam was relieved to hear him speak English, he'd been worried for a minute. His own attorney had referred him to the agency that did private investigations in Paris, of a delicate nature. Sam had been told that they were good at dredging up old history that was hard to find. Their silence since June had led him to believe that there was no history to dig up on Maxine, she was just an ordinary, although talented, gold digger who had gotten lucky with Christophe. Sam felt a responsibility to protect Camille, after Phillip told him how badly she was being treated by Maxine and her sons. He wanted to make sure there was no criminal activity there, but the agency's silence had been reassuring. If there had been something really bad, they would have found it and called him. So he was expecting a banal report now, apologizing for not contacting him sooner.

"Monsieur Marshall?" a deep male voice said at the other end of the line, and sounded serious. It was six o'clock in Paris, still office hours in France.

"Yes, Sam Marshall here," he confirmed. Predictably, the head of the agency apologized for the long delay, and said it had been very difficult to get the information Sam wanted. "It is possible to get a criminal record erased in France after five years, so we had to do quite a lot of digging and checking. And we wanted to see if perhaps there were no criminal records on Madame Lammenais," he did not refer to her as "Countess," which she still used whenever it suited her, "but perhaps she only has a disagreeable reputation." It seemed a funny way to phrase it to Sam, and he smiled. "She does in fact have an interesting history." He went on. "She had three husbands in France, before she married Mr. Lammenais. One from her youth, a man who died recently, only two months ago, in a motorcycle accident in the South of France. He is the father of her two sons, and had a second family in England.

"We were able to speak to his sister, who was young when her brother married Madame Lammenais, and she barely remembers her. She said her parents didn't like her, speak ill of her, and said she was after money, and her brother never speaks to her. She had forgotten that he had two children by her and has never seen them. He had five children with the woman who is now his widow, and they had a very long marriage."

He consulted some papers on his desk and went on a moment later. "She seems to have had a relatively brief second marriage. Her second husband committed suicide a long time ago, two years after they divorced. We were unable to discover anything about him except that he worked for a publishing house. He had no living relatives and they had no children. He appears to have had a small life, and was not a wealthy man.

"She then married the Count de Pantin, about twelve years ago.

She was his mistress for two years before that. He married Maxine when his wife died, and according to the count's daughter, their affair drove their mother into an early decline, and she died of cancer. She said her father was completely besotted with her. He was forty-three years older, and extremely generous to her. His children are older than she is and were opposed to the marriage. They had no children together, and his children blame her for estranging them from their father, allegedly all to get money from him, without the knowledge of his children. They say he gave her whatever she wanted. And they had quite an extravagant lifestyle once they were married. Haute couture clothes, expensive jewelry, yachts they chartered for vacations, luxurious trips. He had an important collection of Dutch Masters, and they are convinced that she coerced him into giving several of them to her, some of which she sold after his death. When his health failed somewhere in his mid-eighties, she moved him to his family château in Périgord and prevented his children from seeing him. We were able to contact two of their servants only recently, who confirmed that was true. She allowed no one to see him, and kept him sequestered. We contacted Count de Pantin's physician, and he declined to comment, but he didn't deny what the housekeeper and houseman had said. Apparently, she kept him away from everyone, and the housekeeper said she was quite brutal to him at times. They found him in his wheelchair in a closet on one occasion, after an argument about a painting she wanted him to give her, which he eventually did." The description of Maxine was one of greed, unkindness, and abuse, to the point of cruelty, extorting valuable objects from a sick old man.

"One of the more disturbing things we were told by all of his children is that they believe she killed him in the end, but there is nothing factual to support their allegations. He died of heart failure in his sleep, according to the death certificate. He was almost ninety-one years old, his death at that age after years of poor health does not arouse suspicion.

"After his death, his children tried to reclaim their family château, and she refused to vacate it, until they paid her to leave. She apparently got quite a lot of money from them. He left her one-quarter of his estate according to French law, but she wanted a great deal more from them. She wanted half of their share as well, which would have given her more than half of her late husband's estate. And she fought them for the house in Paris as well. His daughter said she attempted to blackmail them, and expose facts about their father to the press. Apparently, he had had many mistresses while married to their mother, who had been an alcoholic. She threatened to expose every unsavory thing she knew about the family including the fact that one of the count's married sons is gay and the president of a respected French bank. They chose to settle with her for what they felt was a large amount, rather than risk disgrace for the family, and scandals in the press. They are very bitter about her.

"I think their allegations that she killed him are false, and we cannot know his state of mind at the time of his death. Perhaps he had reached a point of ill health where he no longer wanted to live, and asked for her help. But there is nothing in the death certificate to indicate foul play. He had not seen his children or his grandchildren for four years at the time of his death. And they still seem very sad about it. They feel that she robbed them of their final years with their father, in order to control him. The houseman corroborated it, and that the count often said how much he missed his children when the houseman bathed him. Sometimes he would cry about it."

As Sam listened to the dispassionate account, he felt sick. The image of an old man, lonely, shut away, at the mercy of a greedy controlling younger woman, kept from his family, locked in a closet to punish and extort money from him, was heartbreaking. Even if she hadn't killed him, she had been unimaginably cruel, but Sam could easily believe it of her. All his instincts had warned him of danger every time he saw her. And he couldn't help wondering if Christophe would have believed a report like this, with his willingness to think the best of everyone, even a woman he barely knew and who had him in her thrall.

"She appears to have been in debt quite severely before she left France. She rented an expensive apartment, traveled, and entertained a great deal. No doubt trying to find a new husband. She had to sell several paintings and some jewelry to clear her debts, before she left for the States. I believe that her stepchildren saw to it that her reputation preceded her in Paris, and the doors were firmly shut to her among the people she was seeking to pursue. It's a very closed society here. I assume she thought she'd have better luck in America, where no one knew who she was.

"There is no record of any criminal activity in her case, not that anyone could ever prove, which is not the case of her son Alexandre Duvalier, or her younger son, Gabriel, both from her first marriage. The oldest, Alexandre, was expelled from five private schools in Paris and one boarding school in Switzerland for cheating, and stealing in some cases. He was also expelled from university. He had a job in a bank, which his stepfather apparently got for him, and was accused of fraud and embezzlement at the age of twenty-three. He would have been prosecuted but his stepfather intervened. He was fired, and has not been able to find employment since. His mother appears to support him.

"The younger boy is still enrolled at university, and has a history of drugs at school. He has had minor arrests for possession of marijuana and hashish. He appears to be typical of spoiled boys his age who are on the wrong path. His mother supports him too.

"She also has a quite elderly mother in her high eighties, who lived in a poor neighborhood in Paris, in indigence. The concierge in the building said that the countess never visited her, and before she left, her rent hadn't been paid for months, until the countess cleared her debt too. They had never seen her in the building, and said that her mother was a very nice woman. She never saw the grandsons either. The mother's name is Simone Braque. We're not sure what happened to her. She may have died in the meantime, we didn't pursue it since we couldn't locate her to interview her, and we didn't want her alerting her daughter to our investigation."

"Actually, she's here in the Napa Valley too," Sam said quietly. "So are her sons," who were definitely bad news. And so was Maxine. She was not like the famous Black Widow, with a string of dead husbands behind her, whom she had killed. But she had used, abused, extorted, and done whatever she could to get money from the men in her life, no matter how cruel she had to be. His gut had been right about her, she was a dangerous woman, and no man was safe in her company once she got her hooks into him. He was only grateful that Christophe hadn't lived to experience it. He would have been a lamb led to slaughter with Maxine. He was no match for her, nor was Camille. Phillip had been right too, and Sam was seriously worried about his friend's daughter now, and putting her out of the château to live in a drafty horse barn, and trying to extort money from her, was nothing compared to what Maxine was capable of when she put her mind to it. And according to Christophe's will, Camille had another nine months to put up with her. The thought of it made Sam shudder, and he was going to do everything he could to stop her. The fact that she would inherit everything if something happened to Camille before next June put Camille in real danger and was alarming.

"Thank you for your very thorough report," Sam said quietly, still digesting everything he'd heard.

"We have it in writing for you, both in hard copy and electronically, but I wanted to speak to you first in case you had any questions. I'm sorry it took us so long, but in Madame Lammenais's case it was painstaking work, as so much of it is hearsay, and she has no criminal record."

"It sounds like she should, for elder abuse if nothing else," Sam said fiercely. He was furious about what he'd learned, and what Camille had been unwittingly exposed to.

"That's how her stepchildren feel about it. But these things are hard to prove, and he might have been afraid of her and denied it, even if questioned about her. Both of the servants in the home said he loved her right to the end. She appears to be one of those women who know how to manipulate men for their own benefit. There were many of them in the French royal courts, human nature doesn't change much over the centuries. There have been women like her since the beginning of time. It's only unfortunate when good people fall prey to them. The Count de Pantin sounded like a nice man from what everyone said about him. He was a very important financier in Paris when he was younger, but he was already quite old when she met him, and probably vulnerable to her then, and flattered by her

attentions, given the disparity in their ages." It was easy to recon-
struct what had happened. She had been able to get less out of his
estate than she hoped to undoubtedly, with the resistance of her
stepchildren, but she had gotten enough to satisfy her needs until
she met Christophe. She probably would have bled him dry, or tried
to get him to disinherit Camille, which was legally impossible in
France, but entirely possible in the States. Foolish old men did it all
the time when they met some twenty-two-year-old gold digger and
disinherited their children. But Sam couldn't see Christophe doing
that at any age. He loved his daughter too much to ever let Maxine
manipulate him to that degree. But she was certainly a pro at working men over, and he was going to do everything he could now to get
her and her sons out of Camille's life forever.

He thanked the man in Paris again for the full report, and was
frowning as he walked down the hall and ran into Phillip just leaving
the house. He had come to get a playlist he had made for the DJ to
play during the orchestra's breaks. Phillip had been a DJ in college
and still did it once in a while for friends. He was happy and relaxed,
and surprised to see his father so somber.

"Something wrong?" Phillip had a date for that night, a girl someone had fixed him up with, and he was looking forward to it. He
worked hard and played hard, but he had promised to look for Camille when she arrived, and keep her with him. She had said her evil
stepbrothers weren't coming to the party, and she was nervous about
standing around alone. She said her "fairy grandmother" had convinced her to come, and Phillip was glad she had. He was going to
see to it that she had a good time, and treat her like the little sister
she was to him.

"Actually, yes," Sam said in answer to his question. "I just got a call from Paris, from the detective agency I contacted in June. They took their time about it, and I figured they didn't come up with anything. Your instincts were good and so were mine about the 'countess,'" he said in a scornful tone. "I don't have time to talk about it now, but let's have breakfast tomorrow. We need to give Camille a hand and get that witch out of there. Camille can't handle it on her own." Phillip looked instantly concerned, as his protective instincts were aroused, a trait he had inherited from his father. However much Phillip liked to have a good time, when things got serious, so did he.

"Does she have a criminal record?" Phillip asked him, worried.

"She doesn't, although she should. But she and her sons are a bad lot, all three of them. They're like vultures, she'd have tried to clean Chris out eventually when she found a bigger victim. I'm just glad it wasn't me," he said and Phillip smiled, he knew his father better.

"You're too ornery for a woman like that, Dad." He smiled and Sam laughed.

"You may be right. Elizabeth called me a curmudgeon yesterday."

"But a benevolent one at least." There was no man on earth kinder than Sam Marshall, but he was allergic to dishonesty and dishonest people, and had a strong early detection system for them. He'd had to protect himself for years. "We'll talk about it over breakfast tomorrow, and figure out what to do. Are you going to say anything to Camille today?"

"Not before the party. And I want to talk to you first. You know her better. I don't want to terrify her, I want your thoughts about how we should proceed." He had a deep respect for his son's judgment, which was why they did well in business together. They admired each other mutually.

"Try not to worry about it tonight. We'll get on it first thing tomorrow. Nothing's going to happen tonight, I'm sure the countess is busy getting her outfit ready, and figuring out who to put the make on." Sam nodded, and was taking what he'd heard that morning very seriously. "Is everything on track for tonight?" Phillip asked him, and Sam assured him it was. As Phillip left the house with the playlist for the DJ, Sam noticed that he was more mature these days. The engagement to Francesca had been futile but it seemed to have taught him something, the kind of woman he didn't want.

Phillip was increasingly independent and took his dating life less seriously. He had fun with girls he went out with, but he no longer fooled himself that they were going to be more than a casual evening or a weekend. If Christophe had been able to be that way, they wouldn't have to worry about Maxine now, and instead she was deeply embedded in Camille's life, and Sam suspected she'd be hard to get rid of, and only at a price. But he and Phillip were going to talk about it tomorrow. There was no point worrying about it now on a day when they were so busy.

Maxine had spent the whole day getting her costume ready. The dress had been steamed to perfection and was hanging in her dressing room. It was a pale sky blue, and she had satin shoes with antique buckles to match it. The wig and mask were ready, and she lay down for a quick nap to refresh herself before she got dressed. She thought about Sam Marshall as she lay there. She couldn't imagine his being able to resist her. Her waist was small, her breasts were full. She had recently had Botox shots and her face looked perfect. She had seen the woman Sam went out with, when they'd been at parties together. Her waist was thick, her face unremarkable, she was fifteen pounds overweight, and she was badly dressed and un-fashionable whenever Maxine saw her, in clothes that were sexless and more suitable for a political campaign or a library. He deserved so much better than that, and Maxine was sure that given the right opportunity, she could ensnare him. He had never had a woman like her, and like all the others, once he tasted of her pleasures, he would want more. It was inconceivable to her that he wouldn't.

"Do you want something to eat before you go?" Simone asked Camille as they walked in the garden with Choupette that afternoon. They had just collected the eggs from the henhouse in a little basket.

"No, thank you," she said, smiling at her. "There will be lots of food there." She was planning to leave after Maxine left the house, so she didn't run into Camille and she would avoid her at the party. She was glad the boys weren't going, she didn't have to worry about them.

They heard Maxine drive away in a limousine she'd rented. It was a white Rolls with a driver, which Camille thought looked vulgar. She was planning to drive herself in one of the unmarked winery vans, which was hardly elegant, but it would get her there, and looked in-nocuous enough not to draw attention.

Simone stood and waved at her as she drove away after they got her dressed. She looked like a fairy princess, and the sparkly shoes Simone had lent her were the perfect touch. They had crystals and rhinestones on them and what looked like a glass bow, and they flashed little rainbows from them, whenever the light hit them. She was thrilled to be wearing them, and Maxine's beautiful pink dress.

"Try to avoid your charming stepmother," Simone warned her

again. The boys had gone out to dinner. Simone waved as long as she could see Camille on the driveway, and then turned and went back into her little house, with Choupette following. It made Simone's heart sing to see such a pretty young girl going out to have a good time at a masked ball. She couldn't think of anything better. She settled down in a comfortable chair with a book, happy that she had convinced her to go.

Chapter Eighteen

There were twenty valet parkers waiting to take cars when Camille drove up to the entrance of the party. She took the ticket stub and put it in her purse, and made her way across the gravel and into the garden where people were entering. It was like traveling back in time to the court of Louis the Fifteenth, and the garden that had been installed for the evening was meant to look like Versailles. Women were managing their enormous skirts, men were adjusting their wigs, guests held up their masks to cover their faces, and Camille took out her cellphone to call Phillip and find out where he was.

"Where are you?" she asked him, when he answered.

"I'm at the bar, of course. My date bailed on me. She has German measles, she got them from her little cousin."

"That's what you get for dating twelve-year-olds," she teased him, and he laughed.

"She's older than you are, but not by much. Hurry up, I'm bored." He hadn't seen any of his friends yet, the guests were mostly the established people in the Valley of his father's generation.

"Where's the bar?" Camille asked him. "I'm wearing a pale pink dress by the way. Maxine is in light blue, warn me if you see her."

"I'll send you a text. The bar is all the way at the back. There are three or four others, but the caviar and foie gras are at this one." Sam went all out for the Harvest Ball every year, and he and Elizabeth were greeting guests at a central location.

It was another fifteen minutes before Camille found Phillip, holding a glass of champagne for her, which he handed her. She took a sip. The party was so elaborate that it was almost like a wedding, with two or three hundred brides.

"You look gorgeous," Phillip said, admiring her. She really was exquisite, and it struck him when he saw her all dressed up in the spectacular gown. "Where'd you get the dress?"

"Don't ask," she said as she twirled for him. "My fairy grandmother gave it to me," and as the skirt moved, he saw the sparkly shoes and smiled.

"Now you really do look like Cinderella. Am I going to turn into a pumpkin at midnight, or a white mouse?" he teased her.

"No, you're the handsome prince, you don't turn into anything. You just run around looking for the other shoe for the next ten years, trying it on ugly women with big feet."

"That sounds about right." He laughed. "And what do you do?"

"Scrub the castle floors until you find me. Or in the modern version, maybe I go out and get a job."

"You have a job," he reminded her. "You run a winery."

"Oh, that," she said, laughing behind her mask. And at that exact moment, she saw Maxine in the distance and hid behind Phillip. Maxine was heading straight for Sam, who was talking to Elizabeth. She had on a very pretty dress, and Sam looked happy. "Do you think

Liz and your father will ever get married?" she asked, always curious about them.

"Who knows? Maybe not. They seem to like things the way they are, and my dad couldn't spend all that time in Washington. He has to be here for the winery."

"Maybe she'll give up politics," Camille said and Phillip laughed.

"Not likely. My dad thinks she ought to run for president. I don't think she will, though. Vice president maybe." They walked slowly toward the dinner tables then, and Phillip had had her seated next to him, with his date on the other side, which was now an empty place. He didn't miss her and he was having fun with Camille. They greeted all the guests they recognized, and he danced with her before dinner started. They noticed Maxine at a table nearly in the parking lot, as far away from Sam's table as he could place her. She was sitting at a table of old people, intently engaged in conversation with one of them.

"She could talk to a rock if she had to," Camille commented.

"Only if the rock has a lot of money," Phillip said and they both laughed.

They danced to the band and the DJ and after a while, they'd both had enough of greeting people, and snuck off to the garden where she and Phillip used to play as children. It wasn't being used for the party, and only close friends knew where it was. It was deserted when they got there, filled with roses and a little gazebo. There was a marble bench that looked like it was from an English garden, and a set of swings. Camille walked over to them, drawn to them by memories. She remembered being there, with their mothers sitting and chatting on the bench, while they played tag and Phillip chased her through the trees.

"I used to love coming here when we were kids," she said, and he smiled and walked behind her to push her on the swing.

"You were very brave," he said, lost in his own memories. "I knocked you down once and you scraped your knee, and you told your mother you'd tripped."

"I remember that," she said, smiling, as she stuck her feet out to pump, and admired the sparkling shoes that peeked out from under her enormous skirt. "You were always nice to me. Except the time you put a frog in the picnic basket." He laughed when she said it and she did too. It all seemed so long ago now, and had been part of the happy childhood they had shared, with parents who loved them, and sheltered lives. And then as they grew up, inevitably, real life had intervened. "Do you suppose we should go back to the table?" she asked him and he shook his head.

"I like it better here. We can see the fireworks when they start, and everyone is so drunk by now, and having a good time, they won't care where we are." Camille took her shoes off when she got off the swing so she wouldn't hurt them in the damp grass. They went to sit on the bench their mothers had sat on, and she put the shoes under it, as they looked up at the stars together. And then the fireworks started, and they were better than ever this year. They went on for more than half an hour, and Camille looked at his watch nervously when they ended.

"Simone told me to keep an eye on Maxine, so I could get home before her, and she wouldn't see me come in wearing this dress. I have to walk past the château to get to my house." And they had no idea where Maxine was. They had been in the private garden for well over an hour, enjoying the intimacy of it, their memories, and peace from the other guests. "Maybe we should go take a look and see where she is," Camille suggested, and he chased her down the length of the garden as he had when they were children, and it was only when they got back to the table that she realized she had forgotten her shoes under the bench.

"I can go back and get them," he offered gallantly, but just as he said it, Camille could see that Maxine was leaving, and waiting for her car in the long line of departing guests.

"It's okay, I'll come for them tomorrow. I have to get home." She looked panicked, and wondered how she could now without Maxine seeing her and knowing she'd been at the party in her dress. She explained her dilemma to Phillip, and he grabbed her hand and headed through a small side gate with her.

"I know where they parked the cars. They're supposed to leave the keys on the seat." She followed him in bare feet down a long grass path, and they came out in a huge parking lot, normally used for winery vehicles, which had been removed for the night. They found the winery van she had come in, and she stood next to it.

"Thank you for taking such good care of me," she said, "I had so much fun with you. It was like being kids again, sitting in the garden," and had reminded her of her mother.

"I enjoyed it too," he said and kissed her on the cheek, as she noticed a pair of rubber flip-flops someone had left in the backseat and she put them on, and he laughed at her again. No matter how grown up she was, or how elegant the dress, he always had a good time with her. "I don't remember hearing anywhere that Cinderella went home in flip-flops," he said.

"She did if she forgot her shoes in the garden." She hoped Simone wouldn't be mad at her for leaving them, but no one would find them where they were.

"I'll bring them to you tomorrow. Drive safely." He waved as she pulled out, and took a back exit on the property that she knew well to get on the St. Helena Highway to get home. With any luck at all, Maxine was behind her, still stuck in the gridlock of guests leaving, and she could make it home before her. The evening had been a huge success, and she was glad she had gone.

She was only a mile or two from home, hoping that Maxine wasn't there yet, when she smelled fire from the open window and saw smoke in the sky. The smoke obscured the stars in some places and looked very black, which she knew meant it was an active fire that hadn't been controlled yet. Because of the heat and dry summers, fire was one of their great fears in the Valley, and there had been some devastating fires over the years.

The smoke got worse as she approached their property, and she pressed the pedal to the floor once she reached the driveway. She could hear the fire by then, like the sounds of rushing water, and as she turned the last bend in the road, she saw a wall of flame behind the château, stopped the van, and leaped out. The fire seemed to be coming from Simone's cottage, and when she got there, she saw flames surrounding it, which extended all the way up to where her barn was, and they were moving into the vineyards. And then she saw the small figure through the flames. It was Simone, trying to decide how to get through, with Choupette in her arms, and Camille couldn't see how to get to her either. The flames were higher than the cottage and sparks were flying everywhere. Camille had her cellphone in her hand by pure instinct, she called 911, and as soon as she'd given them the address and her name, she unlaced her dress and took it off. She knew that if she tried to get through the flames in the gauzy dress she would set it on fire, so she stood there in flip-flops and underwear, trying to figure out how to get to Simone and the dog, and then she saw Alexandre standing off to the side leering at her, and she pointed to Simone and shouted at him over the roar of the flames.

"Your grandmother! Get your grandmother!" she screamed at him. He just stood there and laughed at her and she wondered if he was drunk again. There was no sign of his brother or Maxine, and Camille kept waving to Simone to move back and not stand so close to the flames, and then she ran over to Alex and shouted at him. "For God's sake, get her out of there!"

"Are you crazy?" he shouted back at her. "No one can get through that," but Camille was going to. She couldn't let her be burned alive. The back vineyards were already burning, and the flames were moving toward the château, but all she could see was Simone, bravely standing there, waiting to be rescued with Choupette in her arms. The smoke was overwhelming, and as Camille looked for a hose to create an opening so she could get her, she heard sirens in the distance, and in less than a minute, a string of fire trucks had come up the driveway, stopped at the château, and firemen were rushing toward the flames with hoses. She grabbed one of them by the arm and pointed to Simone, and he slipped an oxygen mask on and nodded, just as two men in asbestos suits joined him, and the three men walked through the flames, put an asbestos blanket over Simone and carried her out. They deposited her as far away from the flames as they could, and Camille rushed to her, as she emerged from the blanket, holding Choupette who was stunned. Camille was still in her underwear, and one of the firemen handed her a jacket and went back to fight the flames.

"What happened?" Camille shouted at her over the uproar. Simone looked shaken but still lively and alert.

"I don't know, I smelled gasoline, and then Choupette started whining and barking, and I saw flames outside the windows and coming down the road from your house. My poor chickens . . ." she said, looking distressed, and Camille put an arm around her as they watched the firemen fight the blaze in the cottage, while others ran into the vineyards, and they were told to go down the driveway as the fire moved toward the château. And then Camille remembered Alex, and the terrible expression on his face as he'd watched his grandmother walk back and forth trapped behind the flames. But he had disappeared, and Camille didn't see him anywhere.

They were standing between two fire trucks, as Maxine came home in her rented Rolls. They told her driver to park on the side of the road, and Camille saw another car behind her she didn't recognize, and she went back to watching the fire approach the château. She wondered if they were going to lose everything that night as a thin snake of flame rushed down the hill through the vineyards, and other firefighters rushed to put it out.

"My God, what's happening?" Maxine said as she came running up the hill, still in full costume from the party. And with Camille in her underwear under the fireman's coat, she didn't realize that Camille had been there too. She had left her wig and mask in the van on the way home. "Where are the boys?" she shrieked at Camille who said she didn't know, but she knew she would never forget Alexandre's face as he was prepared to watch his grandmother burn alive and just laugh at her. It was seared into Camille's mind forever, as Maxine ran toward the château, and two firemen stopped her.

"You can't go in there," they said. They were hosing down the roof, and it was at risk to burst into flame at any moment.

"My sons are in there!" she shrieked at them.

"There's no one in the house, we checked," and as they said it, Alexandre and Gabriel came around the corner of the château and walked toward their mother. And as they approached, their clothes reeked of gasoline and were stained with it.

"What did you *do*?" she screamed at both of them, and Alexandre looked at her angrily. The firemen were too busy to pay attention to them, but Camille was watching them closely.

"We did what you told us to do," Alexandre said to Maxine.

"I told you to get rid of her, as in chase her away, I didn't tell you to kill her and burn the house down." There was no question how the fire had happened. The stench of them alone told the whole story, and Camille was looking at them in horror as Phillip ran over to the group with a panicked expression and immediate relief when he saw that Camille was all right. He had been in the car behind Maxine, and had grabbed the first one he could find to get there.

"Chief Walsh was leaving the party when he got the alarm. He told me and Dad where it was. I came as fast as I could," he said to Camille and looked at Maxine in a rage. He had heard what she just said, and had fully understood from the gasoline on the boys' clothes how the fire had started.

"You almost killed your grandmother!" Camille shouted at them, and Maxine looked at her sons in a fury.

"You're idiots, both of you, do you know what kind of trouble you caused?"

"You inherit everything if she dies, Mother," Alexandre reminded her, speaking of Camille as though she wasn't there. But she heard every word they said, and so did Phillip and Simone. As Alexandre said it, Phillip hauled off and punched him as hard as he could, and the two men got into a brawl, as Gabriel stood to the side and looked like he wanted to run, and Alexandre kept shouting at his mother, "You told us to get rid of her." Two firemen had to stop what they were doing to break it up, and the police and sheriff arrived shortly after, with Sam and Elizabeth right behind them. Gabriel tried to make a run for it then, jumped in the car he'd been using and tried to drive through the vineyards, but one of the sheriff's cars stopped him. And the chief on the scene confirmed that it was arson. There was gasoline all around the château and the cottage.

As Phillip, Simone, and Camille watched them, Maxine and her sons were handcuffed and arrested for arson and attempted murder. Maxine hadn't been there when it happened, as she kept explaining to the police, and she said she knew nothing about it. But her sons had already said in front of witnesses that she had ordered them to do it. It had been her idea. She kept insisting that it wasn't what she meant, as though terrifying Camille into paying her off was more acceptable than attempted murder. The three of them were put in two police cars and taken to jail. The Marshalls, Elizabeth, Simone, and Camille stood in the driveway watching firemen hose down the château and the nearest vineyards. The cottage was badly damaged, and the horse barn where Camille lived was gone. The side of the château closest to the flames was blackened as they all stood there praying that the house, the vineyards, and the winery didn't go up in smoke that night. It all depended on which way the wind would turn.

Chapter Nineteen

It was a long night watching the vineyards burn at Château Joy but the firefighters managed to confine the blaze to one section. Some small outbuildings and sheds were destroyed, along with the cottage and the horse barn. The wind shifted and the flames never made it down the hill to the winery. And by some miracle, the château had been spared. One side had been blackened by smoke, but it could be cleaned and nothing had been burned or damaged. It had been a shocking night for all of them, especially Camille, who knew how it had happened, who had done it, and why. That was the most upsetting piece of all. Maxine and both her sons were being held on arson and two counts of attempted murder in the first degree, premeditated murder. And it could so easily have gone so very wrong, and Camille and Simone would have been dead then.

Elizabeth and Sam left two hours after they'd arrived, the situation appeared to be in control by then. Phillip stayed until five in the morning when Camille and Simone were allowed to take refuge in the château, and Camille made Simone lie down in Maxine's room.

She had been through too much that night. And Choupette was whimpering and coughing from the smoke and laid down on the bed next to Simone.

Camille sat in the kitchen alone after that, thinking about what had happened. The firemen had stayed to continue hosing down the vineyards in case the wind changed again, and to make sure the last embers were out.

Phillip stayed for a few minutes, and then left after telling Camille to get some rest, and promising to return in a few hours. There was too much to talk about and they were both too tired and shocked by the realization that Alexandre and Gabriel had tried to kill her, and she had almost lost the château and winery. And Simone had nearly died too.

Despite the fire the night before, and only two hours' sleep, Phillip made time to talk to his father in the morning about the result of the investigation in France. In light of what had happened, nothing his father told him was surprising. Maxine was a dangerous, evil woman, and Phillip was sure that she had wished Camille would die mysteriously, so she'd inherit everything, and her sons had taken her literally and tried to achieve it clumsily, but almost effectively. It had been bumbling and crude, and the plan, whoever's idea it was, had backfired on them. They were all going to prison for a very long time. Maxine's tenure at Château Joy was over, and she and her sons were gone. Finally. And they could never harm or torment Camille again.

Phillip and Sam talked for a long time about what had happened, and how foolish and naive Christophe had been, and too good-hearted. It could have all turned out so much worse than it did. But what had happened was bad enough, and terrifying. If the winds had been different, Camille could easily have been killed or lost everything.

After breakfast, Phillip was going back to the château to see what he could do to help Camille. They would have much cleaning up to do and eventually replanting of the burned section of vineyard.

He stopped in the garden first, and retrieved her shoes of the night before from under the bench. He stood looking at them for a long minute, and remembered them playing in the garden as children, and then shoved the shoes in his jacket pockets, and went back to Château Joy.

He found Camille making scrambled eggs in the kitchen, and Simone sitting at the table looking slightly dazed, and Choupette running around the kitchen barking. He walked in and Camille smiled at him.

"Have you had breakfast?" she offered, as she set the eggs down in front of Simone, who seemed to have a healthy appetite, despite their adventures of the night before. She'd been lamenting her chickens before Phillip arrived, and Camille had promised to buy more.

"I just had breakfast with my father," Phillip said seriously. He wanted to share with her what his father had told him about Maxine and her sons, but not just yet, she had a lot to digest as it was. And then he remembered the shoes in his pocket and handed them to her. "I believe these are yours, Cinderella," he said with a low bow, and she smiled, remembering sitting in the garden with him the night before.

"Actually, they're Simone's," she said as she took them from his hands, and handed them to their rightful owner, who smiled when she saw them.

"In that case," Phillip said to Simone, "you must be my fairy princess, and I'm your Prince Charming," he said and all three of them laughed.

"You might be a touch young for me. Do you have a grandfather?" she asked him innocently.

"Actually, I don't," he said apologetically, and she rolled her eyes, looking very French, and lit a cigarette as soon as she finished her eggs and then turned to Camille.

"Thank heavens you wore the shoes last night or I'd have lost them in the fire. I've saved those shoes for seventy years," she said nostalgically. Everything she'd had in the cottage had been damaged by smoke, water, or fire, but at least she and Choupette were alive. And everything Camille had at the horse barn was ash, but she hadn't taken anything of value there, except photos of her parents, and her father's favorite jacket was still there. But given the possibilities, they had lost very little. Simone had spent the night, thinking of her grandsons, and the unthinkable act they had committed, and her daughter, who had spawned it. Camille had called the insurance company that morning, and they were coming up during the week. They had good insurance, but it was upsetting anyway, particularly since it was arson, and a fire set by people they knew, who wished them ill, wanted Camille dead, and were willing to sacrifice Simone too.

Camille had inspected their rooms in the château that morning, and all she wanted to do was get rid of every shred of evidence of Maxine and her sons. She wanted to throw it all away, and erase them from her life forever.

Simone was looking sad as she sipped her coffee and smoked her cigarette, and Camille felt sorry for her. Her only child and two grandsons had turned out to be criminals and tried to kill her. Camille knew it must have been an awful feeling for her, even if it was no surprise to her that they were evil, but to a much greater degree than even she feared.

But her sadness was for a different reason, she explained to Camille when Phillip went outside to look around and survey the damage.

"I'm going to have to leave you now," Simone said with tears in her eyes. "I feel so terrible about what Maxine and the boys did. I can never make it up to you, Camille. Your father was a good person, you didn't deserve any of this. And I have no reason to be here now. My horrible family won't be living here, and I'm happy for you. And every time you see me, it would remind you of Maxine. I can't do that to you. I'll go back to France as soon as I can get organized. I have a little pension there, I'll get a room in someone's house in the country. I don't want to go back to Paris."

"I don't want you to leave," Camille said to her, with tears in her eyes. "You're my fairy grandmother. You're the only family I have." Camille looked sad as she said it, and Simone was deeply touched.

"You're the only family I want," Simone said, "except for Choupette of course. She's my family too." The little dog wagged her tail as though she agreed. She was filthy from the smoke and falling ash the night before, and Simone had said she wanted to give her a bath in the sink.

They both knew they were going to have to give statements to the police about Maxine and the boys. And if there was a trial, they'd have to testify, but Phillip thought they would plead guilty and make some kind of deal. It was going to be a great step down for Maxine to go to prison in the United States. This wasn't what she'd planned or the way she expected it to turn out.

"Where would I live if I stay here?" Simone said, thinking about it. "I don't want to intrude on you at the château."

"You're not intruding. I want you here, Simone. Besides, who will make cassoulet and blood sausage for me, and rognons?"

"You have a point." She smiled. They had grown so fond of each other, both of them taking refuge from Maxine.

"We can redo some of the rooms upstairs." There were plenty of attic rooms, storerooms, and rooms that no one ever used and could be turned into bedrooms, and a suite for Simone. "We can remodel the top floor and give you a lovely bedroom and sitting room," Camille said to her.

"And a kitchen?" Her eyes lit up at that.

"If that's what you want," Camille said quietly. She wanted Simone to stay, whatever it took. They had come to love each other, and had survived hardship together and near-death.

"I just don't want to get in your way."

"I'd be lonely here without you." They'd been having dinner together every night for nearly a year.

They were still talking about it when Phillip came back from walking through the fields and vineyards. Francois, the vineyard manager, had come in, and several of the workers to help them clean up. And Camille couldn't wait to start getting rid of Maxine's things. She was going to send anything valuable to storage and throw the rest away. She felt as though her home had been poisoned by her, and she had cast an evil spell on it, and Camille wanted every last shred of her cleared away now. The spider was gone and her web had been removed. She was going to move into her parents' room and give Simone the guest room until Camille had a suite for her built upstairs.

"Do you want to go for a walk with me?" Phillip asked her when he came back. He had left his boots outside, covered with mud and ash, and Camille put on her own heavy rubber boots to walk through the vineyards with him. She had found an old pair of her jeans in a closet in her room and a work shirt of her father's and had put them with her old rubber boots from a tool shed at the château. She had lost most of her clothes when the little barn burned down. And so had Simone in the cottage. It seemed unimportant compared to their lives.

When they went outside, the acrid smell of smoke was still heavy in the air. Firemen were still hosing down some areas, and there were police inspectors checking around the house and putting soil samples in plastic bags where the gasoline had been as evidence. And they were taking photographs of the scene. There was yellow police crime-scene tape cordoning off certain areas. It was a crime scene now. Camille had gotten a desperate text from Maxine when they first got to jail, asking her to find them attorneys immediately. As far as Camille was concerned, she could use her own money and connections to get what she needed. The countess was out of her life. And they'd have to use the public defender if they were out of money.

"I'm so sorry this happened," Phillip said sympathetically as they walked. They stopped and looked at the remains of the drafty little horse barn. There was nothing left. Camille was going to come out later with a rake and a shovel, and see if she found anything senti-mental she had forgotten. And Simone wanted to do the same in the cottage, and Camille had promised to help her. She was relieved that she was staying. Camille didn't want to lose her now.

"It was nice last night," Camille said quietly about the ball, "until the fire. I had a good time at the party."

"I loved being in the garden with you. I haven't been in there in years. I remember when you used to love swinging there. I sat there thinking for a while, when I went back to get your shoes this morning . . . or, sorry . . . Simone's shoes." He smiled at Camille and she laughed. The notion of Simone as Cinderella was sweet. "I realized something there today. Maybe I'm not so different from your father. He was fooled by all that dazzle and sophistication, all that slick artifice that Maxine wooed him with. I've been doing the same thing with every woman I've dated since I got out of college. I had the right idea with Francesca, just the wrong woman. She would have driven me insane.

"I think our parents had it right the first time. They didn't want flashy or fancy. They wanted to build something together. You and I didn't grow up with all that showy crap people fall for. They were hard workers, so are we. They had real marriages and were real people. Your father may have been a bit of a dreamer, but he was a straight shooter, so is mine. Your dad turned his dreams into something real. Look at all this, look at what he built for you, the legacy he left you. My father has done the same thing, it just grew bigger than he expected. But none of us are caught up in the pretense or the show."

"Does this mean you're turning in your Ferrari for an SUV?" she teased him.

"Immediately. What it means is that I finally figured out what I want. I don't want a showpiece or a trophy. I want a real person, and I want to be real with them. That's the fairytale for me." He was ready for a *real* life now, and he knew it. He hadn't been until then. The night before and everything Camille had been through had woken him up. His father would have been proud of him to hear his words. Sam always knew he'd get there, he just didn't know when.

"It's funny," Camille answered him. "I always thought my parents had a fairytale life, and that's what I wanted too when I grew up. Just what they had. And then everything went wrong. Mom got sick, and died. My father went down on that plane. They're freak things, but they happen to people. I don't think I've trusted that good things are going to happen since my Mom died. And Maxine was like having poison pumped into our life. No matter how charming she acted at first, I knew she was fake and she hated me. Papa never believed it. He didn't want to see it. I could feel it. And who do you trust after this? How do you believe in happy endings if the handsome prince and the fairy princess die in the end?" She was thinking of her parents.

"You don't know how it ends," he said gently, as they sat down on a bench overlooking the Valley. Her vineyards stretched for miles, and farther up the Valley, so did his. They were a prince and princess in the tiny kingdom where they lived and had grown up. "But you have to believe in something. Yourself first of all. Each other. And if you're lucky, the prince and princess live to be very old. Our mothers died young, and so did your father. That doesn't always happen. Look at Simone. She's chugging along at full speed, even with those disgusting cigarettes hanging out of her mouth. She'll probably live to be a hundred." Camille smiled, thinking about it. She liked that idea. She wanted her fairy grandmother to live forever. She needed her. She was magic in a way, and had been for her. And Simone needed her too as compensation for her family.

"I want that to happen to us, to live to be very old together," Phillip said to her, looking her in the eye. She made him brave. And he wanted to protect her. She was a very courageous woman. She had been through a lot and hadn't let it ruin or damage her. She was as pure and sweet and honest and open as she had been when they were children. No amount of bad luck or heartache had spoiled her. And it made him feel like a better person being with her. She made his life bigger and better, instead of smaller and worse, which was what his father had always told him to look for. Phillip knew he had found it in Camille. It had always been there. He just didn't know it, until now. "I love you, Camille," he said in the earnest voice she remembered from her childhood. She had trusted him then, and she still did. That had never changed. "I'm sorry it took me so long to figure it out. I don't know what I've been waiting for. I should have known years ago how much I love you."

"I wasn't ready for you yet then anyway." She had only figured out the important things herself recently, about what she wanted, who she needed, who she respected and who she didn't. "So you turn out to be the handsome prince after all." She smiled and he kissed her, and they sat on the bench for a long time, looking out over the Valley they both loved, where they had both been born.

"It really is like a fairytale, isn't it?" she said softly, smiling, with his arm around her. "The wicked witch is gone. The handsome prince turns out to be you."

"And I get the fairy princess . . . even if Simone owns the glass slippers." They both laughed at what he said, and walked slowly down the hill hand in hand. They were in no hurry. They would replant the vineyards together, and repair whatever had been damaged. The fairytale had just begun. And without saying it, they both knew they would be a happily ever after. All they had to do was build it together. In the magical valley they loved and where they had grown up, their time had come. And best of all, it was real.

HOME. FAMILY. FRIENDSHIP.

There was a bond between the
two families now, that even time
could not displace . . .

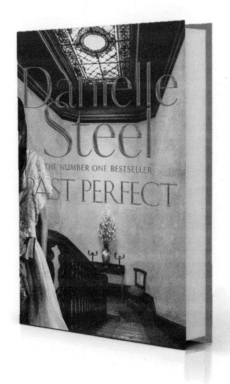

AVAILABLE FOR PRE-ORDER TODAY

#PureHeartPureSteel